THE ORDER

The two women exchanged a glance, then Kalya clapped her hands together twice. As if on cue, the trembling mass of flesh sprang into life. The kneeling men began to buck their hips fiercely, completing their violation of greased, receptive rectums. At the same time, they extended their tongues to lap at the open quims of the women before them. All around the heaving edifice, mouths widened and tongues protruded: lapping into pussies, tugging nipples, teasing pricks and sucking balls.

Darné and Kalya prayed their Mistress would be pleased with their offering to her. If not, their punishment would be dreadful indeed.

THE ORDER

Nadine Somers

This book is a work of fiction.
In real life, make sure you practise safe sex.

First published in 2000 by
Nexus
Thames Wharf Studios
Rainville Road
London W6 9HA

Typeset by TW Typesetting, Plymouth, Devon

Printed and bound by
Cox & Wyman Ltd, Reading, Berks

ISBN 0 352 33460 6

Prologue

Valdez fell to his knees, his hands clenched tightly together. He stared up at the vision in black, a dark blur filling his tear-stained world. His eyes widened fearfully, and his bony arms trembled.

'Please, Mistress!' he wailed. 'One mistake. Only one mistake, Mistress! Forgive me! I beg you! I'm so sorry! Please!'

His Mistress gazed down at him with cold, hooded eyes. She felt no emotion, no pity. Valdez had failed her. His task had been a simple one, and he had been found wanting. The entire project was now at risk, and all because of his stupidity.

'There can be no mercy,' she breathed. 'Those who betray their Mistress must be punished. As an example to all.'

Valdez prostrated himself at her feet, his arms and legs flung wide. He pressed his face into the dungeon floor and wept.

Above him, the Contessa di Diablo raised a black, leather-clad hand, and her fingers curled. From her left, a naked, copper-haired woman emerged from out of the shadows; a blonde, nude Amazon advanced from her right. Had Valdez looked up he would have recognised them at once: Darné and Kalya, the most trusted of the Faithful. But he did not look up. Instead, he clawed at the dirty stone flags, mumbling incoherently, huge sobs of fear convulsing his body.

The Contessa stepped back, her black cloak rustling like crumpled crêpe.

'Cast him into the Darkness,' she commanded. 'My Angels need feeding.'

Valdez lurched violently into life. His head came up and his jaw dropped open. Silver teeth twinkled like so many stars in the dark cavern of his mouth.

'No!' he screamed, as the women seized hold of his legs, dragging him across the cold stone floor.

The Contessa had already turned away. Valdez's incompetence was the least of her concerns. What mattered more was this business at Dorford Haven. She had miscalculated. Forces had been unleashed. Forces she had sought to control. She must think again. The Order was so close to success now; she could not afford a second slip. She would have to redouble the measures already in place. Success would be hers. It *must* be hers.

She suddenly felt very tired. It had been too long since she herself had fed. The likes of Valdez were not for her. She liked her man-meat firm and well-endowed. She would have some of the younger slaves brought to her; half a dozen or so of the more expendable males. She was in no mood to be tender at present; it was unlikely that all the men would survive a night between her legs.

A familiar voice broke through the dark curtain of her thoughts.

'Mistress! No! For mercy's sake, no!'

She closed her ears to his screams. They were not the first she had heard when condemning a wretch to the Darkness, nor would they be the last. Her Angels would put an end to his pitiful pleadings. In time. But he would suffer first, and deservedly so.

The Contessa smiled. Valdez would know a thousand delights before his ordeal was over; and a thousand torments, too. A man could die of pleasure in the Darkness. She might choose to end his suffering before it was too late; or prolong it past all caring. Valdez, too, could end his punishment with a single word. But he would not; no man ever did. Though they prayed for mercy, wept, implored and begged, none ever chose his freedom willingly. The Angels ensnared not merely a victim's body,

2

but his mind and heart, also. Each soul destroyed itself in ecstasy, as would Valdez. But not before he had screamed a little longer. Perhaps later, when she had slaked her own lusts, she would visit the lower dungeons and watch her Angels at work. They had not feasted for some time. They would be hungry, and when they were hungry their victims always suffered that little bit more.

Poor Valdez. He would not fail his Mistress again.

If, indeed, there was anything left of him to fail her.

One

Tamara leaned forward and examined the screen for several moments. The latest in a long line of unknown faces stared back at her from a chamber several floors below. Seated at the console, Commander Trask savoured the sight of two large breasts straining against the thin fabric of a black bolero. Tamara's long auburn hair tumbled forward, masking her features, allowing him the luxury of a brief, stolen leer. Her hips swayed dangerously close and it was all he could do not to reach out and cup her tight rounded buttocks in his huge, hairy hands.

'He's the one,' she said quietly.

'How can you be sure?' asked Trask, averting his gaze with considerable reluctance. 'You haven't seen them all yet.'

Tamara turned to face him, and her emerald-green eyes sparkled in that way that always made his tummy tighten, and his penis stir.

'Have I ever been wrong?' she asked.

Trask was forced to shake his head. 'No,' he admitted. 'But there are some good men here. Creed is a new boy. He doesn't have the experience.'

Tamara's breasts rolled like warm oil as she straightened up. Trask felt his blood pressure rise in sympathy with his penis. He sometimes suspected she flaunted herself on purpose.

'Then it's time he gained it,' she replied.

Trask responded with a resigned shrug. If Tamara had made up her mind then it was pointless attempting to

dissuade her. He reached forward and pressed a flat red button. 'Bring Creed to level four,' he ordered. He might have added, *lucky bastard*, if not for the fact that he was aware that he had just condemned the young man to a fate that he would not have wished on anyone, short of his worst enemy.

Max Creed seemed a little on edge. He stood in front of the large, mahogany desk, arms loose, two fingers of his right hand drumming lightly at his thigh. He was tall and well-built, with short, honey-blond hair; good-looking, but not – Tamara had already decided – quite handsome. Not that it was important. He was the one. That was all that mattered. She knew. She always knew.

In his smart, pressed suit, Max looked more like a middle-management executive summoned to explain declining sales, than a government agent trained to kill. Tamara had glanced at his file in the short time it had taken two sombre-faced men in black suits to escort him from sub-level nine. Max was 27, barely a year or two older than Tamara herself. Two years, one month and six days according to his file. She stretched out her hand.

'My name is Tamara Knight,' she said, introducing herself.

Max nodded. His grip was warm and firm. His eyes were a dark, dark blue: diamond pinpricks in his pupils captured the reflection of the bright overhead lights.

'You're new to Department Omega,' began Trask, rousing himself from behind the desk.

'Yes, sir,' replied Max.

'Two years in Baghdad; the last six months as an attaché in St Petersburg. A facility for languages, I believe?'

'Russian, Arabic, French, German –'

'Yes, I know,' Trask broke in irritably. His long, thick finger tapped the file. 'Birthmark on your right buttock, knife scar on your left forearm; favourite dessert, lemon and mint bavarois.' He paused. 'Sounds disgusting.' Then looked up. 'It's all in here.'

Max said nothing. Tamara was staring at him, her eyes

5

cold and focused. 'How familiar are you with Department Omega?' she asked.

'Not very,' he confessed. 'It's top secret. That's partly why I applied. Always been the curious type.'

Trask interrupted again. 'Curious or not, once you join us, there's no going back. We choose carefully because we choose for life. The same goes for you.'

Max nodded. 'I understand, sir.'

Trask threw himself forward with such force that it seemed for one moment he might leap across the desk.

'No, sir!' he roared. 'I don't think you do. Up to now it's been fun and games.' He prodded the file fiercely. 'It says here you've been shot at twice, stabbed once and survived at least three attempts to garrotte you.'

'Yes, sir,' confirmed Max proudly.

'It's nothing to be cocky about, lad!' admonished Trask. 'You think you can handle yourself. Well, listen: the people we're up against in Omega don't make mistakes. And neither do we. It's the only way we survive.'

'Yes, sir,' repeated Max, his bubble well and truly burst.

Trask fell back into his chair, a suddenly spent force. He looked up at Tamara. 'Are you absolutely sure?' he asked.

Tamara was still gazing quietly at Max. 'I'm sure,' she replied.

Trask transferred his attention back to the young man. 'Ours is a thankless task. No plaudits, no medals, and you can kiss goodbye to a life outside these four walls. Is that what you want?'

Max appeared to consider this dismal prospect for a moment or two. 'No, sir,' he replied. 'It isn't. It sounds bloody miserable.' He paused. 'But I'd still like to do it. Whatever it is.'

'When Commander Trask says there's no way back, he means it,' Tamara reminded him.

'Then no way back it is,' replied Max.

'Very well. We investigate the occult,' Trask announced loudly. 'Black magic, vampires, poltergeists, witches, things that go bump in the night.'

'Would that be witches who fall off their broomsticks, sir?' asked Max, with a grin.

'No, agent Creed,' retorted Trask. 'It's more likely your head falling into a fucking basket!'

Max swallowed. His Adam's apple bobbed up and down.

'What are your views on the occult?' asked Tamara.

'I've never really had any,' answered Max honestly.

'You graduated in archaeology at Cairo University. You must have studied some aspects of the spiritual world.'

'I did,' Max admitted. 'I keep an open mind. There are some things no one can explain. The occult's as good an explanation as any.'

Tamara and Trask exchanged a brief glance. The latter gave a lethargic nod of his big, balding head and Tamara turned her attention back to Max.

'It's time I broke him in,' she said, looking at Max but addressing herself to the man sitting beside her.

Max frowned but kept silent. Trask pushed himself back from the desk, stood up and crossed to the far side of the office. 'I'll leave him to your tender mercies,' he grunted, casting a final lingering eye over Tamara's hips before closing the door behind him.

Tamara walked over to a second exit. 'This way,' she announced.

Max followed her into the adjoining room. Tamara heard the young man's sharp intake of breath. They were standing in an airy, sparsely furnished chamber. It was dimly lit and heavily mirrored; banks of warm, low-wattage lights ranged haphazardly around the walls. A large bed dominated a far quarter of the room, its red satin sheets turned neatly down at one corner.

Tamara twirled round to face her companion. Her short skirt flipped up, revealing a sudden flash of thigh above her sheer black stockings. Max looked perplexed but that, she reasoned, was hardly surprising. She remembered the look on Guy's face when she had first brought him here, four years ago. She shuddered. Had she really been with Omega that long? But Guy was history. She closed her mind to the memories. To dwell on them now would only bring her pain. She hoped Max would be more fortunate.

'When Commander Trask said Omega was for life, he meant it. From now on you have only one friend, one confidante, one lover. Me.'

Max stopped dead in his tracks. His face creased and his lips narrowed. 'I'm sorry?'

'No one else can be trusted. There are no exceptions. Our faith in each other must be total, and it begins now.'

Tamara unclipped a fastener at her waist and her skirt fell to the floor. Max caught his breath a second time. Transfixed by the tight black V of her panties, he scarcely seemed to notice Tamara unbutton her top and drop it on to the bed. Her plunging, black bra matched her high-cut knickers. His eyes danced excitedly; from the tiny, dark triangle of silk between her thighs to the lace-edged spill of her big, creamy breasts.

Max looked up and shook his head. His face was a mask of confusion. 'I don't understand.'

'If we're to be partners, we need to be sure of each other. Absolutely sure,' continued Tamara. She reached behind and unhooked her bra. It fell away, exposing her heavy, rounded bosom.

'Bloody hell,' Max whispered hoarsely.

Tamara smiled, and felt the blood begin to pump through her veins. A surge of warmth flooded her belly as Max's eyes feasted on her breasts. Pink nipples, long, hard and thick, thrust from the broad, rosy rounds of her areolae. She watched Max as *he* watched *her*, savouring the near-childish grin of delight on his face as she hooked her fingers beneath the elastic of her panties and eased them down over her big, flared hips. Only her stockings and suspender belt remained, and these she swiftly discarded, standing naked before him.

'Your turn now,' said Tamara matter-of-factly, crossing to the bed.

'Is this some sort of wind-up?' asked Max. He looked around. 'There are hidden cameras, right? Everyone's having a laugh at my expense.'

Tamara slipped beneath a red satin sheet and stretched herself like a tired kitten. 'There are no cameras. We just need to fuck. That's all.'

'Just like that?' asked Max stupidly.

Tamara sat upright, the sheet around her legs, her big, milky breasts melting across her knees. 'Yes, just like that. Do I have to wait all day?'

Max hesitated, as Tamara knew he would. But only for a moment. She had expected that, too. It was not reserve that stayed his hand, but curiosity. It may have killed the cat; it had probably killed Guy. But if ever Omega were to investigate its way out of existence, it needed all the curiosity its agents could muster. It was an unusual situation. Only a sex-mad cretin would have jumped her straight away. Max was weighing up the options. Not that there were any. His hormones had programmed him to fuck her, whether he liked it or not. That was another reason she had chosen him.

She felt her tummy tingle as Max discarded his jacket, shirt and tie, then reached down to unbuckle his belt. Their partnership was underway. Her eyebrows rose a fraction at the sight of the tiny black jock-strap that came fleetingly into view as he stepped out of his trousers.

'Nice cock,' she remarked as he removed his pants. His pubes were light and curly, like his hair. Funny, she'd imagined they'd be dark and bushy; still, even she couldn't anticipate everything.

Max returned her compliment with a cheeky, boyish grin. His shaft was long and marble-smooth; thick and lightly veined. It was already unfurling and when he reached down to close his fingers around the stem, it rose to a right-angle, bobbled for a moment, then climbed rapidly to its stiffened apex.

'Excellent,' whispered Tamara. 'Nought to sixty in seven seconds.' She laughed lightly. Her pulse had quickened and she felt her heart thump loudly beneath her breasts. Pressing one hand between her legs, she dipped a testing finger into the dampness oozing from her oily sex. She was ready for him.

Max mounted the bed and knelt beside her, his penis parallel with her upturned face. Tamara had never been one to resist temptation. Lowering her head, she extended

her tongue, stabbing him gently between the balls, tickling the underside of his shaft with the tip of her nose. Max covered her head with his hands, fingers smoothing through her hair, steadying himself against her. Tamara dipped lower, her teeth nibbling at his scrotum. Framing one of his large, distended balls with her lips, she opened her mouth wide and drew him in.

'Oh, God!' His body shook lightly, his hands locking around her head. Tamara released the aching sphere and ran her lips around his other ball, sucking it home with a loud, greedy slurp. Max swore, his fingers pulling tightly at her hair. Discarding the tight sac, she turned her attention back to his penis. Raising herself on one arm, she traced a delicate trail with her tongue along the length of his shaft from root to tip.

Her lips plunged over his glans with a force that clearly took him by surprise. He emitted a low, animal grunt and Tamara felt his body stiffen for an instant. She wondered how long he could control himself in this position and how fiercely his penis would unleash itself within her mouth when the time came. But this was not the time. Today, his prick was destined for her pussy. Her mouth would have to wait. She released him suddenly, pulled away and lay on her back, her big green eyes shining, her chin damp with her own saliva.

'Your turn now,' she told him, peeling the soft, satin sheet to one side, parting her legs crudely, fully exposing herself for the first time. She looked down at her bare cunt, aware that it now had Max's undivided attention. Below the neat, golden-red V of her pudenda, her engorged labia were clearly visible; prominent pink wedges of flesh dimpled with droplets of sap. Good enough to eat, she thought, and, for one brief instant, lamented the fact that, supple though she was, even *her* head couldn't reach that far.

Tamara reached down across her smooth, rounded belly, fingers dancing through her curly pubes, feathering the hooded pink pip of her clitoris. She bent her head back and gave a low, shimmering sigh.

'Come on, Max,' she whimpered softly, 'where's your tongue when I need it?'

She arched her back and raised her hips, propelling her cunt towards him. Max shifted position, moving between her thighs, scooping her tight arse-cheeks into his hands. He lowered his face and she heard him breathe deeply, savouring her smell before touching his lips to her waiting labia.

'Oh, yes,' she trilled. 'That's good. That's very good.'

She felt the flat of his tongue wedge itself into the runnel of her sex, opening her up, drawing a sudden rush of juices into his mouth. Squeezing her hardened buttocks, he tugged her hips from side to side, using the motion of her own body to excite her. Tamara growled her pleasure as his tongue-tip stung her clitty, prising it free of its swollen hood. It was almost all too much and she was forced to shut her mind to the animal lust boiling in her belly.

Abruptly, she pushed him away, swung over on to her tummy and lifted her bottom into the air. 'My arse!' she squealed. 'Kiss my arse!'

Unfazed, Max lowered his head a second time, pressing his lips to each of her cheeks in turn.

'Lick my bumhole,' she demanded, wriggling her buttocks from side to side. A pungent raft of scents wafted up from between her legs and she breathed them in. Max must have smelled it, too: the heady aroma of dripping sex. Tamara's mind was suddenly awash with manic, wildly obscene images. It was a long time, she realised with some surprise, since she had felt this turned on.

'Nice and gently,' she counselled. 'Around the edges . . .' She was struggling to retain control. 'Then . . . then into the hole . . .!'

Max's serpentine lips slithered into her dampened cleft. The tip of his tongue circled her opening: once, twice, three times. Tamara's insides boiled and melted as his warm breath scored the delicate little mouth. She buried her head in the pillow and mewed with delight when he finally narrowed his lips around the taut nut-brown eye of her anus.

'You're very obedient,' Tamara sighed. 'I like that in a man. Oh yes! You're in! Oh, God, that's lovely! You've done this before, haven't you?'

He was taking her close, too close. With a supreme effort, she pulled away once more, rolled over on to her back and sat upright. Max rocked back on his heels. His face was damp – with effort and with her. Silvery trails of female sap threaded his cheeks and chin.

Tamara's lungs were aching. Her breasts rose and fell, scored with sweat. 'On your back!' she ordered. 'Now!'

Max rolled on to his side and sprawled across the bed. Tamara swung one long, nimble leg across his chest. 'You mustn't resist me,' she told him. 'Do you understand?'

He nodded mutely as she climbed across his body, nails bared, her green eyes dark with lust. When she dug her fingers into his flesh, he arched his back and howled like a startled wolfhound. Reaching down with one hand, she took hold of his penis and guided it towards her open cunt.

It was time.

Max closed his eyes and shuddered as she pulled him inside her, sitting back and engulfing him in one fluid movement. Tamara felt him twitch inside her, his balls hard and fat against her buttocks. She began to rock; gently at first, then faster; then faster still.

'Fuck me!' she yelled. 'Fuck me, Max!'

He stretched out his arms and took hold of her hips, pulling down, locking their bodies tight. His mouth closed over the huge balloon of one breast, his lips anchored to the teat, milking the nipple gently. She grabbed his head, tugged it away from the tight, quivering orb and forced him on to its sweaty, voluptuous twin. Hugging him fast, she began to squeeze with the muscles of her pussy, demolishing his last line of defence. He thrust: once, twice. They came together; clawing and scratching; cursing and sobbing. Tamara felt his seed splatter her insides and tumbled forward, spent but happy.

She knew she had chosen wisely.

She always did.

* * *

The Contessa, too, had chosen wisely.

She closed her eyes and allowed her mind to wander. She saw the man only dimly at first. He was tall, well-built, good-looking: Dr Marsilio Quellorozata, Professor of Graeco–Roman Studies at the Santa Maria Institute of Advanced Learning. Not at all her idea of a towering intellect. He was standing over a young woman. She was naked, half his size, very petite and very brown. She was hunched forward, her arms stretched out towards a metal frame, her wrists cinched into thick leather hoops holding her fast. Her backside was raised provocatively, the cheeks crudely splayed and exposing both her dark, wrinkled anus and the deckled pink maw of her cunt. Doctor Quellorozata was naked, too. His penis was huge, its purple knob slick with semen. Pearls of spunk had gathered on the Brazilian's balls, evidence of his recent enjoyment of the young woman. He had fucked her four times already, in the space of less than twenty minutes. Each bout had cost him dearly: Violla was the most expensive whore in Santiago. She was also the best.

'Again!' she yelled. 'Take me again, you son of a bitch! And harder this time! Like a man, not a boy!'

His cock stiffened in response to the woman's demand. He pushed at her cunt and watched as the glistening meat of her sex expanded to admit his glans. He leaned forward and impaled her with his shaft, riveted by the sight of her vulva drawing him home, swallowing him by degrees until his balls pressed against her warm buttocks. He began to move inside her, slowly at first, before gradually increasing the tempo of his thrusts. He had nothing left to give, the last of his semen still dribbling idly down his thighs. But his cock swelled with lust, and the need within him felt as urgent as ever. He dug his fingers into her hips and renewed his assault. Violla swivelled her arse from side to side, a maddening wriggle of flesh that tugged at his penis and encouraged him to push deeper into the damp velvet of her sex.

'Help me ...' he moaned, pumping her hard now, blotting out the pain as she squeezed the muscles of her

cunt and drew an impossible spurt of liquid from his exhausted cock.

'Fuck me!' she screamed. 'Fuck me, bastard! Fuck me!'

As he thrust in a delirium of lust and pain, the Contessa, far away and yet so near, savoured the heady swoon of joy that filled his soul. She felt herself move within him, trembling as excitement seized his guts and he emptied the last of his essence into Violla's greedy cunt.

And as she felt his pleasure turn to pain and then to further longing still, she left him to his torment, for there were others whose souls she must touch before her night was over.

Erica Stanislav was a small woman, not quite petite, with strawberry-blonde hair, blue eyes, pink lips and a dimpled chin. Her skin was pale, the result of too many hours sat behind a desk in a dry, dusty room, poring over books, and haranguing idle students.

She was in such a room now, with four of her class lined up in front of her. They were insipid young men; one too tall, one too short, one too fat and one so nondescript that she could not even recall his name. Not that it mattered. They knew why they were there. She had made it plain enough. Their grades were poor; too bad to ensure a further term at the prestigious Budapest College of Antiquities. She had checked their backgrounds carefully; done what they had patently failed to do: her homework. None of them could afford to fail. They would, she was sure, do whatever she asked them in return for a second chance.

Erica locked the door to the classroom, pulled down the blinds to ensure privacy, and crossed back to her desk. The four young men fidgeted nervously. They began to fidget even more when she reached up and unbuttoned her blouse. Sweat broke out on the face of the fat boy when she unzipped her skirt, wriggled free, kicked off her shoes and removed her bra. Her breasts were not large, but they were round and firm: her nipples pink and shaped like tiny cherries. Four pairs of eyes watched as she tucked her

thumbs beneath the waistband of her big, satin panties and eased them down over her soft, sculptured hips. Light brown curls adorned her sex, darker roots snaking down between her legs.

Straightening up, she looked into four flushed faces. When she spoke, her voice was very calm and very serious. 'Please take off your clothes.'

No one moved. Her eyes narrowed. She spoke again, though not in Hungarian this time. The words she used were unfamiliar to the four young men, which was hardly surprising, for few had ever heard them uttered. But their effect was electric. Reluctance vanished as they hurried now to remove their trousers, shirts and pants. Erica smiled as the fat boy stumbled for a moment, his feet entangled in his big white boxers. When they had finished undressing, she stood for a few moments and admired the assortment of naked male bodies. It was clear from the way they continued to fidget that the young men still harboured some misgivings. That pleased her. To take a virgin was always special. The prospect of deflowering four at a single sitting caused icicles of raw excitement to form in the pit of her stomach.

Four hardened shafts bristled with youthful arousal. She walked the short line, trailing one hand carelessly across the top of her students' cocks and was gratified by their childish whinnies of delight. The fat boy's penis was by far the thickest; the nondescript lad the longest and the other two were fair to middling. No matter: they would do for what she had in mind.

'Down!' she told the chubby lad. 'On your back. Now!'

He obeyed her immediately, floundering into place, his cock bouncing like a length of salami against the curve of his belly. Erica quickly orchestrated the movements of his three companions. She pushed two of them into a standing position near the fat boy's head, then stationed their nondescript friend to one side. Satisfied with her arrangements, she straddled the chubby lad's midriff, took hold of his cock and guided it towards her cunt. Her labia were already slippy with arousal, sap dribbling from the

folds of her sex. She sank down, engulfing the boy's shaft in one smooth movement. She felt him twitch inside her and knew she would have to act quickly. She doubted whether any of these young men would be able to hold back for long. Without turning her head, she addressed the boy behind her.

'On your knees, lad, and across my back. I want you to take me in the arse.'

It was a difficult manoeuvre for the young man to accomplish. He got down on all fours and tried to push his cock into her cleft. The fat boy yelled as a stray knee dug into his thigh. Erica ignored the inexperienced fumbling at her rear and bent her face towards the remaining duo. Reaching out, she took hold of their pricks, tugging the two men close together. With astonishing dexterity she stretched her lips around both cocks, drawing them into the tight oval of her mouth. Behind her, she felt something hard and round nudge against the dry hole of her anus. Her would-be buggerer had finally located his target. She pushed back with her arse and felt her sphincter spasm for an instant before opening up around the invader. Sucking greedily on the captured shafts, she drew their combined girths towards the back of her throat, her hands clawing into tight young buttocks. She felt both boys tense when she wriggled her fingers between their cheeks and began to push into their bumholes. The fat boy was breathing loud and fast and she felt his cock twitch dangerously. A convulsion seized her rectum and she felt her narrow channel contract around the cock within her arse.

A cluster of nerves exploded in her groin, sending spikes of pleasure bursting through the walls of her cunt as she came. All four cocks erupted simultaneously, filling her body with spunk. She screamed around the penises inside her mouth and wriggled her hips to extract the maximum pleasure from her spasming sex.

Seed overflowed from her lips and dribbled down her chin. She continued to rise and fall over the boy beneath her, milking him with her muscles until he began to squeal in discomfort. The boy in her arse had stopped thrusting

but had not withdrawn. He lay across her back and grunted stupidly into her ear. His hips wriggled as if a weak electric shock were passing through his body. She tightened the muscles of her anus and sucked the final drops of sperm from his squashed, exhausted cock; and smiled as his tears dribbled on to her cheek.

Oh joy! Oh sweet, sweet joy!

Far away, the Contessa pressed three fingers into her cunt and beat a firm tattoo against her clitoris. Her body shuddered gently but she did not come. Not yet. It was too soon. If she reached orgasm, she would lose contact with those souls she must command. There would be time for pleasure soon enough.

The Brazilian and the Hungarian were an interesting pair, she reflected, as her mind resumed its wanderings. Their lust had lain dormant till she had entered their lives. Though, of course, that she had entered their lives was a fact that as yet remained unknown to them. No matter. They had done their work, and they had done it well. As had Gioseppi. But he remained an enigma. The man who paced his study even now, his mind, perhaps, the most active and brilliant of the three. So strange! She could not fathom it. She felt his emptiness; the dark pool of nothing that lay at the heart of his being. Was that the reason he had failed her? It was a puzzle she had not yet been able to untangle.

Gioseppi turned his mind to his recent discovery. Incredible! Something so original, so diverting in its shape and form. He shook his head and stared out of the window. Night had fallen. A necklace of stars lit up the familiar Roman landscape. He was a happy man. But happy only in his own way. Others would have run from the happiness that filled his heart; it was a dry, arid joy that few would have recognised as being joy at all.

He blinked and in the shadows something seemed to move. He blinked again and the moment had gone. Funny, he was sure he had imagined – no, what was he thinking?

17

What a thought! The image had been quite obscene. Fascinating, really, that it should have come to him of all people. He looked away, yawned and crossed back to his desk. It was time to call it a night. He had a long day ahead of him tomorrow, and very soon a trip to London. He was looking forward to it: a chance to meet with overseas colleagues and share successes. Well, not all successes, of course. He allowed his fingers to stray over the sheaf of notes on his desk. He really should put these away in the safe. If anyone set eyes on what he had discovered – heavens! – it did not bear thinking about.

He pulled up short a second time. He had closed his eyes for an instant and there it was again: a thought so obscene, so twisted in its perversity. He must be tired. Time to go home. Time to rest.

Far away, and yet again so near, the Contessa felt the tightness in his head. Gioseppi had denied himself once more. It was a mystery, but no matter. He would know pleasure soon enough, whether he cared to or whether he did not. She would make sure of that.

Everyone must know pleasure.

And soon, everyone would.

Two

Darné and Kalya set about their task with relish. The Contessa had given them free rein for the project, and they were determined not to disappoint her.

Failure, of course, was unthinkable, even for the most trusted of the Faithful. Today they were members of an élite inner sanctum of free-willed disciples: women chosen for their intelligence and their beauty; for their cunning and their strength; but most of all for their unswerving lust and loyalty, a devotion beyond life itself, to the body and to the spirit of their Mistress, the Contessa di Diablo. One slip, one tiny fall from grace and they could be banished to the lower dungeons, to the Darkness and the realm of the Angels. It was a prospect to chill the most debauched of hearts: even those of Darné and Kalya, whose depravity over many years had won them their most favoured status.

With several dozen oiled and naked bodies at their disposal, they believed their scheme was feasible. Had they not believed it so, they would never have asked permission to begin construction. Ten of the Contessa's Minions – docile male slaves whose fealty to the Contessa was the equal of their own – nestled together on all fours. Darné had arranged them in a semicircle so tight that it resembled more a three-sided square than a crescent. Ten further Minions were positioned at the rear of this first group. Minions were ever erect: it was the means by which the Contessa exercised her sexual dominion over their weak and fatuous minds. It was both the source of their immense strength and yet, perversely, the means of their undoing.

19

Erect, a Minion possessed the strength of ten; dormant, he slept like a child.

The second group knelt close behind the first, their penises pressed up against the arses of their comrades. Kalya had personally oiled the shafts of each of the kneeling men, while Darné had liberally greased the anuses of those who were to be violated. Both had enjoyed their work, Darné a little too much, for she had inserted her finger too far into one Minion's rectum and had come perilously close to making him spend.

When they were happy that the men were arranged as closely as possible, Kalya gave the order to mate. Each kneeler took hold of his partner's hips and pushed forward so that his greasy glans opened the latter's sphincter to admit him, but no more. Now a third group was called forward, women this time: volunteer Faithful eager to serve their Mistress in the new undertaking. Each woman mounted a buggered Minion, feet astride his raised buttocks, hands resting on the shoulders of a kneeler, her oiled and shaven pussy level with his face.

So far so good. Ten more Faithful now entered the proceedings. They lay on their backs and slithered snake-like into the heart of the growing human tableau, legs criss-crossing in the centre. Each woman positioned her head beneath the cock of a buggered Minion. She raised herself on her forearms and opened her mouth around his balls; but otherwise remained as still as possible. At a sign from Darné, each Minion then carefully raised first one arm, then the other, transferring his hands to the bare breasts of the woman sucking at his scrotum.

The last four women, the largest and the strongest of those Faithful who had volunteered for the task, now approached. Forced to exercise more care than any of their predecessors, they squeezed themselves into the congested middle of the arena. Wriggling forward on their backs, across a tangle of shifting flesh, each woman raised herself on arms and legs into a shallow wrestler's bridge. She lowered her head until it rested over the shaven cunt of one of her prone sisters; each of the latter then raised her hips

in turn so that mouth and pussy were locked tight. At the same time, each buggered Minion stretched his neck and tongue to their fullest extent, eagerly claiming purchase on a choice of taut, trembling breasts.

Kalya snapped her fingers and the final participants, four powerfully built Minions, scurried forward and dropped to their knees in front of the four athletic women who had preceded them to the fray. Each slipped his hands beneath the buttocks of his female partner, helping to steady her for a moment before pushing forward with his cock and spearing her distended cunt.

Darné and Kalya examined their handiwork from every conceivable angle, prodding thighs, readjusting buttocks, steadying arms and legs. The entire human construction could be entered at only one point – dead-centre between the last four copulating couples – without shattering its perfect balance.

They stood back and admired the shimmering arrangement one last time: four dozen oiled and straining bodies, muscles tensed, sinews stretched to breaking point. The two women exchanged a single word of agreement, then Kalya clapped her hands together twice. As if on cue, the trembling mass of flesh sprang into life. The kneeling men began to buck their hips fiercely, completing their violation of greased, receptive rectums. At the same time, they extended their tongues to lap at the open cunts of the women straddling the men they cruelly buggered. All around the heaving edifice, mouths widened and tongues protruded: lapping into pussies, tugging nipples, teasing pricks and sucking balls. At the entrance to the structure the last four Minions used their powerful hands to hold and probe their partners' tightened buttocks, while scything into cunts that gushed with sap.

Darné and Kalya prayed their Mistress would be pleased with their offering to her. If not, their punishment would be dreadful indeed.

Max couldn't help himself. He rubbed his tired eyes and yawned. Tamara pressed the projector's remote control

and the latest in a long series of now familiar images flashed before him. He knew their faces and their names by heart: Maria Fencenzi, a Colombian drugs baron with suspected terrorist links; Henri Rousseau, a French porn millionaire; Olivia Hernandez, head of several Central American industrial giants; Dostev Onskeya, a Russian arms dealer; Rochelle Hoffmann, a US publishing mogul; Aubrey Manners, the Home Secretary (the only one that had made him sit up in surprise); and last, but by no means least in his opinion, Allessandra Favelli, Managing Director of Diablo Communications (UK) Inc. She had made him sit up, too, but for an altogether different reason.

'Remember every detail, Max,' Tamara told him for the umpteenth time. 'One day it may save your life.'

He prayed she was right. Something had to make this tedium worthwhile. So far the only thing to grab his attention had been the size and shape of Ms Favelli's deliciously extravagant breasts. That aside, he now knew everything there was to know (which in truth was very little) about the seven men and women who made up the board of Diablo Worldwide.

Another image filled the large white screen. No face, no name this time. Just a plain and simple D. He suddenly realised that Tamara was speaking again.

'Diablo Worldwide is the holding company for an international conglomerate controlled by one person: the Contessa di Diablo. She is never seen in public and we know almost nothing about her: background, family, even her real name. Though we assume the directors report to her on a regular basis, we don't know how or when –'

Max interrupted. 'So how do we know she even exists?'

'We don't. Not in the sense that we can prove it with hard evidence. You'll just have to take my word. There have been leads, of course. Her people have slipped up from time to time. The last case my partner and I were on –'

Max cut her short. He had to satisfy his curiosity. 'What happened to your partner? If you don't mind me asking.'

He was pretty sure she did, but he needed to know all the same.

Tamara's face clouded over, and her large green eyes dimmed for a moment.

'His name was Guy Mastermain. We were together for four years.' She paused as if momentarily sidetracked by her memories. 'We'd been trailing two Romanian businessmen we suspected were vampires. There was just one small flaw in our theory: they were able to go about in broad daylight.'

'So you were mistaken?' ventured Max.

Tamara shook her head. 'No. They were vampires all right. That's what made it so serious. Up to now, vampires have been fairly easy to deal with. But if they'd found a way of coping with sunlight, we knew we were in trouble.'

Max nodded. It was a frightening prospect.

'We tracked them to Kracovo, a small village on the Romanian/Bulgarian border. Castle Lénzói.' She smiled unexpectedly. 'Very gothic. Straight out of a 50s B-movie.'

Tamara took a deep breath. Max watched as the circles of her breasts rose, fell and gently quivered. He imagined himself sucking on a hard nipple and considered for an instant how delightful it would be if he could draw sap from her teat as well as her cunt. He would never be out from between those big, delicious orbs. The fleshier ones up top, or the tighter, meatier ones below.

'We'd had them under observation. They'd let slip they were meeting the Contessa. We thought we had her at last. But it was a trap. They were leading us on.'

'Never trust a vampire,' said Max lightly, and immediately regretted it.

'The Castle was wired from top to bottom. We'd guessed it might be.' She held his gaze and smiled weakly. 'You were right. Never trust a vampire.'

This time Max kept silent.

'Guy managed to hold them off. It gave me time to get out. He didn't make it. The whole shebang went up and took the three of them with it.'

'I'm sorry,' said Max.

'We knew the risks,' replied Tamara.

Max nodded with the assurance of a man who now knew where he stood. 'So, we're after vampires, then?'

'No.'

Bugger. Wrong again. He gave up.

'The vampires can wait. This time the Contessa is up to something far more serious.'

Tamara squeezed the remote. A new image filled the screen. It was a book, a very old book from the look of it. Max hadn't seen this one before.

'The *Ghis'kra* – the Devil's Bible,' explained Tamara. 'The original is in the Vatican. Omega has the only known copy.'

'I've never heard of it,' confessed Max.

'Few people have. It was suppressed in AD 98. In this version, the serpent didn't just tempt Eve with an apple in the Garden of Eden.'

Max raised his eyebrows. 'No wonder it didn't catch on.'

'To cut a long story short, Eve gave birth to a daughter, Mádrofh – Spawn of Lust. She was banished to Hell, along with Lucifer. Born of the world; banished from the world. Half-human; half-devil.'

'A kid with a depraved childhood,' joked Max lamely.

'The Devil's Bible begins with a different version of events, and it ends with one, too: the Book of Chaos.'

'Sounds grim,' Max ventured.

'It is.' Tamara's tone changed abruptly. She was clearly quoting now: ' "Mádrofh was born in Lust and in Lust will she return".' The projector whirred, gave a loud click and finally shut down.

'The *Ghis'kra* proclaims that a Final Chaos will descend upon the world. "From Order will come Disorder and the Select of Mádrofh will walk the earth." Mádrofh herself will return and usher in a thousand years of debauchery.'

Max whistled. 'You think the Contessa is one of the Select?'

'She's the Arch-Select. The means by which Mádrofh communicates with her disciples. They call themselves The Order – the last thing they're dedicated to.'

'At least they've got a sense of humour,' ventured Max.

'The Contessa's every scheme has one purpose, and one purpose only: to create a climate of lust which will throw the world into the Final Chaos predicted by the *Ghis'kra.*'

'And we have to stop her?'

'Yes,' replied Tamara. 'Because if we don't, no one will.'

Max frowned for a moment then grinned broadly. 'Piece of cake,' he said.

A pair of massive, oaken doors groaned open, pushed back on either side by four naked, crawling Faithful. A cold, damp wind screamed into the chamber, swirling into every corner of the room, snaking around every rotten, splintered rafter. Darné and Kalya fell to their knees, their heads bowed reverently as the Contessa di Diablo strode into the Great Hall. Her spiked, leather-booted feet resounded across the dry, stone-clad floor. A long, coal-dark cloak flapped loudly in her wake, riding the currents that numbed the air. Sweeping waves of sable-black hair cascaded about her broad and powerful shoulders; loose, fleecy strands of jet curling down around her heavy, gourd-like breasts. Her areolae were inky-dark against her tawny flesh, nipples proud and taut like sharpened crests. Beneath the flowing mantle, her dark flesh quivered and flowed, barely restrained by a tightly sprung lattice-work of silver chains and ancient, creaking leather. Her labia hung open between her legs, the pink wedges of her flesh already swollen with arousal. The forest of hair that matted her sex snaked out along her thighs and up across her lower belly towards the narrow circle of her tightly girdled waist.

She stopped abruptly at the narrow opening to the seething tangle of oiled, pulsating flesh. At a snap of her leather-gloved fingers, Darné and Kalya leapt up, stepped to her rear and relieved her of the cape. The angry squall fell silent and the Contessa's clear, strident voice echoed around the chamber.

'You may pay me homage,' she declared.

The two women fell to their knees, either side of the

Contessa's wide, muscular haunches. Leaning forward as one, they pressed their lips to the hardened flesh of her buttocks, kissing and licking her softly.

'Enough!' she cried and they immediately removed themselves.

Otherwise naked beneath a bewildering array of flesh-hugging harnesses, the Contessa turned about and seated herself on the writhing welter of bodies. All around her flesh met flesh; juices flowed and semen surged; cocks were thrusting, balls were aching, cunts were weeping. She breathed deeply, her head light with the aroma of carnal arousal. She smiled fondly at Darné and Kalya and they knew that they had done well.

The Contessa closed her eyes. She felt her own sap rise in her belly and leak from her dark, hairy vulva on to her big, meaty thighs. She was a queen on her throne. On her Living Throne. She felt truly revived. It was time to plan again. To scheme.

It was time for Chaos.

Three

Allessandra Favelli surveyed the morning papers. With the
exception of one of the grubbier tabloids, which chose to
dwell on the carnal weaknesses of a vicar from Reading,
her company was front-page news. Its proposed takeover
of its largest satellite TV rival had stunned the business
world. Shares in Diablo Communications (UK) Inc. had
risen 42 points on the Dow Jones, with London expected
to follow suit when trading opened.

The whisper of a smile escaped her plum-dark lips. The
Contessa would be pleased. Which was just as well. After
the débâcle at Dorford Haven, The Order was in need of
some good news.

She could not recall the last time she had seen her
Mistress so angry. It was unusual to be summoned to the
Lair at such short notice. This was the second setback in
the past month; first the affair in Romania with those two
Omega agents, now this. No wonder the Contessa had
decided to intervene more directly in today's business.
Allessandra had assured her that she could close the
takeover smoothly, but the Contessa's mind was made up,
and Allessandra was not about to defy her. Not after
Dorford Haven.

Valdez was her responsibility; Allessandra knew she
must take the blame for his appointment. She had
delegated too much to fools who, in their turn, had
delegated to even bigger fools. She deserved to be
punished; as she would punish those who had failed her,
too. But the Contessa had struck a bargain. The use of her

body for a short time. Allessandra knew the risks, but anything was preferable to the alternative: the Darkness in which Valdez now languished.

She closed her eyes and recalled the look on his face when, in the early hours of this morning, she had accompanied the Contessa to the lower dungeons. His screams had been audible from some way off. No opera by Puccini had ever sounded as sweet! It had certainly helped to lift the Contessa's dismal spirits. And hers, too. She had particularly enjoyed that moment when Valdez had spotted them and imagined, poor fool, that relief was at hand, that his torment was over. The Angels had allowed him to break free. It was deliciously wicked of them, because it gave him hope; and hope dashed was the cruellest of punishments. His hands had clawed through the bars and he had screamed, 'Mistress! Mistress!' over and over again, as if it were a magic word that would release him.

She had not realised how spindly Valdez was. It was the first time she had seen him naked: a wiry wriggling of skin and bones, his long thin cock wrinkled and raw. It had not been a pretty sight; yet his suffering had scarcely begun. He had forced his arms and legs out of the cage, twisting furiously as if he might somehow squeeze his way to freedom.

'Feed on, my Angels,' the Contessa had told them, her cold, dark eyes never leaving his. Allessandra knew then that the Contessa had wanted to gorge herself on the man's despair, to taste his terror; and he had not disappointed her. His pupils had dilated, the whites of his eyes filled with blood, and he had screamed. How he had screamed. Especially when they came for him out of the Darkness. It had been a delicious moment.

Allessandra slipped her hand into the slit of her dress and felt between her legs. There were no knickers to impede progress through the thick black curls of her pudenda and into the hot mouth of her sex. Her pussy was weeping softly at the memory of Valdez's distress: his open mouth, his sad, imploring tear-stained face. Raising her fingers to her lips, she saw that the pads were wet and

28

running, silvery pearls of sap dripping into her curled palm. She sighed, and gently licked them clean, savouring the sweet, pungent taste of her own arousal.

Shaking herself free of her daydreams, Allessandra pressed a button on the desk console and spoke to her secretary in the outer office. 'Bethany, any word from Jarvis Trevelyan yet?'

'No, Madam. Nothing. I'm sorry.'

'No matter,' replied Allessandra. 'Let me know when he arrives.'

'Of course, Madam.'

Allessandra flicked the intercom to off. Trevelyan was over half an hour late; doubtless some childish ploy of his to show her who was boss. How tiresome! When he finally showed up he would tell her his company was not for sale after all; the shareholders giving him hell; new contracts signed; long-term trends distinctly rosy. But if she could see her way to increasing her share offer? He would do his best to sway the undecided.

Allessandra Favelli was not a woman to be kept waiting. 'Poor Jarvis,' she growled beneath her breath. She had been prepared to make him a half-way decent offer for his business. But not any longer. Global Cosmos was an essential addition to the Contessa's growing multimedia empire. Crucial, indeed, to her current plans. It would be hers before the end of trading.

Together with the soul of its dour and discourteous soon-to-be ex-proprietor.

Both Allessandra *and* the Contessa would see to that.

Max had always hated hospitals. He hated the inevitable misery that made them necessary; he hated po-faced, overbearing, overworked doctors; he hated nurses with their stern, matter-of-fact manner and their skirts that were never as short as they should be; he hated the heat; he hated the quiet; but most of all, he hated the dry, clinical stench.

He was not in a hospital now, not as such. He was in a small, single-bedded room; but the smell was the same.

There were wires and bottles and sharp, pointed things; and though Max could not be certain where they all began, he could see where they all ended up.

The occupant of the bed was a white male, in his mid- to late-forties, with short, ginger hair and a rough, curly beard. His eyes were closed, and though presumably alive – but self-evidently not well – his breathing was so shallow that his chest seemed not to move at all.

'Who is he?' Max enquired, breathing through his mouth, trying not to absorb the smell that he knew would cling to his clothes and his skin long after he had fled from this place.

Tamara was holding a small blue clipboard, reading silently, and occasionally frowning. 'His name is Hugo Morgan,' she replied, returning the board to its hook at the foot of the bed. 'Professor Hugo Morgan. He's been here for the past two days. He's in a coma. We don't know if he'll recover, though his vital signs are stable.'

'So what happened to him?'

'We're not sure. Not exactly. Hugo is – was – part of an archaeological team working on a site in north Cornwall: Dorford Haven.'

Max nodded. 'I've read about it. Ancient Roman burial site. One of the big American colleges is running the show, with private funding.'

If Tamara was impressed with Max's knowledge, she chose to hide it.

'The team operates a rota system for night work. Hugo was part of the evening shift on Thursday last. It seems he couldn't sleep and went for a walk. There was no sign of him the following morning.'

'So where did he turn up?'

'In one of the site holes, close to where they'd been digging the day before.'

Max nodded towards the silent sleeper. 'Like this?'

'Almost. He's been cleaned up.'

'Why did he need to be cleaned up?'

'Because his body was covered in something no one could recognise at first. The police were called in.

Fortunately for us, the surgeon on call, Dr Phillips, is attached to one of our watching brief teams.'

Max frowned. 'What are they when they're at home?'

'We can't be everywhere at once. There are people we rely on – Watchers – people who operate solely on a need-to-know basis.'

'A need-to-know-as-little-as-possible basis?' ventured Max.

'Exactly. They have no idea of the exact nature of our work. However, if they come across anything unusual, something they think might interest Omega, they call a special number. We take it from there.'

'So why did the good doctor think we might be interested in Professor Morgan?'

'Ancient burial site, a naked comatose man covered in goo. That was almost enough on its own. When he realised what the goo was, it clinched matters.'

'So what was it?' Max wasn't sure he really wanted to know. But there seemed little point in delaying the inevitable.

'A sheen of female ejaculate.'

'What?' Max's voice rose several notches. It was not the answer he had expected.

Tamara ignored his shrill response, reciting the facts quickly and methodically. 'Professor Morgan had indulged in recent sexual intercourse. Or so it seemed. That much Phillips could tell.'

'What do you mean, "Or so it seemed"? Surely he had or he hadn't.'

Tamara ignored the interruption. 'Our own medical team has completed a thorough examination of the body.'

Max flinched. He didn't like the way Tamara pronounced the word 'body'. It made it sound as if Morgan was dead. Death might be an inevitable part of Max's work, but it didn't mean he had to like it. And he didn't.

'DNA tests were positive. Morgan was covered from head to toe in vaginal emissions. Every inch of his body, every nook, cranny and orifice: ears, nose, mouth, rectum, the lot.'

31

'Holy fuck,' whispered Max incredulously.

'Probably more of an unholy fuck,' countered Tamara. 'And that's not all.'

'Not all? What the hell else can have happened to him?' queried Max.

'His body was completely drained of semen. I don't just mean he was empty because he'd reached orgasm. No man ever spends himself completely. There are always traces.' She looked down at the crisp, white sheets. 'But not this time. There was nothing on or in his penis, nothing in his testicles, nothing anywhere. And his body hasn't produced any since.'

'You mean he's been completely drained? Permanently?'

Tamara nodded. 'It would seem so. Yes.'

'What could have done that?'

Tamara turned her dark, green eyes on him and smiled. 'That's what we're going to find out, Max. It's what we're paid for.'

Jarvis J. Trevelyan was not a happy man. He jumped up out of his chair.

'You must be joking!' he bellowed.

On the other side of the desk, Allessandra Favelli's eyes shimmered like two dark coals. She sat upright in her chair, the lapels of her black silk jacket parting like curtains around her large, undulating breasts. The top four buttons of her blouse were undone, so that when she leaned forward, as she now did, Jarvis found his attention hopelessly drawn to the dark swell of her bosom. The way her flesh moved so freely, he could swear that the bitch wasn't wearing a bra. This was no fucking way to do business, he told himself, and felt his cock stiffen. He sat down again quickly, to avoid any immediate embarrassment.

'I never joke about money,' she replied. 'That's my final offer. Take it or leave it.'

'Global Cosmos is worth twice what you're suggesting and you know it!'

'Of course it is,' smiled Allessandra. 'But it's all I'm prepared to pay. It will teach you to keep a lady waiting.'

He eyed her with a mix of lust and anger. Her breasts were advancing again, testing the few remaining buttons that held them captive. The left side of her jacket fell back further, and it became disturbingly obvious that the blouse was see-through. A dull, brown circle stained the crisp white cotton, a plug of nipple distorting the surrounding fabric into an eye-catching diaphanous crest. His balls began to ache with longing.

'You're no lady!' Trevelyan snorted, trying hard to ignore the warm, tickling sensation in his cock. 'And if I'd known this was how you do business, I wouldn't have wasted my time.'

He leaned forward abruptly, reaching for the documents scattered across her desk. Allessandra's long, blood-red nails clawed sharply across his hand. He yelped and pulled back.

'What the hell was that for, you stupid bitch!'

'Oh dear,' she breathed, her dark eyes narrowing. 'That really won't do at all. First you refuse my offer, then you insult me.'

She stood up and, for the first time, he realised how tall she was. She towered over him, her face a dark mask, her features obscured by the room's low lighting. Jarvis knew it was only the shadows cast and his imagination working overtime, but for one brief moment it was not a woman bearing down on him, but a huge, black raven.

'Look, Favelli,' he blustered. 'You may scare others with your breasts – threats!' He corrected himself quickly, though aware that the damage to his credibility was done. 'But not Jarvis J. Trevelyan the Third.'

'Of course not,' she smiled back. 'You Americans are so big and brave. A little woman like me couldn't frighten you.'

He shuddered. She was no little woman. Far fucking from it. Was it him or had it suddenly gotten very cold in here?

'And you want to do something about your lighting, too,' he complained, scratching around for something to say. 'And get some goddam central heating in. Why the hell you don't have a proper office –'

'Oh, but this is my office, Jarvis J. Trevelyan the Third.'
She was mocking him now and he knew it.

Allessandra leaned forward and bared her teeth. Her face suddenly seemed to brighten, as if the dark coals of her eyes had flamed into fire. They were no longer her eyes. He knew that was crazy, but there was something different about her. Something not very nice. It frightened him and Jarvis didn't frighten easily. He tried to look away, but something gnawed at his guts and he felt his chest tighten. Between his legs, his penis continued its treacherous plot to finish him off completely.

'When I said, this is my offer, take it or leave it, I was being less than accurate. What I meant to say was: take it. Leaving it is not, in fact, an option.'

Jarvis recovered himself. They were talking money again. Sex was dodgy territory; money he knew about. He was back on safer ground. He stabbed a defiant finger into the air. 'Yeah, well spin on it, Duchess!

'I'd quit now, while you're only a long way down,' muttered Allessandra darkly. 'You don't want to make matters worse, do you?'

It was no longer her voice. It was harsher, colder too if that were possible. Jarvis shook his head. What the hell was he thinking? Try as he might, he couldn't drag his eyes away from hers. Goosebumps crawled across his skin.

Allessandra moved round to the front of the desk, and perched herself on one corner, deliberately crossing her legs and allowing her black, slitted skirt to fall provocatively open, exposing her leg from her ankle to her buttock.

Jarvis's eyes widened like saucers. His cock began to fight its way free. What the hell was the crazy bitch playing at?

'Do you like what you see?' she asked him calmly.

Jarvis fingered his collar. It had gone from being very cold to being very warm. He managed to tear his eyes away at last, but they were no longer his to command. Now they wandered slowly up over her thigh to her exposed, marble-smooth hip; then higher still, until they reached her

large, free-flowing breasts. He stared, unblinking, utterly entranced as she began to unfasten the few remaining buttons of her blouse.

'Holy shit,' he murmured, as she popped the last retainer. The blouse fell open and two huge, richly tanned orbs spilled into her scooping hands. She cupped them tight and squeezed each breast until the nipples stood out like two large stalks. Jarvis swallowed hard, his heart thumping, his pulse quickening. A thin trickle of sweat ran down the side of his face. He was finding it difficult to breathe, let alone speak.

'What the hell are you playing at, sister?' His blood was turning schizoid, dividing its attention between his flushed red face and his hard, sticky cock. He looked into her eyes. It was a mistake. She held them with her own.

'Oh, Jarvis,' she purred. 'Don't try to resist. You want me, don't you?'

His heart had become a hammer; the pounding loud and painful in his ears. Of course he wanted her. Who the hell wouldn't want her? She was tall and she was dark and she was goddam beautiful. He wanted her all right.

'What would Mrs Jarvis J. Trevelyan the Third say, I wonder?' breathed Allessandra.

He was too far gone now to register the cynicism in her voice. His vision was clouding over, too. His penis had risen several notches in his pants and the muscles in his groin were trembling. There was a dark curtain falling all around him. He wasn't bothered. It felt warm and nice and altogether free of care.

Before he knew what was happening, she sat on his knee, leaned forward and offered him one of her big, friendly breasts. She smiled sweetly, her eyes never leaving his for a moment. 'Would you like to suckle on me?' she asked him.

Jarvis nodded stupidly. This was like a dream; one of those odd, sleepwalking affairs where only half of him knew what he was doing, and the other half didn't really care.

Allessandra pushed his head down, forcing his mouth on

to the dark swell of her areola. His lips dragged at the long, fat plug of her nipple, while her hands moved like claws through his grey, thinning hair. She held his nose and mouth tight against her flesh, scratching his scalp with her painted nails, drawing blood.

His breath began to thud against her teat, the hermetic seal of flesh on flesh making it difficult, if not impossible, for him to breathe. She hugged him harder, pressed her lips to his ear and whispered softly; in a voice that was no longer hers. She seemed so far away and so did he.

'Mistress needs you to do something for her, Jarvis. To prove your loyalty. Do you promise to obey?'

Jarvis's head trembled between her fingers and her breasts, and a muffled squeal, prevented from leaving his mouth, reverberated in the back of his throat.

Allessandra smiled and pressed still harder at the back of his head. 'I want you to die, Jarvis. I want you to die between my breasts. Will you do that for me? Will you promise not to struggle as I smother you with my living flesh?'

Another squeal, another subdued, rattling shudder of his ribcage and Jarvis's hands closed behind the chair, fingers locked together. His lungs were bursting now, his skull throbbing with blood. He wanted to scream and claw his way to freedom, but this strange, seductive woman had asked him not to fight her and her word was law. Had she allowed him a moment's air, he would have asked her to tie his wrists together so that he could not give in to weakness and struggle at the end. But she held him closer still and the knowledge that he would not resist – could not resist – filled his collapsing heart with love and pride. Darkness began to close in on him; rich and warm; deadly yet welcome.

Allessandra suddenly released him and stood up. Able to breathe once more, Jarvis's self-restraint crumpled and he tumbled forward, off the chair on to his knees. His first instinctive intake of air echoed round the room like the scream of a wounded pig. Allessandra crossed to her desk, opened a drawer and extracted a small, transparent container.

'Stand up,' she ordered, addressing herself to the shuddering heap on the floor. Jarvis struggled to his feet, still wheezing loudly.

'Take your pants off,' she told him, returning to the far side of her desk.

Jarvis unbuttoned his waistband and let his trousers fall around his feet. Stepping out of them, he blindly and without hesitation pulled down his brightly coloured boxer shorts. His podgy penis bobbed erect, as if sniffing the air for something.

Allessandra took him into the warm hollow of her palm, her fingers closing sheath-like around his sticky shaft. She began to work him up and down. Jarvis let out a short, happy yelp as his seed gathered at the base of his cock.

'You will remain completely still and make no sound,' she told him, and watched his features contort with the effort of obeying her command. 'Hold back until I give you permission.'

Jarvis screwed up his face; his eyebrows rose and met. He could feel the jism boiling in his shaft, his balls fat and heavy. He hoped he wouldn't let her down. It was so difficult to concentrate, with her long, powerful fingers coaxing more semen from his scrotum. He felt her weigh his sacs in the palm of her hand, as if judging his state of readiness. Then she gripped his cock again and this time began to pump him rapidly.

'You may spend yourself,' she commanded, her expert fingers stroking fast and hard. He gritted his teeth and felt his penis tense for one short, exquisite moment. Then his seed rose like mercury in a thermometer, surging along the heated rail of his shaft.

Thick, white gobbets of cream spat into the air, or would have if Allessandra had not, at that moment, pressed down hard on Jarvis's cock, forcing his knob into the mouth of the small, plastic container. His legs threatened to collapse beneath him and he whimpered stupidly with the effort of remaining upright. Allessandra continued to milk him steadily until his seed was reduced to a thin, languid dribble. Then, cruelly and deliberately, she ran the nail of

37

her index finger along the underside of Jarvis's still erect shaft, tracing a thin red line from root to tip. Jarvis, his body still shaking in the aftermath of orgasm, closed his eyes as if to shut out the awful pain; but otherwise remained silent and unmoving.

Allessandra pushed down on his penis, allowing the blood to drip slowly into the container and mix with his semen. Then, turning her back on him, she placed the jar on the desk, picked up a thick, black pen lying close by and unscrewed one end. Taking great care, she upended the jar and teased the pink, viscous liquid into the open end of the cartridge. She replaced the cap and shook it vigorously.

'Put your clothes back on,' she told him, returning to her chair, sitting down and speaking into the desk console.

'Bethany,' she said. 'Please bring in the contract documents. Mr Trevelyan is ready to sign.'

By the time Bethany entered, an armful of closely typed A4 sheets clasped to her small bosom, Jarvis had restored himself to some semblance of decorum and was seated quietly. Allessandra, for her part, remained gloriously dishevelled, her blouse unbuttoned, her breasts still rolling free. She smiled at Bethany, who looked splendid as always in her plunging halter-neck top, obscenely short skirt, suspendered stockings and high-heeled shoes. Allessandra reached up, slipped her hand beneath the hem of the girl's skirt and squeezed her bare buttock, fingertips straying into the curve of a tight, deliciously sticky crack.

Withdrawing her hand, Allessandra handed Jarvis the pen which she had so recently filled with his own essence. Within less than a minute, he had signed over his entire media empire to Diablo Communications (UK) Inc.

Allessandra shook his hand as they both stood up. 'It's been a pleasure doing business with you, Jarvis J. Trevelyan the Third,' she smiled.

'Likewise,' he replied, content in the knowledge that though he didn't have the foggiest idea what she was talking about, if it was what she had wanted then he was happy to comply.

After he had left, Allessandra Favelli sat back with a

heavy sigh. She closed her eyes and shivered as if exposed to sudden cold. The Contessa's invasion of her body had exhausted her. But it had been well worth it: her sense of excitement had been quite extreme. Jarvis had escaped rather lightly. She remembered the last time the Contessa had made use of her like this. They had almost had to scrape her victim off the walls. The Contessa had departed now. Allessandra's strength was gradually returning. She felt her blood begin to flow again and her eyes opened.

'Bethany,' she whispered softly, to the long-legged girl at her side.

'Yes, Madam?'

'Remove your clothes, please. I'm suddenly in the mood for a little fun.'

'Of course, Madam,' replied Bethany, standing up, reaching down and unzipping the short skirt that concealed her shaven, panty-free and very – very – wet pussy.

Far away, in her Lair, the Contessa sprawled happily upon her Living Throne. Oily humans squelched around her; the smell of frenzied coupling, of raw, forbidden pleasures, filled the air. She had enjoyed her brief sojourn into the outside world. Allessandra's body was a fitting tabernacle for her lust, though sadly too weak and human for her to linger long. Had Trevelyan not been quite so old, so ugly and so sexually inept, she might have been tempted to enjoy him fully, to empty him and break him with another's body. But the flow of a disciple's blood could not be halted for long. Allessandra was too important to risk. She had taken her close once before. Never again. Still, Trevelyan had served her briefly and might serve her in the future, too, albeit in a subtler fashion. Commercially, he was a far from spent force. Like her, his fingers were long and buried knuckle-deep in many pies. What was important was that he was hers now; as one day soon all men would be. For when Chaos came, her lust would carry all before her.

Sweet dreams!

She reached out and stroked a pendant buttock, worming a long, nailed finger into the tight aperture between a pair of broad, female cheeks. Knuckle-deep, she felt the young girl's rectum pulse and quicken. Pushing down with her other hand, she forced her arm through writhing flesh until her fingers closed around the penis of the Minion on whose back she lay. Probing with the one hand and pumping with the other, she wondered which of her servants would be the first to succumb to the flames she was stoking in their bellies. When that moment came, the carefully constructed human edifice would collapse around her. Then she would gorge: on breast and arse; on cunt and cock. None would be spared; her pleasure would devour them all.

Only when she was fully sated would they be allowed to leave; to tend and nurse the wounds she had inflicted.

Then her Living Throne would rise once more.

And the pleasure would begin again.

Four

Traffic was moving at a snail's pace through central London. Tamara thumped the horn furiously as a large black cab pulled out in front of them and forced her to brake.

'Bastard!' she railed, as the driver poked two fingers in the air. 'We should have used one of the Undercors.'

'What the hell's an Undercor?' asked Max, extending his feet towards imaginary pedals.

'Underground corridors,' explained Tamara. 'They run all over London. Unfortunately, only about half of them are mechanised so we'd have had to walk. Mind you, at this rate it would have been quicker.'

'You still haven't told me where we're going,' complained Max.

'Great Russell Street,' replied Tamara distantly, checking in her rear-view mirror before skewing across the path of a second black cab. 'Got you!' she cried.

'Yes, but why?' asked Max.

'British Museum. Professor Abigail Crayshaw.'

'Another professor,' muttered Max, with little enthusiasm. 'This case is becoming clogged up with profs. She another Watcher?'

'No,' replied Tamara. 'One of our advisers. The best. What she doesn't know about the occult isn't worth knowing.'

'You think she'll be able to explain Morgan?'

'I hope so. Or if not, she should be able to tell us where to look.'

'So what's she like, this Professor Crayshaw?' asked Max idly.

Tamara smiled. 'You mean, is she a looker? Or a wrinkled old bag?'

Max shifted uncomfortably in his seat. That was exactly what he meant, though he didn't really care to admit it.

Tamara grinned. 'You'll see,' she replied unhelpfully.

Another black cab. Another furious thump on the horn.

'You were right,' muttered Max, giving his seat belt a precautionary tug. 'We should have used one of the Undercors.'

Professor Crayshaw was not a looker. Nor was she a wrinkled old bag. She was in her early to mid-fifties, her tumbling biscuit-brown hair streaked with grey, her face round and not unattractive. She was also large. Very large. Probably the largest woman Max had ever seen. She didn't so much move as roll across the floor to greet them.

'Tam!' she screamed hoarsely, her friendly grip absorbing half of Tamara's arm. 'Long time no see!' Her big blue eyes danced the length of Max's body, top to toe and back again. 'This must be your new feller! Greetings!' Her hand flashed out a second time, her huge fist devouring Max's fingers.

'Sorry to hear about Guy,' she added quickly, bowling back behind her desk, waving them towards two leather armchairs. 'No word, I suppose?' she gasped, squeezing herself into her seat. She flopped forward as if spent with effort, her huge breasts threatening to pour across the table and engulf them.

Tamara shook her head. 'No,' she answered matter-of-factly. 'But I don't think there's much hope.'

'You never know!' bellowed Crayshaw. 'Stranger things and all that! Vampires that walk in the daylight! Who'd have thought? Whatever next?'

'You've read the file?' Tamara was anxious to proceed. Crayshaw had a brilliant mind, but she could talk until the proverbial cows came home. It was best to get to the point as fast as possible. If not, they might be there all day.

42

Crayshaw nodded furiously. Waves of fat crashed around her body. 'Fascinating! Absolutely fascinating!' she roared. 'Had me foxed for a while, I don't mind telling you.'

Tamara's eyes lit up. 'But you think you've found something?'

Crayshaw shook from left to right. 'Can't be certain. Call it an educated guess. Nothing more.'

'It'll do for openers,' replied Tamara. 'Anything to get us started.'

'Ever heard of the Nhaomhé Chalice?'

Tamara shook her head and looked blank. Max kept quiet beside her.

'Thought not,' continued Crayshaw. 'Hadn't myself till a few hours ago.' She rolled a thick pink tongue around her lips and winked at Max. 'You're a big strong feller!' she chuckled, and Max shifted uncomfortably in his seat. Crayshaw turned her attention toward a tall bookcase just behind him. 'Fetch us that book?' she asked. 'The big green bugger!'

Max stood up, turned round and scanned the shelves. The book in question was on the very top one and he had to stretch to reach it.

'Nice bum!' Crayshaw chuckled.

Max gave a weak smile as he slid the tome across the desk, then sat down again.

'Nhaomhé was a pagan high-priestess. AD 10–20. Can't place her closer than that. Cut a long story short, ran a cult: Dauwteys Desyres. Roughly translated: Daughters of Desire.'

'Devil worship, free love, the usual sort of thing?' ventured Tamara.

Crayshaw nodded and the lower half of her head appeared to merge with her chest. 'But more serious. Got out of hand. Overstepped the mark in a big way.'

'How exactly?'

'Nhaomhé worshipped Vanjja, pagan goddess of lust. Seems Vanjja had crossed one of the smaller cheeses, Zaltaire. Raped his son, Dolmo, the god of virtue. After

43

she had finished, she tied the poor bugger to a rock and let her daughters loose on him. All seven of them. They'd never had a man before, so it was a sort of coming-of-age rite. Took him every which way. Biggest celestial gang-bang on record. You can imagine the brouhaha. Anyway, they were all banished to Vhalgoor – the Underworld.'

'And Nhaomhé wanted to summon them back?' Tamara was speculating now, but she wanted to get to the point quickly.

'Exactly!' confirmed Crayshaw. 'But more than that. She wanted to *be* Vanjja. Or at least allow Vanjja the use of her body on earth. That way she'd be top dog. She organised her own cult. Seven acolytes to represent the seven banished daughters. The idea was that they'd all be taken over, when Vanjja and her man-eating brood returned.'

'So what happened?' asked Tamara.

'They embarked on a veritable rampage,' explained Crayshaw gleefully. 'Sex with anything that moved, not to mention anything that couldn't get out of their way in time!' She sighed dreamily for a moment. 'They had a ready supply of men at first: well, who wouldn't, eh?' She threw Max another filthy wink, and he edged back a few more inches.

'Then the saps cottoned on to the fact that once they'd had sex with a Daughter they were crow fodder.'

Tamara frowned. 'You mean they were into human sacrifices?'

Max shifted position again. He hoped this story wasn't going to turn all gory on him.

Crayshaw nodded. 'The well ran dry. They began kidnapping men for their ceremonies. Terrified the locals silly.'

'So what happened?' asked Max. He felt it was time he made some effort.

Crayshaw's eyes narrowed a little. 'Ever heard of the Hedwynne?'

He shook his head. 'No.'

She looked thoughtful for a moment, opened her mouth

44

and licked her lower lip. 'Hardly surprising,' she said. 'Bit of a mystery even then. They were white witches.'

'The good guys? Girls, I mean,' ventured Max.

'Something like that,' replied Crayshaw. 'Seems Nhaomhé was gearing herself up for Ghalvas Night – one of the unholiest dates in the pagan calendar. That was when she planned the Final Sacrifice, the one that would summon Vanjja and her daughters back from Vhalgoor.'

'And the Hedwynne planned to stop her?' asked Max.

Crayshaw nodded. 'Managed it, too. With a little help from the locals. Caught 'em just in time. Forced one of the girls to confess. Tortured her. Nasty business. Name of Ettae. They still believed Vanjja would turn up to save 'em at the death. Didn't, of course.'

Tamara gestured toward the table. 'So what's in the book?'

'Ettae's confession,' explained Crayshaw, patting the thick dust-encrusted volume. 'Fifteenth-century transcript, mind. Not the original. But all we've got.' Delving into a drawer she extracted a small, silk cloth and dabbed at the cover, her fingers moving deftly across the dark leather binding. Max read the upside-down golden, gothic script with some difficulty: *Pagane Cerymonies: Nhaomhé Evile: Witneffe Off Ettae, A Dauwtey Chosene*.

'It's not for the squeamish,' warned Crayshaw, opening the volume. 'Pretty nasty in places. But, by jove, quite something!' Her small bird-like eyes scanned the first few pages. 'Won't bore you with all the details, just enough to give you the gist.' Hunching low over the book, she found what she wanted and began to read, pronouncing each word slowly, and with care:

*Inne plesure dyd wie tayke hym inne ower sacrede playce
/ e'en thoe he' crie to hev'n ande begge uff stoppe forr
mercie ande forr lovve . . .*'

Crayshaw looked up. 'Sorry, should have explained. Victim was roped to a stone block. Altar if you will. Probably to replicate Dolmo's seduction.'

She blinked rapidly, then added as an apparent afterthought, 'They used ropes made from virgins' hair, you know. To enhance the magic.' Her lips twisted into a broad red slash. Max took it as a smile at best, a smirk at worst. No, on second thoughts, definitely a smirk.

'Right,' he muttered absently, not sure why he felt a need to fill the momentary silence.

Crayshaw's smirk blossomed into a full-scale nuclear grin. It was scary. The woman was crazy, Max decided. Completely stark staring bonkers. March hares and mad hatters didn't get a look in.

'He was stripped, of course, and possibly oiled, though we can't be sure. The accounts are a little vague.'

It occurred to Max that being buff-naked and oiled were probably the least of the man's concerns at that moment. But the professor was speaking again:

'They took it in turns to straddle him.' She paused to repeat the opening words of Ettae's account, ' "*Inne plesure dyd wie tayke hym inne ower sacrede playce*." By her "*sacrede playce*", of course, she meant her vagina. Many pagans saw the genitals as receptacles of the soul.'

'You mean they *raped* him?' Max wanted to be clear about what was being described. It all seemed pretty far-fetched, even to his overactive imagination.

'It was their *modus operandi*,' confirmed Crayshaw. '*À la* Vanjja and her daughters. The victim was drugged beforehand – some exotic potion not handed down to history, I'm afraid.' She looked momentarily wistful. 'By all accounts it not only rendered the penis unstoppably erect but also dramatically enhanced the victim's libido. Sent all their inhibitions right out the window. Ettae describes one occasion where a man actually broke free of his restraints in an attempt to bring himself to a climax.'

Max frowned. 'But if he was being raped, surely –'

Crayshaw foreshortened his enquiry with a wave of her fat hand. 'The drug intensified the man's need for sexual release, but perversely it also rendered him incapable of reaching orgasm.'

She allowed Max a moment or two to digest the

information, then smoothed her palm across the hard, creamy page. 'Can you imagine how the victim must have suffered? The ceremony could last for up to three hours.'

'So what about the women?' asked Max. 'Did they hold back, too?'

Crayshaw shook her large, mobile head; several chins wobbled down to her chest like mini-waterfalls of flesh. 'Far from it!' She turned a leaf and stabbed her fingers halfway down the next page: '. . . *thuffe seated wie as queenes uponne ower throwne / do spende owerselves inne joie uponne hys man / while he do screeme uff forr to lette hym saite hysselffe / inne vaine!*'

Max felt his blood run cold.

'What happened then?' Tamara was speaking now, her bright, green eyes focused on the professor.

'Once each girl had climaxed,' explained Crayshaw, carefully flicking to another page, 'she would relinquish her place to the next in line. But instead of immediately dismounting, she would slide forward, smearing the sacrificial body with her secretions.'

Something stirred at the back of Max's mind and he almost missed the professor's next words.

'While the second girl mounted the victim's penis, the first would straddle his face and arouse herself all over again.'

'Did the men struggle?' asked Tamara. It seemed an unnecessary question in Max's opinion.

'You'd have thought so,' replied Crayshaw. 'But, no. They were happy to be used. The drug, you see. As I said, it removed all inhibitions. They couldn't get enough. The only drawback was the fact that the poor buggers couldn't climax.'

'Where was Nhaomhé while all this was going on?'

'Kneeling to one side, according to Ettae, praying to Vanjja.'

'So let's get this straight,' said Tamara. 'Each girl would rape the victim, reach orgasm, then make way for the next in line?'

'That's right. By continually moving forward across his body, they would soak him with their own ejaculate.'

'Just like Hugo Morgan,' concluded Tamara quietly.

Crayshaw nodded. 'Exactly. Only after the last girl had topped and tailed him, would the high priestess herself enter the proceedings and bring the opening ritual to a close.'

The professor's eyes misted over. Max was unable to shake off the distinct impression that she was enjoying herself a little too much.

'We have no surviving description of Nhaomhé,' Crayshaw continued, 'though doubtless she was a beauty. Pagan priestesses were invariably chosen for their looks as well as for their, shall we say, earthier qualities.' Again, she read from the faded parchment:

> *. . . thenne woold ower Mifftreffe crie uff staye ande do he thynke hys tormente atte an ende / oh emptie hope! / forr nowe inne nayture nakedde woold shae mounte hersselffe uponne hys hedde / ande thuffe hys finalle struggall do beginn . . .*

Tamara crossed her legs and her skirt rode up a little, exposing the top of her thigh. Max cast a furtive sideways glance and felt his penis stir gently as she spoke.

'She sat on his face?'

Crayshaw's jowls shook vigorously. ' "*Inne nayture nakedde.*" ' She grinned at Max, wobbled and winked. 'That's bare-arsed to you, young man!'

Unlike her heaving flesh, Max did his best to appear unmoved. Crayshaw sitting on a man's head was too obscene a prospect to contemplate for long. It would take a crane to lift her off again.

Tamara crossed and uncrossed her long, creamy legs. She was struggling to frame the question. Crayshaw came to her rescue.

'She smothered him: as a sacrifice to Vanjja. A broken neck would have been kinder, and quicker, too. But doubtless not as arousing.' She flicked through several more pages, chewed her lip for a few seconds, then said, 'But there's more.'

There would be, thought Max.

'Nhaomhé would skim the Chalice across his chest, so as to gather an offering of the women's juices. There's a drawing. See!'

Tamara and Max leaned forward as Crayshaw shifted the book sideways on. The sketch was rudimentary: a small rectangle of an altar on which lay the matchstick outline of a prone figure. Straddling its face was a crudely drawn caricature of a nude woman, her buttocks and breasts curiously out of all proportion to the rest of her body. Though rough lines across the victim's body suggested the presence of restraining ropes, its pencil-thin arms and legs poked up at odd angles, hinting at a vigorous struggle.

Crayshaw's face darkened. 'Eventually, the drug wore off. This is where it becomes more interesting.'

Max felt her use of words was less than choice.

'Ettae puts it thus: "*Ower offeryng to Vanjja thuffe performéd / nowe do he wilte at laste / stones heavie wyth hys owné manné-milke.*" I don't think I need to explain what that means, do I?'

'You said there was something interesting,' said Tamara, wanting to keep Crayshaw on track.

'Did I?' she replied absently. Then suddenly her face lit up as if she had been awoken from a trance. 'Oh, yes! Of course! The Sacred Prayer!'

'What's the Sacred Prayer when it's at home?' asked Max.

'By all accounts, once the drug wore off the victim recovered his senses and began to struggle for real,' explained Crayshaw. 'Hardly surprising, of course, with two hundred pounds of hot totty clamped to his face.'

She licked her lips lasciviously. 'Wouldn't have stood a chance, mind. Even untied he'd have been no match for a woman like Nhaomhé. As it was . . .' She made a slicing motion across the bulge of fat that passed for her throat.

Crayshaw paused for a moment, to catch her breath. Max closed his eyes and drifted away, lost in a fantasy: Tamara was bare-bottomed and sitting on his head, bouncing up and down and giggling like a naughty

schoolgirl. It was lovely and he felt his cock begin to swell. Crayshaw's voice dragged him back to reality.

'That was when she began to recite the Sacred Prayer. Look here,' she continued, stabbing her finger at a part of the page they couldn't actually see, and reading on regardless:

> *. . . to Vanjja woold Nhaomhé crie haer sacrede prayere/oh sweete delighte! / ande howe he strugall! / inne vaine! / thow he woold crie haer mercie ande woold begge haer noe yette woold Nhaomhé holde hym faste untille noe brethe remane inne hym / thenne woold he saite hysselffe atte laste inne joie.*

Max frowned. He felt he'd lost the plot a little. Crayshaw caught his eye and grinned.

'She'd hold up the Chalice and recant the magic mumbo-jumbo. At which point, according to Ettae, the man would finally ejaculate. Quite spontaneously. Won't bore you with all the details, but it seems Nhaomhé would scoop up the man's seed in the Chalice, allow the essences to mingle, then drink from the cup while continuing her prayer to Vanjja.'

'And they did this every time?' asked Max.

Crayshaw nodded vigorously. 'Although the final ceremony was to be held on Ghalvas Night, they believed that Vanjja and her daughters drew strength on each occasion they performed the ritual. They were convinced that on the night itself one more sacrifice would be enough.'

'But it wasn't,' said Max.

'We'll never know,' replied Crayshaw. 'Fortunately, they were stopped. Their final victim survived. He corroborated everything Ettae said. As much as he could at any rate.' She flicked back a few pages, to the drawing she had shown them earlier, then swung the book around.

'Though it's only a rough sketch, you'll notice there are vague markings around the sides of the altar.'

Tamara nodded, though she couldn't see the point, and said so.

'The point is,' explained an effulgent Crayshaw, 'that it may represent the wording of the Sacred Prayer.'

'But we don't know what it says,' said Tamara.

'Unfortunately no,' admitted Crayshaw.

Max shifted uncomfortably. He was embarrassed to admit it, but Crayshaw's story had given him a powerful erection. He hoped she wouldn't ask him to return the book to its shelf.

'Be that as it may, the Chalice is what you're looking for,' concluded the professor. 'And no doubt that's what *someone else* is looking for, too. Someone who'll make a better job of things than Nhaomhé ever did.'

Tamara seemed to consider this for a moment. 'You're probably right,' she said.

Crayshaw sat back in her chair and rubbed her chin thoughtfully. 'The Prayer's the key. That's my thinking. Have to do some digging. See what I can come up with.' She paused and chewed her large lower lip. The silence lasted so long Max began to think she'd forgotten what she wanted to say.

'Yes?' Tamara leaned forward, anxious as ever to proceed.

Crayshaw stopped chewing. 'There's an international symposium here in London next week. Pagan culture. Usual stuff. Experts flying in from everywhere.' She paused. 'Arranged for by you-know-who.'

'The Diablo Foundation?'

Crayshaw's innumerable chins chased each other down her face. 'Got it in one,' she replied.

Max looked puzzled. 'What exactly is the Diablo Foundation?' he asked.

'A charitable association set up and funded by Diablo Worldwide,' explained Tamara.

'So is this thing out of the ordinary, then? The timing, I mean?'

'Not as far as I know,' admitted Crayshaw. 'My point is there'll be people there. People in the know. Could be wrong, of course, but it might be worth looking into.'

'Anything will help,' said Tamara. 'We don't have a lot to go on so far.'

51

'Let me do some snooping,' suggested Crayshaw. 'I'll get back to you as soon as poss.'

'Thanks,' replied Tamara. 'What would we do without you?'

'I aim to please.' Crayshaw's shoulders shook and her huge breasts shuddered like giant captive jellies beneath her blouse. 'Anyway, I think that just about concludes our business. My usual payment?'

Tamara looked suddenly uncomfortable. 'I thought perhaps on this occasion . . .'

Crayshaw's eyes narrowed. 'My usual payment,' she repeated, and this time it was a statement, not a question. She stood up and wobbled around to their side of the desk.

Tamara nodded. 'Your usual payment.'

Crayshaw smiled. 'I was sorry to hear about Guy.' She looked Max up and down. 'But I'm sure your new partner is well up to the mark.'

Max frowned. He had totally lost track of this conversation.

Crayshaw chuckled. 'He doesn't know, does he? You haven't told him.'

'Told me what?' asked Max.

A large, meaty arm reached out and stroked the lapel of Max's jacket. 'You're the payment,' revealed Crayshaw, with a big, happy grin.

Max looked totally bewildered.

'It's the arrangement we have,' Tamara confessed meekly. 'Sorry. I meant to tell you. It slipped my mind.'

Crayshaw was already unbuttoning her blouse. Max wondered what size her cups were: something like 500G, he hazarded. She pulled down the lacy edges of her bra to expose the brown dimpled circles of her areolae: long, cylinder-shaped nipples pointed toward him, like twin gun-barrels, cocked and ready to fire. She could put his eye out if she wasn't careful.

Max was struck by a sudden thought. He turned to Tamara, who had made no attempt to leave. 'And you get to watch?' he asked.

She smiled. 'Call it a perk of the job.'

Max swallowed hard. Tamara leaned in close and whispered in his ear. 'Just lie back and think of England,' she advised.

He took a deep breath and began to unbuckle his belt. 'Thanks,' he replied. 'I owe you one.' Then a second thought struck him. 'Shouldn't we lock the door?'

Crayshaw's secretary, Emma, worked in the adjoining office. Unlike her employer, she was short, lean and blonde. She had remained seated at her desk when they arrived, affording Max a bird's-eye view of her brown, bra-less cleavage, breasts flopping loosely inside a half-unbuttoned blouse. His eyes had lingered a fraction too long, so that she had looked up and caught him out; but instead of cajoling him as he had feared, she had simply smiled and licked a corner of her small, cherry-red mouth. Max couldn't help but wish it was her he was about to fuck, and felt his penis bob inside his pants.

'It's all right,' said Tamara. 'Emma won't disturb us.'

'Not unless it's urgent,' added Crayshaw with a wide, lippy grin.

Max pondered this for a moment, absorbing the full implication. 'You mean she knows?'

Tamara shrugged her shoulders a little guiltily. Max's cock rose another notch. He felt like a performing animal at the zoo, yet for some unfathomable reason it aroused him all the more.

Crayshaw reached behind her and, with a flabby scoop of her fingers, cleared the contents of her escritoire. Leaning further back, she eased her voluminous form on to the desk, before hoisting up her skirt and parting her wide, rippling legs. For a moment Max found his eyes locked on to her big black knickers. Then he realised his mistake. Crayshaw wasn't wearing any knickers. The huge expanse of darkness that covered her thighs and belly was something else altogether: a veritable forest of black, snaking curls. My God, thought Max, a man would need a map to find his way in and out safely. But he felt his balls begin to roll and knew he wanted her. Kicking his trousers to one side, he quickly removed his pants. Crayshaw's eyes

lit up at the sight of his thick, marble-smooth erection. She licked her lips.

'My, my,' she breathed hoarsely. 'How generous, Tamara. You've upped the payment.'

Max stepped forward, divesting himself of his remaining clothes. His penis felt stone-hard, flushed with blood, firm and unyielding. Even so, for one moment he paused. He couldn't get the nubile Emma out of his head. Having Tamara watch him perform was one thing. But the door was slightly ajar and he wondered just how much Crayshaw's secretary could see and hear.

'Don't worry,' cooed the professor, mistaking the cause of his hesitation. 'I won't eat you. Not yet ...' And then she laughed in a way that gnawed at his insides; gnawed with sudden, uncontrollable lust.

Max drove forward, surprising both himself and the woman astride the desk. Her arms came up to meet his hands, fingers locked tightly together as he pushed her back. He felt her fatty legs tremble against his own granite-hard flesh as he pushed between her thighs. His penis lunged into the tropical heart of her pubic jungle, searching for the entry point and finding it like a heat-seeking dart.

Crayshaw's legs closed around his waist, holding him fast as his cock eased into her oily depths, like a plug through syrup. Her big, fleshy arms stole across his back, nails denting his skin as she dug with urgent need. Max felt her shift beneath him, her huge behind cascading from side to side as he moved within her.

He reached down and palmed her massive hips. Crayshaw responded by crushing him closer, biting his ear and mumbling, 'Yes! Yes!' He tried clawing his way between her arse-cheeks, down toward her anus, wanting now to probe her most secret place, but the task proved beyond him. Instead he scooped up wads of mobile buttock, kneading and pinching and making her squeal in pleasurable discomfort.

Pushing up with his arms, Max broke her grip, his back arcing like a taut bow. He gazed down, his face tight with effort, squiggles of sweat criss-crossing his chest.

Crayshaw stared back for a moment, her eyes small and cloudy. Then she lowered her lids, and he saw that her lashes were matted and wet with tears. 'Fuck me,' she whimpered. 'Please fuck me . . .'

Max bared his teeth and let out an animal growl, a primitive grunt of power and possession. Somewhere nearby he thought he heard the sound of a chair being pushed back, and feet tiptoeing across a wooden floor. He wasn't bothered. He was too far gone to care. The more the merrier, he told himself as he bucked his hips and felt his penis tense inside the fat professor. Her flesh seemed to melt around his shaft, like warm, bubbling butter. He drove forward, again and again, as if stabbing at her womb, his eyes narrowed, his chest bursting with short, sharp breaths.

Crayshaw opened her huge, cavernous mouth and screamed. Max felt her body jerk beneath him, her pussy tightening sheath-like around his penis as she came. He allowed her two or three seconds' start, before thrusting one last time and taking himself over the edge, too. He felt the seed boil along the length of his shaft, erupt from the eye of his cock and flood into her cunt. Driving himself forward, he attacked with his hips, straining to enter the deepest part of her yielding flesh; so that when the last gobbet of seed spat from his body it would reach the very limits of her hot, voracious sex.

'I'm impressed,' said Tamara as they walked back to their car. 'Not to mention a teeny bit jealous.'

Max grinned from ear to ear and tilted his head like a cheeky schoolboy. 'Next time you'll have to join in. Mind you, I'll have to pace myself.'

Tamara smiled. 'Try taking on the two of us at once, Max, and you'll have less in your balls than Hugo Morgan.'

Mention of the comatose professor was enough to drag Max's mind back to the job in hand. 'So what now?' he asked. 'Dorford Haven?'

'I think so. Whatever's going on, it's going on down

there. You'll be supplied with an alias. I'm staying here for the present. Too many of the Contessa's people know my face.'

Max was about to ask another question. At the time he thought it was important. After what happened next, he was never able to remember what it was. Tamara pushed him up against a wall and kissed him hard on the mouth. Her hand covered his groin and squeezed. When she dragged her lips away and nuzzled his neck, he felt his penis harden and dig into her belly through his trousers.

'We're being watched!' Tamara hissed, before pushing the tip of her tongue deep into his ear.

'I'm not surprised!' groaned Max who wanted to whip out his cock and take her there and then, regardless of the public laws of decency.

'Not that sort of watching,' mumbled Tamara, rubbing between his legs and nibbling at his lobe. 'It's one of the Contessa's men. I'm sure of it.'

Max whimpered in a confusion of excitement and despair. This couldn't be happening to him. He shouldn't be here. He should be at home, tucked up in bed, with Tamara for a duvet.

'Where is he?' he managed to gasp into her shoulder.

'Phonebox across the road,' she whispered, mashing her breasts against his chest, her fingers fluttering lightly beneath his trapped balls.

'Are you enjoying this as much as I am?' groaned Max feebly, half-heartedly turning an eye in the direction Tamara had indicated.

'What do you think?' she purred, bending her left knee and rubbing her thigh against the outside of his leg.

Max spotted the man at once. He looked like a lost tourist, struggling to read a map that clearly made no sense. Hardly suspicious in London, at any time of year.

'How can you be sure?' His voice rose an octave as Tamara deftly unzipped him and pushed her fingers home, circling him where it mattered.

'He's got an erection.'

'He's not the only one! Christ! You'll make me come!'

'So you left a little cream for the cat, Max,' she purred. 'How sweet.'

He felt her fingers tighten around his lust-hardened flesh.

'Do you want it?' she whispered sweetly.

'Of course I want it!' His voice was hoarse, his every thought concentrated on his cock.

'It might make your pants wet.'

'I don't care! I don't fucking care!' He was a spoilt child now and every day was Christmas. All he wanted was Tamara's present. She was milking him so gently, her palm cool around his shaft, her fingernails tickling the hair at the top of his balls. She tugged once, then twice, and pushed him hard against the wall as he came. He felt his penis jerk several times before he collapsed on to her shoulders, happy to let her hold him there as his strength leaked from him along with his seed.

Tamara removed her hand and tongued her fingers dry. Max knew there couldn't have been much to mop up, but from her exaggerated lapping she seemed to be making the most of what little there was.

She leaned against him and whispered sweetly into his ear. 'You owe me one.'

Pulling up his zip, she took his hand in hers and tugged him behind her down the street.

'Where are we going? The car's the other way,' he protested.

Tamara slipped her arm around his waist, her head against his shoulder. 'The man watching us is a Minion,' she whispered.

'A what?' asked Max. His mind was still on other things. A week with Tamara and he could imagine being stretchered out of the service.

'One of the Contessa's drones. They're completely mindless. They'd walk through fire if she asked them to.'

'You mean, like zombies?'

'Not quite. These guys are willing slaves. The word is, she masturbates them into submission.'

Though his immediate lust had been slaked, Max felt his groin begin to tighten.

'They adore her. Once she's worked her spell on them, they're hers forever. Or at least while they're erect. Which they are – permanently. They're incredibly strong, too. You have to jerk them off to stand any chance.'

Max felt his belly flutter sweetly. Blunt-speaking women always turned him on. 'You must have great eyesight,' he said. 'What if he's just horny?'

'He's horny, all right,' returned Tamara. She glanced into the wing mirror of a Mercedes parked on a double line. 'He's also still following us.'

'So what now?' asked Max.

'We take him on a wild goose chase,' replied Tamara. 'Then we lose him.'

'And then what?'

Tamara tucked her arm around his, leaned close and giggled girlishly.

'Then *we* follow *him*!' she said.

Five

'So what now?' asked Max.

They were seated outside a quiet pub, sipping orange juice, just across the street from a dark, soot-blackened building. Its upper-floor windows were narrow, grey and nondescript; those on the ground-floor, however, were large, wide and opaque. Although there were no external signs as to the nature of its business, it hadn't taken them too long to fathom.

Losing the Minion had been easy; following him, easier still. Tamara had told Max they were incredibly strong. It soon become obvious to him, however, that whatever strength they possessed had been diverted into that part of their body immediately below the neck.

'One of us will have to go in,' decided Tamara.

'It's a massage parlour,' replied Max. 'I suppose that narrows the odds a bit on which of us it is.'

Tamara smiled. 'Just a bit.'

He finished his orange juice and stood up. 'Anything in particular I should be looking for? Aside from the obvious.'

'No idea,' confessed Tamara. 'I'll give you an hour. After that, I'll have the place raided. Just in case you've bitten off more than you can chew.' She lowered her eyes to his groin. 'Or someone else has.'

He winced. 'Thanks, Tamara. It's nice to know you've got my interests at heart.'

'Run along,' she grinned. 'I'll sit here and drink. Sorry – think.'

* * *

The Contessa was walking her dog. Or, to be more precise, she was taking Dog for a walk.

Dog was one of her more docile acolytes. She had never known his real name; not that it mattered. All that mattered was his all-embracing desire to serve. Like all Minions, he had come to her with a willing heart and an aching cock. Masturbating him into bondage, she had gazed into his eyes, and had seen deep into his submissive soul. When he had grovelled before her like a faithful hound, licking at her ankles, and gasping his short, heavy breaths of obedience and fealty, his fate had been sealed. The ensuing arrangement of Mistress and pet had been one which, in its different ways, had suited them both.

The Contessa tugged sharply on a long leather leash, and the collar around Dog's neck tightened cruelly. It was a source of some concern to her that the work at Dorford Haven was taking longer than expected. Speed had always been of the essence; now it was even more so. There was danger in delay. Greater danger than even she had allowed for. Perhaps the team Allessandra had assembled was not as good as she had been led to believe. Its leader, Erskine Santer, was, by all accounts, too much of a ladies' man. If only half the reports were true, it seemed that he wore trousers largely to keep his ankles warm. Still, it would be churlish of her to criticise a man for doing what, in her heart, she wished that everyone would do: to satisfy their animal needs and spread the cause of carnal lust. There was yet time for them to prove her wrong. And if they did not, then her vengeance would be dreadful to behold. She smiled. Vengeance was always such a pleasing thought.

She reached the entrance to the lower dungeons. It was very quiet tonight. She wondered what that portended for Valdez. Perhaps he had given up the struggle; perhaps her Angels had finally dragged him screaming beyond all human limits. Or perhaps they were simply taking it in turns to sit on his ugly face and see who could shut him up the longest. As long as they remembered that a man could only survive without air for a short time. It would not be the first time they had forgotten. Her sweet darlings could

be so careless on occasion, mindful of no other thought than their own degraded pleasure.

Two Faithful knelt at the entrance to the lower dungeons, their heads bowed, their eyes averted. Dog gazed up at his Mistress with a wet, expectant glimmer in his eyes. The Contessa rewarded him with a curt smile of approval. Dog gave a yelp of joy and pushed his head down between the legs of the nearest woman, a plump, voluptuous redhead with gourd-like breasts and stout, muscular hips. Nuzzling into her groin, he tried to force her thighs apart with his head, to open up the secrets of her vulva. The young woman maintained her rigid pose as best she could, offering no resistance as Dog wormed his tongue into the slit of her sex, before withdrawing suddenly and lapping at her shaven, satin-soft pussy. Abruptly, he changed tack, scurrying round behind the object of his desire, and wriggling his nose in between her bare buttocks. She fell forward on to her face, her arse-cheeks lifted high in the air. Dog extended his big wet tongue and burrowed into her cleft, lapping at the taut, rope-like surround of her anus. Dipping his head further, he flattened his nostrils over the nut-brown opening, and began to sniff loudly. Between his legs, his penis jerked and bobbed. The Contessa reached down and felt for his balls. They were round, stone-hard and heavy. When she squeezed them, Dog emitted a loud canine whimper. She slapped him gently on the buttock – her sign that he could mate. Immediately, he lifted up his arms and rested them on the woman's broad back. Then he pushed his cock in between her legs, scything into her defenceless pussy. He fucked without finesse, his bony hips rocking back and forth, his balls squashed up against the lower reaches of her arse. It was nothing more than pure animal lust: no feeling, just base, primeval need.

The Contessa judged the moment of his spend to perfection. Looking on with apparent indifference, it seemed she was happy to allow Dog to complete his violation of the delectable young redhead. But that was simply her way of extracting more selfish pleasure from the

situation. She had never allowed Dog's penis to release itself into a woman's cunt, and she had no intention of doing so now. As his body tensed for one brief, pre-orgasmic instant, the Contessa reached forward, slipped her arms beneath his shoulders and pulled him back. His lust-maddened prick emerged with a loud plop, a big, heavily veined column of flesh, slick with female sap. Falling on to his haunches, he threw back his head and wailed miserably; then slumped against the wall, his penis jumping up and down between his legs, a man in torment. The Contessa watched as the seed spat from Dog's shiny glans. Thick gobbets of cream pumped into the air, spraying his belly, his thighs and the dungeon floor.

Then his eyes rolled, he gave a loud, shuddering gasp and fell senseless to the ground. The Contessa smiled. She left instructions for one of the girls to carry Dog's body back to his kennel. He would sleep for two or three hours. When he woke she would masturbate him back into servitude and dream up new ways to tease him. She knew, in his heart, it was what he would want.

'This is our schoolroom,' explained Chloe, the leggy brunette charged with showing Max around the premises. She had a captivating smile: a sweet, upturned nose, immaculate, even teeth and big, red lips. Her pert, well-formed breasts were squeezed into a black PVC bustier, laced tightly at the front. Her lower half had been poured into a pair of white leggings several sizes too small, so that when she walked, her small, plum-shaped bottom bulged deliciously. Her calves were bare; her tiny feet encased in red stiletto heels.

It was the third room he had been taken to so far. The first had been a hospital ward, which he hadn't liked at all. He had done his best to blot out what was on offer there, from a busty nurse in a tight, see-through blouse, a tiny apron and no knickers. The second had been a modern, fully equipped office, where a bare-breasted secretary in crotchless hot-pants was prepared to take down more than dictation while pummelling his tired torso.

The schoolroom was big and airy. There were four rows of five desks, in front of a raised area on which stood a larger table. It struck him that it was just a little bit excessive. Much as all the other rooms had been.

There was a woman sitting at the table. She wore a long black gown around her shoulders, and a small, tasselled mortar-board on her head. Beneath the gown, as far as Max could tell, she had on nothing more substantial than a tiny, scalloped peep-hole bra. Chloe sat him down at a desk immediately below the table. From there, he could see that the rest of the woman's outfit consisted of suspenders, black fish-net stockings, and leather high-heeled shoes. Her pussy was shaven, and her labia partially distended so that the pink inner lips were prominent. Not for the first time on this unusual tour, Max felt his penis stiffen.

'Bad boys are brought here to be punished,' explained Chloe. 'Sometimes they're made to kneel under the desk and lick out teacher while their classmates watch.'

Max felt his pulse-rate quicken alarmingly. But Chloe was already moving on. She took him by the hand, out into the corridor, and then into another chamber, a dungeon this time. There were racks and pulleys, and body-shaped iron cages; not to mention a bizarre array of whips and cudgels, masks and paddles. An open fire blazed in one corner of the room. A woman was stoking it. Apart from a tiny grey cloth around her groin, and leather-strapped footings, she was naked. When she turned round, however, Max saw that she wore a small black mask around her eyes: there was something about it that made him feel uneasy. She was powerfully built, with big muscular arms and legs. Her breasts were huge, tipped with big brown nipples, her upper half spattered with soot. She was sweating profusely from the heat of the fire, her body streaked with grime. He could smell her from the doorway.

'Here a man can really come to terms with his pain,' said Chloe. 'Madam Zelda won't release you until you give her the password.'

'What's the password?' asked Max, judging it as well to be prepared for all eventualities.

63

'Only Madam Zelda knows,' replied Chloe lightly and led him back into the corridor.

'We've got a lot more rooms,' she said with a smile. 'Unless you've already seen something you like?'

Max had seen plenty he liked. And it puzzled him. There was too much here. And not just in terms of sexual excess. The building was not that big. It couldn't possibly house even half of what he'd been shown so far. Whatever else this was, it wasn't just a massage parlour. As far as he could tell, whatever it was, it shouldn't even be able to exist.

'Perhaps you'd just like a rub-down?' Chloe smiled. He wished she wouldn't; it did funny things to his stomach. What he should really do now was what the Sunday journos always claimed to do: make his excuses and leave. But it seemed such a waste. He couldn't see the harm in staying just a little longer. It might relax him. He glanced at his watch. He'd been here half an hour; he had another thirty minutes before Tamara ordered in the troops.

'That'd be great,' he decided and followed Chloe's tight little bottom back along the corridor. Which was when he noticed another odd thing. He must have been in half a dozen rooms, and they'd all been empty apart from a presiding female. Now the doors were shut and there were noises coming from inside each one: smacking, screaming, laughing and moaning. They were in use; every one of them now occupied! It didn't make sense. Nothing about this place made sense.

They passed through into a room smaller than any he'd been in so far, with peach-coloured walls and a thick, soft carpet. A low, black massage table stood in the centre. A rich, pungent smell filled the air: a blend of aromatic herbs and spices. Max took a deep breath and felt vaguely light-headed. Chloe gestured at a couple of hooks on the wall. 'You can hang your things there,' she said, with her big, friendly, tummy-wobbling smile.

As Max began to undress, Chloe opened a cupboard and removed several items: jars, and tubes and what looked like clusters of broad, pink ribbons.

'Do you want anything in particular?' she asked softly.

Yes, there was something Max wanted in particular. He wanted her in particular. He wanted her across the table, her delectable little bottom in the air, her small, apple-hard breasts filling his hands while he fucked her until neither of them could stand. But he didn't want to sound desperate.

'I can recommend the Double Delight,' she continued. 'It's expensive, mind, but well worth it.'

Max wondered how much of this he could legitimately claim back on expenses. All of it, he hoped. The Double Delight sounded too inviting to resist.

'Why not?' he replied, quickly removing his pants. There was no time for false modesty. The clock was most definitely ticking. Chloe's eyebrows rose a fraction and her tummy-wobbling smile broadened into uncharted territory.

'I'm not sure the Double will be enough,' she grinned, her eyes wandering the length of his cock, as it rose like a thick marble column between his legs. Turning away, she drew back a small hatch-shaped section of wall, curled a finger and beckoned him over. When Max peeked through, he found himself looking into a room full of young, beautiful and very naked women. He counted twelve in all. They were standing in a line, six looking straight ahead and six with their backs to him. What really took his attention, however, was the fact that the girls were manacled and standing on tiptoe, their arms stretched towards the ceiling. Their positions alternated, so that as he ran his eyes along the trembling line of flesh, he could feast on a seductive vista of pussies, breasts and buttocks. A thirteenth woman strolled up and down, examining each of the captives in turn. She wore a plunging black basque, tiny leather thong, thigh-length boots and small face mask. As she moved along the captive wall of flesh, she tapped a short tawse against her thigh, and occasionally pawed one of the women with her gloved fingers.

'Who would you like?' asked Chloe.

Max found it hard to tear his eyes away from the line of bodies. To tell the truth, he wanted them all. But that was being greedy. Besides, Trask would have a coronary if that particular expenses sheet slid across his desk.

'Whoever you choose will be very grateful,' said Chloe. 'They're due to be beaten in five minutes.'

Max looked at her. He wasn't sure how to respond. He could hardly come the heavy and threaten to report her to the appropriate authorities. That would well and truly blow his cover. Besides, he was sure this whole thing was a charade set up for his benefit. If it wasn't, then at least he could spare two of the women from an imminent thrashing.

After a few moments' consideration, he opted for a tall, wide-hipped brunette and a short, rather petite blonde; it felt uncomfortably like choosing fish from a restaurant tank. Chloe shut the hatch and went through into the adjoining room, giving Max a short pause to reflect. So far he hadn't really learned a lot – just that things were not what they seemed. How much ice that would cut with Tamara, he had no idea. Still, he wasn't going to let it ruin his enjoyment of the next half-hour. He took his watch from his jacket pocket and glanced at it. OK, then, seventeen minutes; which left another five to dress and leave before Tamara sent in the stormtroopers.

Chloe returned, followed by the two girls Max had chosen. Close up, they looked even more gorgeous. The muscular brunette had large, cushion-like breasts, a narrow waist and long, circular buttocks. The blonde was very much smaller, with tiny lemon-shaped breasts, narrow, boyish hips, slender legs and delicate, perfectly formed feet.

'This is Raya,' said Chloe, introducing the taller woman, 'and Annie,' she added, her arm around the blonde girl's shoulder. She smiled her lovely winning smile for the last time and said, 'I'll leave him to you, girls. Don't be too gentle.'

Max watched her retreating buttocks jostle each other as she left the room. He offered no resistance when Raya made him lie on his back, then used the silk ribbons to secure his wrists and ankles to metal links at each corner of the table.

Annie, meanwhile, opened up two bottles of clear,

scented oil and proceeded to smear his body from his chest to his feet. She took particular care with his penis, coating not just the shaft, but his balls, too. By the time she began work on his thighs, his cock was straining against his belly, the skin of his scrotum stretched and slippy.

Opening up two larger bottles, the women proceeded to drench themselves, taking several minutes to work the oil into their flesh from head to toe. Max felt his groin tighten with raw animal lust when the girls began to knead their breasts and buttocks, hands circling the swell of their glistening vulvas. If this was part of their design to turn him on, he reflected, it was working.

They began to massage him slowly. Raya started at his chest and worked her way down, while Annie began at his feet and worked her way up. The closer each came to his penis, the more aroused Max became. Though he was desperate for them to get on with it, even he had to admit that delaying that exquisite moment when they would meet at his groin left his excitement balanced on a knife-edge. However, when at last they reached his cock, they chose to ignore it, rubbing his tummy instead and around the top of his thighs. Occasionally, one or the other caught his shaft with the edge of her hand. Each time Max raised his hips expectantly, certain that this was the moment they would take him between their fingers and stroke him to a climax. But they knew what they were doing, constantly postponing his release. He was left groaning feebly, straining against the tightly knotted ribbons that held him in place.

When they finally allowed their hands to stray across his cock and balls, Max closed his eyes and emitted a long, strangled sigh of pleasure. But their touch was too light, and he was again denied that extra nudge of friction needed to take him over the edge. Instead, they changed tack altogether. First, Raya tied Annie's hands behind her back, before securing her feet. Then, to Max's astonishment, she hoisted up the lighter girl and laid her down on top of him, so that their faces touched. Annie turned her head slightly and kissed Max on the lips, pushing her

tongue into his mouth. Max wriggled his hips, in the vain hope of insinuating his penis into her slippery pussy. But she was too short and too far forward; the best he could manage was to nudge the edge of her labia with the tip of his cock. It was enough to trigger a fleeting surge of heat along his shaft, propelling a dot of come from the eye of his glans.

Raya took hold of Annie and swivelled her round, jiggling her small frame, using her like a damp cloth across Max's body. At one point, with Annie's head facing his feet, Raya dragged her backwards, so that for one teasing moment her thighs passed around his head and her pussy brushed against his lips. Max extended his tongue to stab at the tight runnel of her sex, but he barely made contact before it was pulled away. Salt and oil lingered on his tongue; musk filled his nostrils. He was almost at the end of his tether. If this was Double Delight he wondered what Double Distress was like.

Lifting Annie free, Raya quickly untied her. Now she straddled his chest and leaned forward so that her breasts covered his face. She moved them from side to side, soaking his face in oil, always moving just a little too fast for him to catch either of the nipples with his mouth. Behind her, Max felt Annie's fingers cuddle his balls, rolling them in her hand. Then he felt the fingers of her other hand circle his girth. She began to stroke him in a way that suggested he was about to get what he had not yet paid for. Raya lifted her hips and Max could see straight down between her legs; the sight of Annie masturbating him so gently took him that little bit closer to the edge. What he wanted now, more than anything in the world, was for Annie to excite the seed from his cock and then for Raya to engulf him with her cunt and finish both the job and him. Preferably while Annie continued to milk him with her long, pliant fingers.

Nearby, Max heard a door open. Despite himself, he craned his neck and saw Chloe return. She was no longer dressed in her figure-hugging top and sprayed-on pants. All she wore now was a pair of tiny white knickers. Her

breasts were small and hard and barely moved as she walked. Max felt the seed begin to spill from his balls and into his shaft. He hardly knew where to look next or what to think. He wanted to close his eyes and indulge his most obscene fantasies, but he wanted to keep them open, too, in case he missed anything.

Chloe stood over him and he caught a faint whiff of something sweet. It wasn't a female smell. It was something else that he couldn't quite place.

'You've been a naughty boy,' said Chloe quietly.

'What do you mean?' he asked, genuinely perplexed.

'You lied to me. You're not what you seem, are you?'

Raya slid backwards, on to Max's tummy, allowing Chloe to straddle the upper part of his chest, though taking care not to sit on him and grease her thighs. Her vulva bulged in a way that wasn't natural. The smell he had caught grew stronger. It was coming from between her legs. He suddenly knew what it was: chloroform. She was wearing a pair of chloroformed knickers!

Max tried to shift his head but it was a pointless manoeuvre. Chloe lowered herself on to his face, her big crotch covering his nose and mouth. He held his breath. Somewhere out of sight, fingers were tugging at his cock. Chloe looked down at him and smiled.

'I've got all day,' she said softly, though it was obvious she wouldn't have to wait that long. The fingers at his groin were making sure of that. His penis tensed, twitched and spat. Max felt his seed splatter his belly. Then something hot and humid engulfed his penis, and he realised that Raya was fucking him. A minute ago it had been his dearest wish; now it was the last thing he needed.

Max screamed out with the pleasure of release, and then breathed in involuntarily. Chloe stroked his hair gently and smiled. 'That's right, Max, deep breaths. Nice deep breaths. Don't fight me. It'll soon be over.'

She hugged him to her cunt and smiled again. Her smile was the last thing he saw before everything went suddenly and irretrievably black.

* * *

Tamara had left the pub. The sight of an attractive young woman, seated alone, and in a skirt that barely covered her buttocks, had proved an irresistible allure for too many of The Merry Monk's lunchtime regulars. Eventually abandoning all hope of a quiet, uninterrupted drink, she had fled. It was a nuisance not being able to keep watch over the road, but she reasoned, not improbably, that Max was unlikely to emerge until his allotted hour was up. Besides, she had had an idea. It was something of a long shot but worth considering. She needed a quiet, preferably secluded spot in which to test her theory, and a narrow thoroughfare, twenty yards from the pub, seemed to provide it. There was only one door into the street: the tradesman's entrance at the rear of a small boutique. Tamara settled herself on the cold, grey step and removed a small laptop from her shoulderbag. She switched it on and tapped in several long codes. A series of coloured map images flashed across the screen. This part of London, as she had told Max, was riddled with Undercors. It had belatedly occurred to her that there might be one running beneath the massage parlour. An alternative route in – and maybe out – could prove useful if Max discovered anything worth investigating.

At first glance, three tunnels looked vaguely promising. On closer inspection, however, it became clear that though they passed close by and even, in one case, right under the establishment, there were no exit points. Short of requisitioning a pneumatic drill and relying on the entire staff being stone-deaf, there seemed no point in pursuing the idea further. Shame, Tamara thought, and switched off the computer, storing it away in her bag.

It was at that moment that things began to go a little awry.

Something pushed her on to her back. But she was still sitting upright. She was floating on a fluffy white cloud, and there was a warm, faintly tropical aroma in the air; except that the hard edge beneath her buttocks reminded her that she was still perched in an alley doorway. Inside her head, a voice called out to her. Arms circled her body,

70

a finger touched her lips and someone shushed her gently as she opened her mouth to speak.

Guy Mastermain was kneeling between her legs, one hand on her thigh, the other stroking the side of her face. He was naked. His cock was erect, the foreskin drawn back over a familiar plum-shaped knob; a knob slick with semen. It was bubbling out of the eye of his glans and dribbling along his shaft. Tamara had never seen anything like it. She shook her head. It occurred to her that she was dreaming. But how could you ever tell? It didn't seem like a dream, but if it was one, then it wouldn't, would it?

'Guy?' she whispered. 'Is it really you?'

What was she thinking? Of course it wasn't Guy. Guy was dead. She'd seen him blown to pieces in a rather nasty explosion. No, correction, she'd seen a castle blown to pieces. She just assumed, a fair assumption she told herself, that Guy was inside it at the time.

Guy – or whoever it was kneeling between her legs, his penis dribbling like a fat, juicy pear – moved closer. His fingers began to scrabble about beneath her skirt, his hands tugging down her knickers. Instinctively, Tamara raised her bottom, to facilitate their removal. She drew breath sharply when he ripped at her top, tearing it, and exposing her bra. He pulled at the jagged satin cups, freeing her breasts, before lowering his head and enclosing her left nipple with his mouth.

Tamara felt a raw, animal need surge through her belly. She no longer cared what was happening: all she wanted was to fuck. She lifted one leg and curled it around Guy's waist. She looked down through the tangle of their bodies and watched the semen dripping from his cock, coating her pubes and dribbling on to her thigh. My God, she found herself thinking – how much does this man have inside him? As he drove down with his penis, Tamara lifted her buttocks, altering the angle of her cunt so that he entered her smoothly. She bent her back and screamed. Guy's cock seemed to fill her in a way it had never filled her before. His glans touched the neck of her womb, and she felt the hot, rapid spurts of seed splattering against the insides of

her cunt. She was clawing at him, fingers digging into his flesh, her nails ripping at him like a wild animal. Now he pressed one hand beneath her buttocks, wedging his palm into her cleft. She felt first one, then two, then three of his fingers wriggling into her anus. It was as if something warm and wet was filling her rectum, as if feathers were tickling her bowels.

'Guy!' she managed to gasp. 'How? I don't understand! How?'

His tongue-tip darted into her ear, making her giggle and squirm. She screamed as the first orgasm hit her, all thoughts of how or why abruptly banished. A perverse pleasure clawed at her insides. It was so different from anything she had ever known. The rush of excitement didn't begin in her cunt; incredibly, it seemed to burst from the depths of her finger-fucked arse.

Now Guy was gasping, his voice both near and far away all at the same time. She was vaguely aware of something behind the words, too: delight, and longing, but most of all, pain.

'Contessa . . . Help me . . . Contessa . . . Tam . . . Tam . . .'

She knew she should draw back, that she should close her mind to the pleasure welling in her guts. Guy was trying to tell her something. But this was so good. He was so good. He was fucking her harder than ever, driving his cock in and out of her cunt. His teeth were tearing at her breasts, his fingers scrabbling at her bottom. He was still coming, and so was she. A second wave of delight crashed against the rock of her clitoris, making her arch her spine and squirm with pleasure.

And then it was over, as suddenly as it had begun.

Tamara fell back and bumped the side of her head on the door. Her hand brushed her thigh and she felt her fingers slide through something warm and sticky. Guy's semen was spilling from her cunt and pooling across her skin. So much seed. She had never known so much seed.

Nor had she known so much pleasure. The feelings that had swamped her body had been of an intensity she could scarcely begin to describe.

But there was something else, too. Something in the voice that had come to her out of the ether: Guy's voice. In it there had been something that swept away the last shards of sleepy pleasure from her still trembling tummy.

It was fear. No, it was more than fear.

It was terror.

Six

Max knew he was in trouble. He was strung like a bow from the ceiling, suspended by several long metal chains. Broad leather hoops pinched his wrists and ankles, and a fierce heat stung his bare flesh. He was back in Zelda's dungeon. He shook his head. How long had he been unconscious? Where was Tamara? Where was the cavalry?

He was not alone. Raya and Annie stood to one side of him, Chloe to the other. Their naked bodies glistened with oil and sweat, and shadows danced across their skin. To his surprise, Max saw that there was another man tied up nearby. He could just make him out through a narrow doorway to his left. Then he blinked and realised his mistake. He was staring into a tall swivel-mirror. Its gilded, ornate presence seemed rather out of place in a chamber dedicated to darker pursuits than those of vanity. Ugly gold and silver serpents slithered around its rich, mahogany edges, brought to life by the flickering brands. Max felt suddenly and unaccountably cold in spite of the heat of the room. Straight ahead of him, he was able to make out the grey, dirty outline of Zelda, the dungeon-keeper. She had her back to him, stoking up the fire. Though she still wore a tiny, protective girdle around her waist, each time she bent low to prod a coal or rake some ash, the huge, muscular cushions of her backside rose and trembled in the air. A long shadow seemed to split her flesh in two; sweat dribbled from the deep cleft of her arse, scoring her big, meaty thighs. Thick black tendrils of soot and perspiration streaked the insides of her legs.

Chloe stepped forward. 'Awake at last, Max,' she said. 'We thought you'd never come round.'

He had given them his real name because it seemed easier than lying. But that was all he had done. He couldn't see why they should suspect him of anything. Was he really that obvious? Tamara would give him hell for this. Though that, he reasoned, considering his present predicament, was only if he was lucky. Very lucky.

'Who are you, Max? Who do you work for?'

Chloe's voice was soft and friendly. She stroked his face and smiled. Max let his eyes wander over her firm, sculptured breasts, her cherry-red nipples, her tiny waist, her flared hips, her long slender legs. His penis was already erect; it had been hard when he woke. Now, if anything, it grew harder.

Chloe bent forward and kissed him on the forehead. 'If you don't tell us Max, we'll have to hurt you. And I don't want to hurt you. But I can do very bad things when I need to.'

'I don't know what you're talking about.' Suspended as he was, his throat was stretched and it was difficult to squeeze out the words. He hoped they sounded as sincere as they were false.

Chloe smoothed the hair either side of his face, nibbled lightly at her lip for a moment or two and managed to appear very concerned.

'This is your last chance, Max. Do it for me, Max. Do it for Chloe.'

'But I don't know what you're talking about. I'm a salesman, I told you.'

He *had* told her that. He wasn't quite sure why. It seemed a bit silly now.

Chloe frowned. 'Oh dear,' she sighed, then leaned forward and whispered softly into his ear. 'You're in trouble now, Max. Big, big trouble.'

Max had little doubt of that. What shocked him was the way his cock tightened at the thought of what these women might do to him. It felt as if someone was screwing his prick into place.

'What time is it?' he asked.

'Why?' asked Chloe. 'Are you expecting help?' She laughed. 'I shouldn't worry your little head about that. No one's going to find you here.'

She said it with such certainty that he almost believed her. But he knew that she was wrong. He must have been here for an hour at least. Thirty minutes on the grand tour. Fifteen minutes on the massage table. Surely another fifteen minutes out for the count. Any second now the front door would be matchwood and half a dozen stout coppers would arrive to extricate him from this mess. Okay, so it would be embarrassing to be found like this, but he could cope with that as long as they didn't know who he was or where he lived.

Chloe moved to his rear, raised one leg and straddled him. Max felt his spine curve painfully. He wondered how far it could bend without breaking. It was not a particularly cheering thought. He was still thinking it when Chloe lifted her feet off the ground, and transferred her full weight on to his back.

'Let's go for a ride,' she laughed and slapped his rump fiercely. 'Giddy-up!' she giggled, bringing the flat of her hand down several times more on his bare arse.

Raya was holding something in her hand. Max hadn't noticed it before. Now, it was difficult to ignore – it was a large strap-on dildo. She buckled it around her waist, then picked up a small glass vessel from a nearby stand. Removing the lid, she inserted her fingers, scooped out a handful of thick green jelly and began to coat the phallus with liberal amounts of grease. When she had finished, she moved out of sight, still clutching the jar. Bugger, thought Max, then wished he hadn't. He winced as his buttocks were forced apart. A hand pressed up against his anus, smearing it with warm fat, tickling his sphincter so that it convulsed around the fingers that now pushed into his rectum. Chloe's hands overlapped across his mouth, so that when he tried to speak, his words were muffled against her warm palm.

'Hush, boy,' she cooed gently. 'We don't want to disturb the neighbours, do we?'

Max would have swung forward, sideways, anything to save his arse from being impaled, but Chloe put her feet down and held him fast. Raya rested her hands on his buttocks and began to move slowly and rhythmically between his legs.

Annie knelt at his side and felt for his penis. It probed the air, a thick column of lust-hardened flesh. Max grunted into Chloe's hands as Annie's fingers closed around him.

'I think he wants to mate,' she giggled.

Chloe slapped his bum again. 'Is that right?' she asked. 'Is our stallion ready for stud duties?'

Without waiting for a reply, Annie slithered beneath him, wrapped her long arms around his neck, then raised her legs and circled his waist. The fluffy curls of her pudenda tickled his cock, and the deep runnel of her sex smeared his shaft with a sultry wetness.

Max's brain was now on auto-pilot. His body felt as if it were being ripped apart, borne down between two warm, voluptuous weights, while behind him Raya continued to ream his arse.

Chloe leaned forward and pressed her wet lips to his ear. 'Are you frightened, Max?' she whispered, licking softly at his lobe. 'Because you should be. We haven't even begun yet!'

She pulled his head back sharply, forcing his mouth open. Zelda the dungeon-keeper came forward. Max had forgotten all about her. She lifted one of her hefty breasts and manoeuvred as much of it as she could into his mouth. Sweat and dirt mingled on his tongue, her salty essence dribbling into the back of his throat. Chloe pushed hard at the back of his head, forcing his nose into the woman's damp expanse of flesh, making it hard for him to breathe. When he did, the stench of her body was enough to make him gag. The fat plug of her nipple drove against the roof of his mouth as if she were trying to force the whole of her breast past his lips and down his throat.

Another solid spank on his rump from Chloe was followed by a further thrust from Raya. Zelda withdrew her dirty breast, raised her hips and pushed her

evil-smelling cunt into his mouth. Her thick, wiry pubes were hot and sopping. The mix of sweat and musk formed a pungent assault on his taste-buds: a dark, earthy, primeval mixing of raw essences.

'Are you thirsty?' asked Chloe.

It was clearly a rhetorical question, because she didn't wait for Max to answer. Instead she slapped him hard for the umpteenth time, giggled loudly and said, 'Then have a drink!'

Zelda gave a fierce grunt and wriggled her cunt. Warm pee hit the back of his throat and Max gagged. His entire body went into an instinctive spasm. He was hardly aware of Annie easing her humid vulva down over his shaft and engulfing him properly for the first time. She began to work her powerful vaginal muscles, so that her cunt seemed to be sucking on his cock. Max felt the seed flood from his balls and overflow into the base of his prick. His back was awash with liquid heat. Chloe rubbed herself back and forth, grinding her clitoris against the ridge of his spine, from base to neck. She was warbling girlishly, bouncing with excitement, and smacking his rump harder than ever. Behind him, Max heard Raya scream as a final thrust took her over the edge. Chloe yelled happily at the same time, while beneath him Annie sobbed with delight and her oily sex tightened around his cock. Zelda rubbed the bullet of her clitoris against his upper lip and continued to relieve herself into his mouth. Her juices mingled with her pee, some running down his throat, some spilling out over his lips and down his chin.

Max felt he was going to explode. His own orgasm welled up inside him. Deep in his bowels, Raya hit some magic spot. Beneath him, Annie's milking muscles sent the semen surging into his shaft. It was suddenly all too much. Max emitted a mad, muted bellow into Zelda's capacious cunt and surrendered to bliss.

A bliss that died halfway along his cock.

He swung furiously, no longer caring about the fact that he was being raped, buggered, and used as a human chamberpot. All he cared about was that he hadn't

climaxed. Every muscle in his body screamed in pain and protest.

A voice whispered in his ear. 'Oh no, Max. You're not allowed to come. It's against the rules. You can only climax if we let you.'

He shook horribly. Annie had already slithered off his cock, denying him a last chance to reach orgasm.

'First tell us what we want to know, Max. Then we might let you come.'

'Get fucked!' yelled Max angrily.

'Oh we intend to, Max,' cooed Chloe. 'All night long, if we have to . . .'

Tamara had recovered herself. When the grey mist had cleared from her head, she was still sitting on the cold, hard step outside the boutique. Guy had gone. So, she was beginning to feel, had much of her sanity. Her bra – she had thought – had been ripped to shreds, but now it was perfectly intact. True, her knickers were down around her ankles and her cunt was wet and weeping. She knew she had come; the gentle pulsing of her body confirmed that. But there was no semen leaking from her pussy, and none congealing on her thigh as first she had imagined.

None of it made sense. She wondered if she'd had a fit. She'd never really mourned for Guy; there hadn't been time. Besides, though they were close, it was as partners in Omega, nothing more. Emotional attachments were a luxury she could not afford. Perhaps her grief had all welled up in a moment; perhaps this was her mind's way of dealing with the loss. And yet it had been so real. It was as if Guy had really been there. But that was crazy. It didn't make any sort of sense.

She looked at her watch. Damn! An hour and five minutes had passed since Max had entered the massage parlour. It was time she got a move on. Hopefully, he was waiting for her at the pub. She didn't need any more surprises today.

There was no sign of him outside The Merry Monk, so she poked her head through the doors. It was busy but,

again, no sign of Max. That settled it – he must still be inside the massage parlour. But that could only mean one of two things: either he was enjoying himself too much; or he was in trouble. She tossed a mental coin and it came down bad. Taking out her mobile, Tamara hurried back into the street, tapping in numbers as she walked. Then she pulled up dead. She looked across the road and blinked. Looked and blinked again. Carefully, she returned the phone to her bag. There seemed little point in making her phone call now; little point in summoning the local police to raid the massage parlour. After all, they couldn't raid what wasn't there.

Perhaps she *was* going mad. Perhaps it was all the strain of the past few weeks. Perhaps she needed a long break. First Guy, now this.

She looked one last time to make absolutely sure. But there was no doubt about it. The massage parlour had gone. In its place, large as life and twice as imposing, was a small, Tudor-timbered antiques shop. It didn't make any sense. It didn't make any sense at all.

The Contessa held the golden phallus between her long, slender fingers, examining the clouded glans-shaped sphere at its topmost end. Her dark, hooded eyes narrowed and her voice, when it came, was low, sonorous and full of muted anger.

'Where did you go, Guy? Let me read your thoughts. No? You should not defy me. I will not have it!'

She twirled the phallus around in her leather-covered hands. The débâcle at Lénzói had not been without its advantages. True, the accursed Knight woman had escaped, but that was a minor point. She could be dealt with at any time. Capturing the soul of her partner, Guy Mastermain, however, had been a delightful and most unexpected bonus. It was as well that she had been there; as well, too, that Mádrofh had prepared her and taught her this new trick. She twirled the phallus once again. She had imagined that Guy was trapped inside the sphere; caught between this world and another. But it seemed she was

wrong. He had escaped for a short time. Only a short time, it was true, but she had not expected it and it had angered her. She wanted to know how and why. But it was not easy communicating with Guy. If he had been alive, truly alive that is, she would have entered his mind: that was another trick Mádrofh had taught her. If he had been dead, Mádrofh might have brought him to her. But he was neither dead nor alive and it was that which complicated matters.

Now she could only read his thoughts with difficulty. But while she held him captive, she held something which might have its uses. And pleasures, too; for she had discovered a most wonderful fact about Guy's imprison-ment within the sphere. When she held the phallus and suffered pain – as she sometimes did for pleasure – he suffered pleasure, too. Or rather, instead. And when she suffered pleasure, he suffered pain. The more extreme the one, the more intense the other.

The Contessa held the globe-end of the phallus towards her body now, pushing the glans down through the thick luxuriant mat of her pubic hair. She knew that inside the sphere, Guy was travelling through her wiry curls, his entire being centred wherever she centred the phallus. She stroked her labia and forced them open. Then she watched her juices coat the smooth, rounded shaft, and dribble on to the golden sphere. Closing her eyes, she felt Guy's fear as she edged the top of the phallus closer and closer to her opening. With a sudden pull she struck her clitoris and fell to her knees in a swoon. She began to rub furiously, her pleasure heightened; again she felt Guy's pain, felt his every nerve on fire as her excitement grew. She should have drawn it out, made him suffer for his sins, but all she wanted at this moment was to satisfy her own longing. She felt the need boiling in her belly. Sap began to issue from her cunt, running down the insides of her thighs. Guy was in distress, that much she knew, that much she felt, and it made her rapture all the greater.

At the moment of orgasm, she moved the phallus lower, changed its angle and, as she came, pushed it hard into her

vulva and began to fuck herself rapidly. From somewhere deep within her cunt, she heard a long drawn out wail of torment. With every thrust, the scream grew louder, more intense.

The Contessa fell forward, her lust temporarily slaked. She took a deep breath, recollected herself and smiled. It was a cruel smile. A very cruel smile. Now that the initial yearning had been dealt with, she could draw more slowly from the well of pleasure. She would begin again. She would take longer this time; it would be an altogether slower and more delicious form of gratification.

It would give her such delight. Such joy.

As for Guy, her captive human dildo, his agony had only just begun.

Max's, on the other hand, was almost at an end. Zelda struck him hard across the bottom with her tawse. It was a vicious blow, but by now he really didn't care. His rump was raw, the skin covered in angry red weals, his arms and legs aching, his mind far removed from the agonies of his body.

Time and again they had brought him to the point of orgasm, then cut his pleasure short. The ritual seemed never-ending. Chloe would stroke his forehead, smile and say, 'Tell me what I want to know, Max, and I'll fuck you till you come.' And Max would reach down deep inside, ignore the urges welling in his guts and tell her to go to hell.

When teasing hadn't worked, and they had given it a good two hours, they had taken him down and tied him to a chair. It was fitted with a rotating dildo on which Max had been made to sit. Stimulation of his prostate had brought him close to release several times. But they timed each session to perfection, shutting down the power a second or two before Max reached orgasm. When that, too, failed to elicit the desired response, they tried another tack. Each woman took it in turns to physically arouse him, while another talked dirty. The remaining pair lay on their backs in front of him, raised their legs in the air and

masturbated. Next, they straddled his cock for several minutes at a time, pinching the root of his shaft to prevent him from coming. They tried it first with their backs to him and then with their breasts in his face. But that had not worked either.

Their next scheme had involved upending the chair, following which they took it in turns to sit on his head. Each girl had offered him first her cunt and then her arse, while one of the others stroked him so smoothly that he thought he would collapse with lust. But all to no avail.

Finally, they had tied him over a V-shaped trestle and whipped him. Pleasure had not loosened his tongue, so they decided it was time to revert to pain again.

But that had not worked either. Chloe looked puzzled. She turned to Annie.

'He's either very well trained,' she said, 'or he really is who he says he is.' She frowned. 'Perhaps our information was incorrect.'

'If it is,' said Annie, 'then he's still lasted longer than anyone else we've had down here. This guy's not real.'

'Shall I get rid of him?' asked Raya.

Even half out of his mind with pain and frustration, Max caught the meaning in her voice. He suspected that being got rid of did not involve an all-expenses trip to the seaside where he could enjoy a long recuperation.

Chloe seemed to consider it seriously for a few moments. At that point, Max finally decided to go off her.

'No,' she announced. 'I've got a better idea. We'll let the Mistress have him. If he's lying she'll find out for sure. And if he's not, well, he's young and healthy. He might last a night or two with her.'

Raya and Annie laughed out loud. Zelda crossed her legs and giggled.

It was obvious, even to an exhausted Max, that in the girls' view, being got rid of was an altogether more pleasant prospect than being handed over to 'the Mistress'.

But at that point Max ceased to care, rolled his eyes and quietly passed out.

Seven

Tamara had checked and rechecked her facts. There had been an antiques shop on this particular spot for the past forty years. The elderly gentleman who ran it had taken over from his father in 1972. No, it had never been a massage parlour, not even for a couple of hours that morning. Old Mr Lackerty had been most affronted. He suggested that if Tamara were in the market for that kind of work she might note down some numbers from the cards cluttering up every phonebox within a three-mile radius.

There was nothing for it. Tamara had to accept that he was telling the truth. She had seen some strange things during her time with Omega, but nothing quite so odd as a building that was there one moment and gone the next. If she discounted Castle Lénzói, of course, and the explanation for that particular disappearance had more to do with several pounds of strategically placed TNT than with matters magical.

Crayshaw seemed her best bet now, but unfortunately she had disappeared. Crayshaw was always disappearing. She was a law unto herself. Emma had no idea where she was or when she would be back. Tamara left a message to call her on her mobile, then considered her next move.

Max's disappearance had complicated matters. The Minion must have noticed more than she had given him credit for. She cursed her stupidity. Wherever the parlour had gone, it had taken Max with it and thrown her plans into disarray. She had arranged for him to go down to

Dorford Haven and join the dig. An entire cover story had been prepared, but now the plan was shot to pieces.

There was nothing else for it. She would have to go instead of Max. It was risky, the Contessa's people knew her face. But there was no alternative. Besides, if Max was in trouble, the sooner she got moving, the better. She had lost one partner; she had no wish to lose another.

First, though, she would have to make a quick trip back to HQ.

'Me, please, sir! Please, sir! Choose me, please!'

Aubrey Manners MP smiled. The Brimstone Club was a welcome break from the daily parliamentary grind. Not that he didn't enjoy his work. He just enjoyed sex rather more.

Six girls were currently vying for his attention. He was sitting on a tall, high-backed chair, another man to the left of him perched on a slightly lower seat. Aubrey was always keen to ensure that people knew their place. He savoured the beauty of the moment. Though the women were all of legal age (it wouldn't do for him to run foul of the law, after all he *was* the Home Secretary), they were dressed to confuse in satin gymslips, tiny skirts, figure-hugging bustiers and knee-length socks. One girl pulled down her tank-top to expose tiny, lemon-shaped breasts.

'Look, sir!' she shouted. 'Look at my boobies! You can squeeze them, sir. Squeeze them as hard as you like!'

Another girl hoisted up her skirt, tugged down her pants and pushed her hips towards him. A band of tight red curls adorned her small slit of a pussy and she succeeded in drawing his attention away from the girl who was still kneading her breasts.

'A cunt is better, sir! A cunt can give more pleasure! Fuck me, sir! Fuck me with your cock!'

This show of strength drew a rapid response from a tall, brown-skinned woman at the end of the line. She dragged her skirt up to reveal that she was wearing no knickers. Her cunt was in stark contrast to the first girl's. A thick forest of black hair crowned her vulva. Her labia were

long, plump and distended, the inner flesh pink and shiny, like raw meat. Crudely, she ran her fingers over one damp, bloated lip.

'This is a real cunt! This cunt will eat you alive! I'm the one you want!'

The temptations hurried thick and fast. Another woman displayed larger breasts, another still turned her back on the men, bent over and exposed her arse. Aubrey turned to his companion and said, 'So what do you think of my girls?'

The other man stretched a pair of long legs and shifted in his seat. 'I say this for you, Aubrey,' he remarked, in heavily accented English, 'you know how to put on the good show.'

Aubrey smiled. This was more than a show. His companion was the Minister for Trade and Telecommunications of a large, unfriendly state in Eastern Europe. There was a dual purpose to be served here. On the one hand, he hoped to secure a trade agreement that had eluded a Cabinet colleague. It wasn't his job, of course, but it would do him no harm with the PM. Knives had been out for him lately and the Contessa would be furious if he were demoted. She could always intervene and save his skin, but that would involve a loss of face which might prove dangerous. His failure to close down Omega had damaged his standing, though the list of names and photos he'd recently obtained had earned him brownie points. A suspected agent had been apprehended by a squad of Faithful at the massage parlour and was currently undergoing interrogation. That was a lucky break, though not for the man concerned, he reflected.

There was a second purpose to be served, though. The Contessa's multimedia empire had been largely successful in expanding across Europe. Only one country remained outside the fold, though not, he suspected, glancing across at its Minister for Trade and Telecommunications, for much longer. It was vital that Diablo Worldwide be in a position to begin transmission on a global basis as soon as possible: not merely from a commercial point of view, but

for the wider good of The Order. Or should that be the wider bad, he chuckled to himself?

Aubrey put further speculation aside and gave his full attention to the girls assembled in front of him. He would be delighted to fuck them all, and more besides. But he mustn't be greedy. He must share the goodies.

He snapped his fingers and summoned the girl who had bared her backside. If the rumours were true, the Minister rode his bicycle down both sides of the street. This way he might double his pleasure and Aubrey might double his success.

'Show us your bottom!' he told her. 'My friend would like a closer look.'

'Of course, sir,' responded the girl, turning around, bending over and raising her skirt a second time.

Aubrey waved to his companion. 'You may examine her as closely as you like.'

Despite his reputation, the Minister appeared somewhat cautious. 'In any way?' he asked, licking a pair of fat, lascivious lips.

'Of course,' replied Aubrey. 'The girls love to please. Isn't that right, Lana?'

The remark was addressed to the girl bending over in front of them. 'Oh yes, sir,' she replied enthusiastically. 'We only want to give pleasure.'

The black girl cupped her big pussy in her even bigger hand and said, 'You can have me any time. I'll give you a night you won't forget.'

Aubrey eyed her warmly. Joni was one of the newer recruits and seemed particularly keen to impress. He had not enjoyed her yet and made a mental note to rectify that before the evening was over. In fact, he decided, why not now?

'Come!' he ordered, with an imperious waggle of his finger. Joni hurried over and knelt down in front of him. The Minister was momentarily distracted from his task.

'It's all right,' said Aubrey. 'Don't mind me.'

Beside him, the Minister reached out and stroked the young girl's buttocks. His fingers strayed cautiously into

87

her crack. It was not that he was a prudent man by nature, it was just that he had never had sex offered on such a generous plate before.

'Unzip me,' ordered Aubrey. Out of the corner of his eye, he saw the other man look askance. Swiftly and efficiently, the young woman eased his fly down, extracted his penis and squeezed it between her large, brown fingers.

'What would you like to do?' enquired Aubrey. It would have been simpler to tell her what to do, of course, but there was a subtle pleasure to be gained from receiving a service you craved without asking for it.

'I want to fellate you, sir,' replied the girl. She lowered her eyes and managed to look acutely embarrassed by the forward nature of her request. She was a brilliant little actress, thought Aubrey; the type of minx who, with the proper training, would make a first-rate addition to the Contessa's Faithful. He would have to bear that in mind. It would certainly win him further plaudits from the Arch-Select.

'Why do you want to do that?' he asked.

'Because I want to make you happy, sir. To give you pleasure in any way I can. First with my mouth and then as Nature intended I should give you pleasure, sir. With my cunt.'

Aubrey felt the muscles tighten in his groin. His cock unfurled and grew hard. He was in no mood to delay matters further. A curt nod of his head passed for permission and the woman fell on him as if she intended to devour his shaft rather than pleasure it.

Stroking the back of the girl's head, he turned towards his companion. Another conversation was taking place, one which suggested that the Minister was enjoying himself as much as he had hoped.

'You can kiss me on my bumhole if you like, sir. I don't mind. Or push a finger into me if you'd prefer.'

The Minister pulled her backside closer. Excitement seemed to have confused him. He was unsure. Should he employ his hands or his mouth to extract the greatest pleasure from this girl? In the end he decided to use both.

First he wriggled his finger into her anus, watching as his digit vanished up to the second knuckle. He gently eased it in and out and was rewarded with a giggle of delight.

'Oh, that's lovely, sir,' she cooed happily. 'Gosh, you're making me wet!'

Aubrey found himself impressed by this girl, too. Like Joni, she seemed to have a total joy of sex which was somewhat rare. If he could present two new acolytes to the Contessa, his future was assured. Eddies of excitement shuddered along his cock at the thought of the rewards such a gift might procure.

The Minister extracted his finger and leaned forward to lick the girl's rich young curves. Nuzzling her bare behind, he lapped and sniffed and extended his tongue so that its very tip teased the rim of her anus.

Lana wriggled her backside and uttered a long, drawn-out sigh. Her pleasure seemed genuine. 'Oh, give me a kiss, sir, please. Give me a kiss!'

He pressed his lips to her bumhole and sucked her gently. 'Oh, thank you, sir! Thank you!' she trilled, swivelling her little hips. 'You can do anything you like to me now!'

Her words seemed to spur him into action. He unbuckled his belt, stood up and pulled his trousers down. Extracting his erect shaft, he knelt behind her and presented the crown of his cock to her arse.

'Oh nice,' she whimpered and pushed back. The Minister's penis trembled dangerously close to orgasm. Beside him, Aubrey made a silent bet with himself that if he didn't enter the girl in one stroke, the pressure of her ring on his glans would make him spend before he got anywhere near penetrating her rectum.

In the meantime, he closed his eyes and enjoyed the gentle sucking motions that carried his own cock towards its inevitable release. It was going to be a long evening, he decided. And if events so far were any guide, a very pleasurable one.

Erskine Santer was a tall man, with a head of thinning black hair and lean, finely chiselled features. He was

eminent in his field, and head of department at a leading American college. He also had an eye for the ladies. And he particularly liked what he was looking at just now. The blonde with her shiny blue eyes, firm hips and big breasts had greatly impressed him with her figure if not with her brain. No, that wasn't true. It was just that her qualifications were not what he had expected. But then neither was she. For a start she was supposed to be a man.

'Admin cockup!' she giggled. 'It's always happening. I tell them I'm Frankie Laine and they think I'm a man. I mean, I ask you, do I look like a man?'

Tamara pushed her breasts forward and turned sideways in the chair just in case Erskine was in any doubt.

No, he thought, she looked nothing like a man. He wasn't too sure about the way she wore her hair, mind. The tight bun was a little too severe. He wondered if she were trying to impress him with her seriousness. But Erskine Santer, PhD, FAAE ArchDip, etc., etc. was no one's fool. He knew a chancer when he met one, and Frankie Laine was a chancer in spades. She obviously knew next to nothing about archaeology. So what did she want?

Tamara gave a coy grin and lowered her eyelashes. Then she crossed her legs and her short skirt rode up her bare thigh and exposed her equally bare hip.

Erskine tried his best to concentrate on the matter in hand. It wasn't easy. If it wasn't for the fact that they were sitting in the busy and very public foyer of the Hotel Grande, Dorford Haven, he might have been tempted to lean across and pat her on the knee.

'I'm not sure we can offer you the post,' he said at last. 'We really were expecting someone with a – well – little more experience.'

Tamara crossed and recrossed her legs, smiled and moved around so that he could see her breasts from another angle. 'I'd do anything to get the job,' she purred.

Now it was his turn to shift in his seat. His penis had risen several notches and was pushing awkwardly against his underpants.

'Why do you want it so much?' he asked. 'The job, I

mean,' he amplified, and was rewarded with what he decided was a rather naughty smile. He hoped she had a good reason. She had just got his cock's casting vote. But even he needed a better argument than that.

'OK,' she said, 'I'll come clean.' She leaned forward, allowing him to peer straight down into the well of her cleavage. 'I'm a writer.'

The rest of his body caught up with his cock and stiffened. One thing he had been warned to look out for were reporters sniffing around. His employers had already gone ape over Hugo's accident. He couldn't afford another mishap.

'I'm writing a novel,' she said. 'It's a big romance, you know, love under the pyramids and all that.'

Erskine relaxed a little. This wasn't quite so bad.

'Trouble is, I don't know what it's like. I thought this was a great way of finding out. My hero's a bit like you.'

'Is he?' Erskine raised himself in his chair and preened. The girl was a fool, anyone could see that. But she was very attractive. He wondered how far she was prepared to go in order to research her hero.

Tamara smiled and looked around her shyly. 'I don't suppose . . .'

Erskine leaned forward. 'I don't suppose what?' he echoed eagerly.

'I don't suppose we could go somewhere a little more private and discuss this, could we?'

Erskine felt his balls roll and tighten. Somewhere a little more private was just what he had in mind.

Max's eyes fluttered open. They seemed to have been doing that a lot lately. His body ached and his skin stung all over. But at least he was no longer tied up. He stretched his arms and looked around him. He was lying on a bunk in a dark, stone-built chamber. It looked like a prison cell, only somewhat smaller and a little bit nastier.

He was still naked, but he was getting used to that, too. There was a leather band around his neck with a small metal clip at the rear. He wondered what his captors had

91

in store for him next. He also wondered where he was. Only one thing was clear at present: Tamara had not arrived with the troops.

A grill in the wall slid back and a face appeared briefly. Then the door opened and two women entered. Though he didn't recognise them, they made an immediate impression. They were naked: a copper-haired beauty and a tall, blonde goddess. Both women had shaven cunts and he found his eyes skipping from vulva to vulva before they hauled him to his feet and put an end to his obscene speculations.

'Ow!' he moaned, though he was surprised to discover that he didn't hurt as much as he thought he would. There was a funny smell in the air and he realised that it was coming from him. His skin had been coated in a fragrant oily substance, a soothing balm of some kind he imagined, judging from the way his flesh tingled. Well, that was something positive, surely. If they were going to hurt him again, it wouldn't make sense to heal him first. Not unless they were real sadists and wanted it to go on for as long as possible.

He wished he hadn't thought of that.

Tamara was rather pleased with her performance. The dyed blonde hair and the blue contact lenses wouldn't have fooled anyone who knew her, but she was banking on the fact that no one would believe she was daft enough to turn up in person. Acting the silly novelist had not been difficult. She had got the measure of Erskine Santer from the extensive files at Omega. It was hard to tell how seriously embroiled in all of this he really was. But his weakness for the ladies was a bonus.

After she had proposed somewhere a little more private, Erskine had suggested his room. She had agreed with alacrity. They were hardly through the door when he pushed her up against the wall and begun fondling her like a randy schoolboy. They had eventually reached the bed, after grappling up against the wall, on the floor and over a dresser.

By then they were both naked. She had expected him to fuck her straight away, but instead he had lain on his back and made a request. It took her by surprise.

'I want you to sit on my face,' he said to her. 'Will you do that for me?'

Tamara shrugged her shoulders and smiled. 'Of course,' she replied. 'If that's what you want.' She straddled his chest and moved up to his neck.

'No,' he said, 'the other way round. I want your butt on my head.'

Tamara reversed her position. She felt her cheeks open up as she wriggled back. It was a while since she'd sat on a man's face. Not everyone liked it. She was wondering what Erskine would do next, when his tongue stabbed out and tickled her bumhole. He followed up with his nose, sniffing at her arse like a randy dog.

'Sit on me,' he said. 'Properly. Sit on me as hard as you can.'

'So you can't breathe?' she asked, seeking clarification.

'Yes,' he replied urgently.

Something stirred at the back of Tamara's mind. She recalled the Sacrifice to Vanjja, and the way Nhaomhé had despatched her victims. Erskine must know all about that. The randy old goat wanted to know what it felt like. Well, she'd show him. She wriggled her bottom back and lowered herself on to his face, teasing him with delay. The moment her flesh met his, trapping his nose and mouth in her cleft, his cock unwound between his legs. She began to stroke it gently, leaning forward and tickling his balls, but making sure that her contact with his head was not broken.

He began to move around beneath her. Tamara had once subdued a Minion like this. It had been touch and go, but she had managed to masturbate him into insensibility before he had been able to shift her. And he had had the strength of ten. She wondered how Erskine would react if she told him she could probably make his dream come true. His delight, she reckoned, would last for about a minute and a half. Then panic would set in and he would begin clawing at her buttocks. It was lucky for him that he was more use to her in one piece.

He began to wriggle rather desperately now, but she tightened her thighs and held on. At the same time she began to work his penis up and down and watched as his balls rolled and hardened in their big, hairy sacs. Erskine had a long cock, heavily veined, and circumcised. His purple knob looked like a giant plum, and her mouth watered at the thought of taking it inside her. But just at this moment, she couldn't resist the urge to make Erskine spend himself. If this was his particular turn-on, then it gave her a hold she could use.

She pulled his cock sharply and watched huge dollops of cream fountain over his belly. His hips bounced and his hands pulled at her hips as she moved them from side to side. She lifted her bottom briefly, just enough to let him catch his breath then dropped back again. Erskine wheezed and squirmed and moaned in a way that told Tamara she was doing rather well. Good. Things were going according to plan.

Things were not going according to plan so far as Max was concerned. A leash had been threaded into the clip in his neckband. He had then been taken from his cell by the two strong-armed Amazons and led along a long, winding corridor. Now they stood outside a large pair of oaken double doors. The copper-haired Amazon turned to him and said, 'You will kneel.'

She obviously took his hesitation for defiance and struck him roughly across the side of the arm with her short leather tawse.

'Down!' she commanded, and Max wasted no more time in falling to his knees. He felt the handle of the tawse dig into his neck, forcing his head lower.

The other woman spoke. 'In the presence of the Contessa you will not rise until permission has been granted. Is that understood?'

The Contessa! Great, thought Max. As if things weren't bad enough. The tawse struck his back with unexpected force. He yelped. 'Understood! Understood!' he replied quickly.

The doors swung open with a groan. There was a tug at the band and Max was made to shuffle into the room like a dog. The temptation to look up was almost irresistible; but the thought of the tawse held his curiosity in check. He was dragged several yards across a cold, stony floor. All he could see were the women's feet just ahead of him. But somewhere beyond that he could hear noises; familiar noises. He could have sworn it was the sound of men and women making love.

The trio came to a halt. Ahead of him he was aware of the two women going down on one knee.

'Mistress,' one of them said. 'We bring you an offering.'

An offering. Max wasn't sure if he liked the implication. It made him sound like fruit at a harvest festival.

There was a long silence, broken only by the sound of bodies moving. He was sure they were bodies moving. And he could smell something, too. It was the smell of raw, animal sex. Despite his predicament, he felt his penis stiffen.

A deep, sonorous voice echoed around the chamber. 'Bring him to me.'

The women stood up and tugged on Max's chains, dragging him forward again. He scuffed his knees, but reminded himself that that was probably the least of his concerns at present.

'Let him stand,' said the voice and he was pulled upright. Even with his eyes lowered, he was aware of the cluster of bodies all around him. He could see feet and arms and legs and buttocks. A hand reached out and touched him under the chin, raising his head with a gentleness he did not expect. When he looked up he found himself gazing into a pair of large, hypnotic, coal-black eyes.

He was, he decided, staring into the face of the most beautiful woman he had ever seen. She was heavily garbed in chains and black leather and seated on a mass of heaving flesh. It was the most incredible sight he had ever witnessed. All around her, bodies moaned and swayed in a quivering dance of sex. Max was suddenly aware that the vision in black was speaking to him.

95

'I am the Contessa,' she said quietly. 'And you are an Omega agent.'

It sounded like a statement, but could as easily have been a question. Something stirred in the depths of Max's befuddled brain, and for a moment he succeeded in tearing his eyes away. But only for a moment. Lust flooded his groin and he turned back to face her.

She rested her chin thoughtfully on the broad steeple of her hands. 'You would make an interesting addition to my stable,' she said and beckoned him with a long, curled finger.

Max stumbled nearer, stopping only when she raised the flat of her hand. He suddenly felt very tired.

'Join me,' she said, inviting him to sit beside her. She put her arm around his shoulder and pulled him close. Her left hand stole down between his legs and took hold of his penis. Something at the back of his mind told him he shouldn't let her do this. But it felt so nice that he didn't really want to listen to that particular voice. It sounded like Tamara's, but he wasn't sure.

The Contessa began to work him up and down, her fingers dancing around his cock, her long, painted nails scratching at his fat, hairy balls. Max felt the spunk gather at the root of his shaft, and delicious sparks of pleasure sizzled in his groin. She began to pump him faster now and harder, too. His head began to sway, and he nuzzled into her warm, slightly damp armpit. He pressed his nose into her flesh and opened his mouth around the hair that grew there, sucking the moisture from each long, curly strand.

He felt himself drifting away from the real world, his attention torn between the raw essence of her smell and the delicious rise of pleasure in his belly. He wanted her to finish him off and began to wriggle so that his penis rose and fell between her loosely held fingers.

The Contessa moved her arm and tugged his head up to face her. Max found himself staring into those coal-dark eyes again. Fire sparkled in her pupils, radiant flames that tugged at his soul. He couldn't tear himself away.

'You are mine,' she was saying, and he knew it was what

he wanted. Until that damned voice at the back of his head started calling to him again. He blinked and the spell was broken. The pleasure still surged between his legs but his head was suddenly clear. The Contessa's lips twisted into a look of disapproval.

'You defy me,' she whispered. 'Such a pity.'

He didn't know what she was talking about. The Contessa snapped her fingers and Darné and Kalya joined her on the Living Throne. Kalya thrust her hands beneath Max's backside and probed for his anus, pushing two fingers into his rectum. He knew he should resist, but he didn't want to. His head was pulled back and a pair of large breasts swam across his face. Big tawny nipples rubbed at his lips, and warm flesh squashed itself over his nose. Out of the corner of one eye, he was vaguely aware of controlled sexual activity all around him. He saw the Minions for the first time and realised they were buggering each other. A range of flared female arses swayed from side to side, and he saw the dribble that coated their thighs, aware that they were being licked by the men. Then his vision was blocked as Darné's breasts covered his head completely. His arse was being pumped as gently as his cock. Again, a voice at the back of his head told him to fight these women. But how could he? He had neither the strength nor the willpower to struggle free. All he wanted to do was surrender happily to the lust gathering in his belly.

The Contessa was licking his ear. He felt her tongue-tip probe and squirrel its way deep inside, and his entire body shivered sweetly. A honeyed voice began to whisper to him.

'Do you feel the pleasure within? Is it not delightful?'

Max might have grunted some vague response, but he was too busy chewing on a hard circle of breast, his teeth nibbling at a bone-hard nipple. His cock was painfully stiff and his balls ached with longing. He was suddenly aware that he was surrounded by cunts. His fingers pressed into something hot and sticky, while warm heat oozed across his left thigh. The air was heavy with the scent of female excitement.

'Enough!' barked the Contessa. Immediately the two Amazons withdrew. Max felt his heart thump rapidly. He wanted to come, he wanted to thrust himself somewhere warm and wet. Instead, he found himself dragged off the mass of bodies and kicked sharply in the ribs. It seemed a rather gratuitous act of violence.

The Contessa stood over him. She snapped her fingers. The two women took hold of Max's shoulders and hoisted him up, so that his head was directly in front of the Contessa's vulva. He stared into the rich, ruby folds of her flesh. Her cunt was like a gaping wound, her labia engorged and open, her sap dripping on to her thighs. Max had never seen such a crude display of flesh in all his life. It was frightening.

'Lick me out!' commanded the Contessa. Max hesitated for a moment, then a strong pair of arms pushed him down towards her cunt. Close up, he realised for the first time how huge it was. The runnel of her sex was several inches long. He had a sudden, awful thought that if he pushed his face in at the right angle it might swallow him whole. He extended his tongue and began to lick gingerly, mopping up drops of juice that hung from the strands of her pubes. Her essence was like none he had ever tasted; sweet and spicy. It was like drinking wine, heady and infusive. The more he lapped, the more he wanted to lap. He began to attack her vulva with renewed fervour, no longer aware of his own pleasure, but simply wanting to give the Contessa joy. She began to sway unevenly, her fingers digging into the back of his head. Sweat ran down her belly and mingled with her sweet secretions. He tasted the salt on his tongue and it fired him with fresh enthusiasm. Hands danced between his legs, while fingers wound about his cock, pulling at it gently, making him pulse with need. Other fingers trawled across his balls as he whimpered into the gaping maw of the Contessa's cunt.

Then suddenly it was over. She pulled away. Max raised his hand to wipe away her spendings, but Darné restrained him.

'The Mistress's juice is sacred,' she yelled angrily, and struck him across the shoulder-blades.

'I think we should introduce our guest to the delights of the Darkness,' said the Contessa.

Max wondered what the hell that meant.

It wouldn't be very long before he wished he hadn't.

Eight

Darné and Kalya dragged Max down several flights of stone steps. It was a struggle to keep his balance and he stumbled more than once. The women strode on regardless, tugging on his leash, pulling him around corners and across cold, damp flagging with scant regard for his difficulties. The Contessa preceded them. Despite his need to concentrate on remaining upright, Max found it hard to keep his eyes away from her broad, muscular buttocks. He knew now why she attracted such devotion from her disciples. She had the figure of a goddess. He had not imagined such a body existed anywhere. She was huge, Amazonian in stature, yet every part of her was in perfect proportion. No, that wasn't really true. Her breasts were surely too large; her buttocks too long; her labia, when he had caught sight of them, like two thick lengths of pulpy pink melon. And yet it all seemed just right, just perfect. Since she had first masturbated him on the Living Throne, Max's erection had refused to subside. A lust gnawed at his belly. It was a lust that he had never felt before. He desperately wanted to fuck someone, preferably the Contessa, though he had to admit she looked as if she might eat him alive. He wondered how much of this desperate longing was the result of pure animal need for a beautiful woman and how much was down to the Contessa's alleged mesmeric powers. Had he become a Minion? No, that was impossible. He was still in control of his mind, Or was he? He was no longer sure. All he knew was that if the Contessa had asked him to walk

across burning coals in return for the slightest hint of a fuck, he would have done so.

At last they reached a gloomy, lower level. Someone else was there already: another man. He was naked, his body suspended on chains fastened into the black ceiling. A woman stood close behind him. She was tall and big-breasted; long brown hair tumbled over her wide, muscular shoulders. Her hands were on the man's waist, and her big broad hips were moving gently. She wore a small leather belt around her midriff, the base of a thick black dildo visible each time her hips withdrew. Shock registered in Max's befuddled mind. She was buggering her victim. A second woman knelt in front of him. She was sucking on his cock, one hand digging into his right hip, the other pressed between her legs. All the while, he grunted into a gag wrapped tight around his face.

And there was more.

A few feet away, on the far side of a metal cage, stood several naked, mud-spattered women. Max counted half a dozen at least. Their dirty arms clawed through the gaps in the bars, fingers extended towards the trio, mouths open and cursing obscenely. As soon as they saw the Contessa, however, they fell back and huddled on the ground. Looking past them, Max could make out movements in the shadows and wondered who else was there, crouching out of sight.

The prisoner's penis slipped from the second woman's mouth. It bobbed in the air, glistening with her saliva, some of which ran down the shaft and dribbled from the man's dark, wiry pubes. The woman standing at his rear stepped back and dropped to her knees, her head bowed low. As the phallus had emerged from her victim's arse, Max was stunned to see how large and long it was. The man's head slumped forward and lolled from side to side.

Darné and Kalya took hold of Max's wrists and fixed chains to them, tugging tight so that his arms rose towards the ceiling. Before he had a chance to gather himself, a large rubber ball was pushed into his mouth and a leather binding wrapped around his face and secured at the back.

The Contessa turned to him and smiled. 'In all the best stories, the hero escapes. I thought I'd bring you here so that when you return to Omega you can tell them all my secrets.'

Max guessed she was being sarcastic and grunted several inaudible curses into the gag. The Contessa reached out and stroked the top of the other man's head. Sweat ran down his face and his eyes flared with fear.

'You may continue, my darlings,' she said quietly. The first woman stood up, took hold of her phallus and guided it back between the prisoner's buttocks. He threw back his head and wailed. The second woman closed her mouth around his cock. Max looked on, utterly transfixed. It was hard to know if he should feel horror or excitement. In truth, and not for the first time, he registered a little of both.

'Don't worry about our friend here,' intoned the Contessa. 'It is his will to suffer.'

Max found that hard to believe. The Contessa smiled as if she had read his thoughts, turned to the man and pulled the rubber ball from his mouth. 'Is that not so, William?'

His head rocked up and down with surprising vigour. 'Yes, Mistress! Yes!' The woman at his rear thrust deep and his face twisted horribly.

'Or would you prefer to leave my service?' asked the Contessa sweetly.

The man bit his lip and whined as the buggering seemed to reach new depths. His head shook violently. 'No, Mistress! Please, Mistress! I am yours forever!'

She smiled. 'I have promised my Angels some pleasure. Will you serve them as well as you serve me, I wonder?'

The man's eyes opened horribly wide. 'No, Mistress, please! Anything but that! Anything!'

There was a sudden commotion from the far side of the dungeon cell. The encaged women seemed to have recovered their confidence. The Contessa turned to Max, stepped forward and grabbed him by his cock. He let out a yelp of pleasure and surprise. She stroked him gently, and he felt the spunk surge into his shaft. Leaning close,

she whispered into his ear. 'These are my Angels, Max. Say hello to Max, my darlings!'

The Angels' way of saying hello was to bay and shriek and rattle the bars loudly.

'I have to keep them caged, Max. If they could get at you, they would tear you to pieces.'

'Please, Mistress!' screamed one of the women, a wide-hipped brunette. 'Let me have him. I need a man, Mistress.' She thrust herself against the nearest bar, so that her pussy lips parted either side of the warm metal. 'I need a man, Mistress!'

The Contessa smiled again. 'They want you Max. They know you're fresh meat. Better than William, here.'

She called over her shoulder, towards the woman who had just spoken. 'I haven't forgotten what happened to the last man I gave you!'

'I'll be more gentle with this one, Mistress. Please. I promise!'

The Contessa ignored her and leaned close. Max could smell the warmth of her body, and the unusual perfumed sweetness of her breath.

'You can have your pick of the women,' she whispered. 'They all long for you. I'll have one brought out, if you like. She'll have to be tied down, of course, or she'll do you harm. You can do whatever you want to her. What do you say, Max?'

Max tried to shut his eyes to the sight of the women scrabbling at the bars of their cage. They were gorgeous in a wild, primitive way. It was clear that they were strong, eager and sexually excited; frustrated, too. The thought of being able to fuck any one of them made his balls ache.

The Contessa gave his shaft another playful squeeze and he felt his balls roll painfully. 'You can have whichever one you choose. But you must resist me, Max. I know you want to empty yourself into my hand, but you must fight your desires. Do you understand?'

Max nodded his head and grunted into the gag. He understood all right. He desperately wanted to spend himself. It was difficult to hold back, but he knew he must.

If the Contessa made him spend into her hand he was finished. Her words were like poisonous snakes, ensnaring his will.

'The longer you resist, the greater your reward,' she promised him.

Max was confused. What reward? One of these gorgeous women? He wanted that more than anything just now, but he knew it was a trap. Beside him, his fellow captive groaned. Here was the example he needed: a man so desperate to serve the Contessa that he would submit to the vilest tortures. Or would he? Even he seemed terrified at the prospect of being thrown to the women beyond the bars. What did she call them? Her Angels?

The women were snarling now, and stretching their limbs, lifting their legs in the air, reaching out with their hands, fingers clawing towards him. The Contessa leaned close. 'Kara has not had a man for over a month. See how she longs for you.'

Max's penis kicked inside the Contessa's warm fist. On the far side of the cage, a big-busted redhead licked her lips and stretched out an imploring arm. 'Let me have him, Mistress. Please! Let me have him!'

The Contessa's lips grazed the side of his face. 'I doubt you would survive her attentions,' she whispered.

Max felt his cock tremble against her fingers. Blood surged through his shaft, and his balls tightened. The Contessa gestured towards a pair of lean, gangly blondes who stood aside from the group, stroking each other.

'Evie and May work well as a team. When they mount a man together, he had better say his prayers.'

Max's body stiffened. He was approaching the point of no return.

'Or do you desire me, Max?' she purred into his ear. He felt her warm breath tickle his cheek and he shivered with need. He turned his face towards her. His eyes narrowed with lust. She smiled and squeezed gently. 'Then resist, my darling,' she murmured. 'Resist for me.'

Max closed his eyes and concentrated hard. The Contessa's voice remained insistent, forcing its way into his

thoughts. 'This is where I bring those who have failed me, Max,' she whispered. 'When you are in my service and displease me, this is where I will bring you. These women are savage. They will show you no mercy.'

Another woman raised her voice. Max couldn't help himself, he opened his eyes and looked in her direction. He saw a tall, russet-haired girl squirming against the cage bars. Her juices began to dribble down the metal. A dreadful longing snagged him in the stomach.

'Has he been bad, Mistress?' she asked. 'Will you let me punish him for you?'

'Have you been masturbating again, Ailsa?'

'I can't help it, Mistress. If you won't give me a man to satisfy my needs, what else can I do?'

'Who wishes to feed?' asked the Contessa loudly.

A clamour of voices filled the air. Their Mistress looked around her briefly, then said, 'You may share him.'

A sudden burst of joyful screeching filled the chamber. The Angels giggled shrilly, like a horde of randy schoolgirls. Max was horrified. The Contessa snapped her fingers and Max heard a whirring sound somewhere in the ceiling. He looked up and saw that the chains around his wrists were attached to a pulley. Wheels began to turn and he felt himself being shunted towards the cage. The women licked their lips, hooted and yelled madly. The Contessa glared at them for a moment and they immediately shifted back a few feet. Max considered struggling, but there seemed no point. Besides, at the back of his head a little voice was telling him not to fight it, but to surrender happily to his fate. After all, he was being offered on a plate to half a dozen naked women. It was hard not to get excited at the prospect, even if that same voice kept warning him that it was a mistake.

The Contessa pushed Max's erection between the bars of the cage. The women edged forward, spittle dribbling down their chins, limbs coiled, and ready to pounce. The Contessa pressed herself up against Max's back. He felt her breasts flatten against his shoulder-blades and her bullet-firm nipples dig into his skin. Her hard, hairy mound

grazed his bottom, and he sighed with pleasure when she began to rotate her hips. The Contessa tightened her grip on his shaft and began to pump him smoothly. She tickled his balls with the fingers of her other hand. They were heavy and hard and he knew that he would come at a moment of her choosing. She pushed out her forefinger, wriggled it between his cheeks, and scratched at his anus. Max twisted in a delirium of agony and delight. He felt his body stiffen one last time. Pressing her mouth up against his ear she whispered, 'They want you, Max.'

It was too much. His penis erupted, his hot white semen arcing into the warm air. The Contessa pulled his shaft from side to side, directing his spunk from one woman to the next. It spattered their faces and their bellies, their arms and their legs. They pushed out their tongues and tried to catch his seed in mid-air. When it fell on them, they licked at themselves and at each other, like cats cleaning their young. The last thing Max saw was the women advancing on him and then, not for the first time recently, his world went mercifully black.

Erskine Santer's on-site headquarters were more luxurious than Tamara had expected. A large prefabricated unit had been installed which ran to several rooms: an office, two utility sections, a kitchen area, living space (with three-piece suite and drinks cabinet!) and an unusually well-appointed bedroom, complete with en-suite facilities. A tall mirror stood opposite the big, double bed, curiously out of place, with its delicately carved wooden frame, and gold and silver trim. Peering closer, Tamara had been able to make out a swathe of grotesque, gargoyle-like features. Occasionally, when the light caught the edges of the mirror, the faces seemed to move, as if they were actually alive. It was horrible. And yet there was something about it that stirred a distant memory: something locked away at the back of her mind. What was it? She had seen it before, or something very much like it. She just wished she could remember where.

Unlike the rest of the staff, Tamara had not been

checked into the Hotel Grande. After sharing Erskine's bed on her first night, he had moved her in with him at the dig. She suspected that she was, strictly speaking, surplus to official requirements. Fortunately, she was not surplus to Erskine's unofficial needs, and spending more time on site suited her better in any case. So far, though, there had not been much chance to snoop around. Erskine, it seemed, liked to delegate. As such, he spent a great deal of time in his 'office', regularly raiding the well-stocked drinks cabinet before locking the door to his trailer, kicking off his trousers and chasing Tamara through the maze of rooms. The man seemed insatiable. They had been together for less than 24 hours and already she had lost count of the number of times they had made love. At this moment, they were lying side by side on the bed, at the end of an unusually straightforward session. It was the first time Erskine had made love to her on top. Previously, he had either requested that she ride him, or sit on his face and masturbate him to a climax. Being fucked, rather than doing the fucking, had made a pleasant change. He had taken her with more vigour than she had expected and, for the moment at least, she was glad of the rest. A discarded bottle of warm champagne sat in a nearby bucket of water; a thin satin sheet was coiled loosely around their legs. Erskine's eyes were closed and he smiled contentedly. Tamara looked down at his limp cock. It was large enough even when not erect. The shaft still gleamed with her juices, its foreskin pulled back to reveal the purple-red knob of the glans. On an impulse, she reached down and stroked the underside of his prick. Erskine sighed but kept his eyes shut. Tamara felt an almost imperceptible movement at the root of his penis and watched as one of his balls jerked in its sac.

She pushed back the sheet, wriggled down and nuzzled his cock with her nose. The mélange of smells, of spunk and pussy, was quite intoxicating. Tamara extended her tongue and lapped at the underside of Erskine's shaft, taking the mix of tastes into her mouth, savouring the heady tang of animal spendings. Almost at once his penis

began to tighten. She ran her tongue up to his glans and captured it between her lips. His hips moved gently and he brought one hand down so that it rested at the back of her head, his long, callused fingers trawling through her hair. She began to suck him softly, aware of the blood pumping into his shaft, and his balls rolling in response to her touch. His other hand came down and held her in position. Not that she needed much restraining. Erskine surprised her by suddenly rolling on to his tummy. He was over her head now, and it took a few moments to adjust to the changed perspective. She circled his backside with her arms, wriggling the fingers of both hands into the damp, hairy cleft of his arse. At the same time, she felt his mouth close over her cunt and the tip of his tongue flick against her clitoris. She pushed up with her bottom and wriggled her hips. The index finger of her left hand found the hard rim of his anus and she pushed down into it. His whole body jerked and he groaned into her cunt. The sudden blast of warm air opened up her sex. Tamara squealed as an unexpected ripple of pleasure flooded her vagina. As she came, she pushed her finger deep into Erskine's rectum and he climaxed, too, a weak spurt of liquid tickling the rear of her throat. At this rate, she told herself, she would never find out what was going on at Dorford Haven, or where the hell Max had vanished to. It really wasn't good enough. She must try harder.

In the meantime, she contented herself with pushing her finger deeper still.

Dog was crouched on all fours, his small bottom raised in the air. The Contessa knelt behind him, a thick black dildo strapped around her waist, the smooth, rounded head pressed up against his anus. Of all her male slaves, Dog possessed the greatest self-control. Most men could not withstand prolonged buggering. It was never very long before the pressure on their prostate had its inevitable effect and they emptied their balls over the dungeon floor. Dog was different, and it pleased her. Whether his restraint was physical or mental mattered not. He lived to please

her. She took a firm hold on his hips and drove herself forward, scything into his arse in one clean movement. Dog lifted his head and emitted a loud howl of delight. As he pushed back to meet her rhythmic thrusts, the Contessa watched the elastic ridge of his sphincter expand around her artificial cock. A series of loose plastic beads gathered at the base of the dildo, tickling her clitoris each time the phallus met resistance. She grunted with delight, thrust deeper still, then threw back her head and yelled obscenely into the otherwise empty room.

A tall, beautifully carved mirror faced her. Clouds formed on the smooth surface of the glass, swirling shapes without true form or meaning. Yet with each thrust of her hips, each spear of delight into her sex, the mists began to clear. She narrowed her eyes as the first swell of pleasure gathered in her belly. Squealing through gritted teeth, she watched the other pair, the woman and the man, as they sucked and licked at each other's bodies. Dog wriggled his buttocks and clawed the stone floor, biting back his urge to spend. She felt between his legs for a moment. His testicles were big and hard, like two heavy billiard balls packed with seed. The Contessa knew how much Dog suffered for her sake. She liked to tease him: toying with his cock and stroking his balls, until the need within him became unbearable. He would nestle at her feet, whimpering softly, aware that his desires were to remain frustrated. Occasionally, she would allow him to reach orgasm. But even then, she would treat him cruelly. She could still recall his shriek of despair when she had pulled his cock from the cunt of her red-headed Faithful down in the dungeons. Release, for Dog, was a rare delight. She much preferred to torture him for the pleasure it afforded her. Such sweet, sweet pleasure! Sometimes she would sit him on her lap, kiss his face and gently stroke him. She would smooth his hair and feather his balls. She would push her tongue into his ear and rub his penis. His struggle was palpable. She could feel him fighting back the urge to reach orgasm. It was his ultimate act of homage to an adored Mistress: to resist her until she chose the moment, which she rarely did.

Dog was weeping now, like a small child. She could feel his body shudder with longing. It was delicious to abuse him like this. When she was finished and had grown tired of the orgasms she would extract from his arse, she might remove the dildo and make Dog lick her pussy. She would hold his head tight against her and flood his mouth with her juices. That would be a most exquisite way to end the proceedings. If she were feeling particularly cruel, she might summon Darné and Kalya and invite them to use him, too. That always enhanced his suffering. One would fondle his scrotum, while the other squeezed his penis. And all the while he would suck from his Mistress's vulva.

In the mirror, it was clear that the frenzied couple were fast approaching orgasm. Erskine Santer was a man after her own heart, she decided. Perhaps when all this was over she would have him brought to her. She would show him the true meaning of lust. She would break him for her own pleasure.

Her cunt felt suddenly very hot. Armies of ecstasy fought their way across her tummy and down into her groin. One more thrust and pleasure would flood her belly.

She stopped suddenly. The man was coming, emptying whatever remained of his thin seed into the throat of the woman he straddled. Her face turned sideways to avoid being smothered by his shaking hips. The Contessa froze in mid-thrust. No! Impossible! It could not be!

But it was. Erskine Santer was a bigger fool than even she had allowed. There was no question about it. Though her appearance was vastly changed, she knew without a doubt that the woman fellating Santer to climax was Tamara Knight.

The Contessa snarled angrily. She bit into her lip and blood ran down her chin. Trembling with rage, she thrust forward again and again, thundering into Dog's backside with a cruel disregard for the pain she was now inflicting.

'Bitch!' screamed the Contessa as the first waves of delight crashed through her body. 'Bitch! Bitch! Bitch!'

Tamara Knight had been a thorn in her side for too long. She would tolerate the woman's interference no

longer. This latest act had sealed her fate. The Contessa drove forward one last time, embedding the phallus hilt-deep within Dog's ravished arse. His bottom wriggled furiously as if he were trying to escape. A confused, despairing gurgle broke from the back of his throat. The Contessa dug her nails into his flesh and held him fast. Dog rarely spoke, but he spoke now.

'Mercy!' he cried. 'Mercy, Mistress!'

'No escape! No mercy!' she screamed as the full force of her orgasm struck like a sudden storm, ripping away the last shreds of self-restraint. She threw back her head and howled.

This time Tamara Knight had gone too far. This time she would die.

Then the pleasure struck again and the Contessa gave herself up to ecstasy.

Nine

Doctor Marsilio Quellorozata opened his eyes and yawned. The cabin was shrouded in gloom, a patchy darkness broken only by the pale glow from a dozen or so overhead TV sets and the occasional reading light. What time was it, he wondered. He pressed a button on his watch. The illuminated dial showed that they were only four hours into the flight. Damn! He had hoped the sleeping draught would have put him out for longer than that. A familiar need asserted itself in the pit of his stomach and he felt his penis harden against his belly. He remembered the girl at the airport: a short, fat Swede with big breasts, a full rucksack and an empty pocket. For 350 *reals* – a ridiculous amount of money, but then beggars could not be choosers – she had agreed to go with him to the men's toilets where they had queued up at one of several occupied cubicles. The astonished looks from his fellow-travellers had lent such a *frisson* to the proceedings that he had almost succumbed to a temptation to pull down the girl's knickers and take her there and then. That would have given his audience a show to remember. As it was, however, he had decided to err on the side of caution. Once inside the loo, he had made her squat on the closed seat with her pants down, her backside in the air and her hands on the cistern. When he felt for the girl's cunt, he found her labia to be warm and wet. He slipped two fingers into her plumpness and was rewarded with a cry of '*Ja!*' and a friendly wiggle of her big fat bottom. He knew then that she was as excited as he was and cursed himself for

112

having already paid her. Entering her from behind, he had proceeded to take her vigorously. It had not been a quiet fuck. She had yelled in Swedish at every thrust, and though he knew nothing of the language, her shrill tone had spoken volumes. He, too, had sworn and grunted and the flimsy walls of the cubicle had rattled rather dangerously. One of the other men had grown impatient and had begun to hammer on the door. But he had been promptly told to desist by his companions, who were content to enjoy the unexpected diversion. One or two had even shouted encouragement. Afterwards, Marsilio had escorted the girl back to the main concourse, but as he had checked into the departure lounge he had noticed with a wry smile that she still lingered near the loos. More power to her elbow, not to mention her hot little cunt, he told himself as he headed towards the plane.

Four hours into the flight and his thoughts turned once more to sex. A dark shadow flew past and a rush of cheap scent offended his nostrils. The female flight attendants were not as young as they used to be, but they were pretty enough all the same. Especially in the dark. He was stationed by the window, with two empty seats beside him. Reaching up, he pressed a button to summon assistance. Half a minute later, a tall, dark-haired, pert-bosomed Latino woman appeared and asked how she might help. Marsilio leaned forward, pushed up the two arm-rests between them and whispered into her ear. She immediately frowned and he felt a pang of fear and frustration. Then her face cleared and she smiled warmly. She sat down on the end seat while he unzipped his trousers and pulled out his penis. His circumcised cock stood proudly to attention, the glans a faint, swollen blur in the darkness. Without a word, she bent forward, lowered her face into his lap and took him smoothly into her mouth. He rested his hands on the back of her head and held her tight as the first of his seed began to pump along his aching shaft.

Tamara scrambled down a muddy slope and into the trench. The entrance to a carefully dug cave lay directly

113

ahead. Three or four heavy posts had been set in place. Broad orange ribbons were strung between them bearing the warning 'Danger! Keep out!' at regular intervals. Thick electric cable trailed everywhere and she had to step carefully to avoid it. It was the first opportunity she had had to nose about. Giving Erskine the slip had not been easy. As she had discovered both to her misfortune and her pleasure, the man was insatiable. If he wasn't touching her up behind the filing cabinet, he was taking her across tables, over carpets and even occasionally on the bed. Even she was beginning to feel the strain. Time was not on her side. The International Symposium began tomorrow and she had decided, in Max's absence, that she would have to attend it on her own. But today, her luck had changed. She had told Erskine that she had to go to London for a meeting with her publishers. She had expected him to be awkward about it, but on the contrary he had seemed relieved. It transpired that he was awaiting the arrival of one of the backer's representatives: Allessandra Favelli of the Diablo Foundation. In the circumstances, a quick look round followed by a swift retreat seemed highly advisable.

'You shouldn't be here.'

Tamara's heart skipped a beat. She spun round in the direction of the voice. A tall, cloudy-faced man with a lazy eye and a limp was standing behind her. She couldn't help but wonder from under which of the nearby stones he had crawled. He wore a badge that read 'Security'. Tamara frowned. Damn! It was lunchtime and the site had temporarily emptied. This was all she needed.

'I'm sorry,' she said. Her mind raced. Only one idea came to her. It was old but it was usually effective. She unbuttoned the top of her blouse and shook the material loose. Even to this cretin, she hoped it was obvious that she wasn't wearing a bra.

'It's awfully warm, isn't it?' she continued, still flapping her shirt. Pulling it out from her waistband, she tugged it high and exposed her tummy. The man's eyes locked on to her belly-button, and he licked his lips, like a greedy child eyeing up a bar of chocolate. Tamara leaned forward and

peered at his name badge. She could see his name well enough from where she was standing, but it allowed her to push her breasts just that little bit closer.

'Stan?' she said, as if she knew the name but couldn't quite recall the face. He took a deep breath and inflated his chest. It was clear he thought this would impress her.

'I'm Mr Santer's new assistant,' she explained.

'I thought you were his secretary,' replied the lugubrious Stan.

This was going to be harder than she thought. Oh, well, decided Tamara, when in doubt, get them out. She smoothed her hand across her blouse and scratched her right nipple.

'It's hot, isn't it?' she said, returning to her earlier theme. 'Shame we don't have a pool. I could do with stripping off.'

Stan made no reply. But she was sure his heart had begun to pump just a little bit faster. Now she unbuttoned her blouse. Stan looked on, open-mouthed. She wasn't wearing a bra and, when her heavy orbs tumbled free of the shirt, Tamara could almost hear his Adam's apple pump up and down in the dry channel of his throat. He tottered for a moment when she unzipped her skirt and tugged it down over her hips. Stepping out of it, she stood there in her black, high-cut knickers and nothing else.

'I just wanted to do a bit of topless sunbathing,' she explained. 'It's nice and sheltered down here so I didn't think anyone would mind.' She paused to let her near-nakedness sink in, then added, 'You don't mind, do you, Stan?'

She stepped up to him, pressed her cool body against his and playfully pulled at his belt. 'You should try it, too,' she cooed. 'Come on, why don't you?'

He tried to escape her grip, but it was a half-hearted effort. It was obvious he could scarcely believe his luck. But it was equally clear, from the glances he kept throwing over his shoulder, that he was sure that whatever he tried now, he wouldn't get away with. There were too many people around, people who might disturb them. Tamara

frowned. She knew she didn't have much time. It wouldn't be long before people began drifting back from lunch. She would have to do something about Stan and she would have to do it quickly.

Standing on tiptoe, she stretched her arms around his neck and kissed him lightly on the mouth. His lips were chapped and dry. She heard the gurgle in his throat and sensed the struggle going on inside him. Letting go with one arm, she pushed her hand down between their bodies and felt for his cock. His trousers were very loose and his penis was already hard. It made it easy for her to form a small half-fist around his sheathed erection. This time he didn't fight her. The pleasure gnawing at his insides was evidently too great for anything more than token resistance. Tamara began to pump him firmly and his legs trembled. She pressed her mouth close to his ear and whispered, 'I bet all the women want you, don't they, Stan? I bet they've all been down here. I bet you've had the lot of them.' She gave his cock a gentle, playful squeeze. 'Mouths, pussies, bumholes even. I bet you've buggered a few women in your time, haven't you?' She was pretty sure he hadn't. In fact, she was willing to bet that precious few women had been anywhere near Stan's cock, which was why he was happy for her to do whatever she liked.

Too late, Stan realised what she was up to. He tried to pull away, but his body had gone too far; he had surrendered too much ground. Suddenly he was ejaculating into his pants, his hot, sticky sperm soaking into his trousers.

'Oh fuck!' he grunted, his knees buckling. He began to sob like a baby and for a moment Tamara felt sorry for him. It was obvious that something like this was a rarity for Stan. Perhaps she should have fucked him, just to show him what it was like. No, that was silly. This was better. Not better for Stan perhaps but certainly better for her.

Stan pulled away. As the post-orgasmic fog began to lift, the cold realisation that his Y-fronts were drenched and his sperm was leaking through the front of his uniform revived what passed for his senses. He looked first at Tamara, then

116

down at his pants and seemed totally at a loss as to how to proceed.

'You'd better go and change,' she advised him.

'I haven't got anything to change into!' he responded angrily.

Tamara shook her head. She picked up her skirt, tugged it on, then reached under the hem and pulled down her knickers. 'Go to the toilet, take off your pants, clean yourself up and put these on,' she told him.

He looked horrified. 'I'm not putting on a pair of women's knickers!'

She thrust them into his face. 'You can eat them for all I care. I'm just trying to do you a favour.' As they wafted across his face, she felt his body still. She pushed them into his hand and noticed that he didn't resist.

'They're a present,' she whispered in her sexiest voice. 'I don't want them back. Now clear off before someone comes.' She smiled at the pun but Stan didn't seem to get it. He studied the panties screwed up in his fist. Would he never go? Tamara asked herself. Much more delay and she would have to opt for plan B, which involved bashing him over the head. Then, just as she was about to abandon all hope, he turned, scurried up over the bank and disappeared.

'At last!' muttered Tamara thankfully. She scooped up her blouse, slipped it back on and turned towards the cave entrance. What was so important here that no one other than Erskine Santer and a few trusted helpers were allowed anywhere near it?

She stepped over the phalanx of bright orange ribbons, extracted a pen-torch from her skirt pocket and passed into the gloom beyond. It was pitch black and she had to tread carefully. The interior went deeper than she had expected, with several small openings leading off. She investigated the first two, but they petered out into dead ends. Her third attempt was more fruitful, though she was forced to crouch for a few feet before the tunnel widened into a larger cave beyond. She kicked around and found some wires. Following the route of one thick lead, she came to a small

wall-mounted box. A large red button sat in the centre and her face lit up an instant before the rest of the cave. It took her eyes a few moments to adjust to the brightness, but when they did she knew she had found what she was looking for. That the main dig was centred here was obvious from the series of neatly excavated niches in the surrounding walls, all marked with tiny coloured flags. But there was something else down here, something she had not expected to find. The mined area was delineated by a thick, neatly chalked pentagram. At each point sat a small golden urn. Tamara squatted down and examined each container. The first held a small ruby; the second a silver scarab; the third a scrap of parchment covered in hieroglyphics; the fourth a delicately carved snake-head amulet; and the fifth a handful of green ash. After six years with Omega, Tamara recognised the significance at once. These were charms – charms to contain an occult force. It puzzled her. If the Contessa's purpose was to free Vanjja and her daughters, why attempt to restrain them too?

A warm breeze fanned her cheeks. Odd. She stood up and looked around for the source. She was still turning things over, when there was a loud bang and the cave was plunged back into darkness. Almost immediately something brushed her thigh and she jumped. It felt like a human hand, which was crazy because she knew she was alone. Fingers closed over her left breast and squeezed. Tamara shrieked instinctively and turned to lash out with her fist. Before she could make contact with whoever or whatever was down here with her, she found herself upended and lying on the ground. No, not lying on the ground: struggling on the ground. Something thrust up between her legs and nudged her pussy. Her skirt blew up around her waist, exposing her cunt, and her legs were forced apart. Hands reached across her body, teasing and stroking. There were fingers at her breasts again, stretching her nipples. She lashed out with her arms, but there was no one there. The unmistakable warmth of a tongue stole swiftly along her sex and stabbed at her clitoris. Behind it came a cock, long and hard, burrowing its way into her

cunt. She twisted left and right and the cock drove deep. In spite of herself, Tamara felt her body tighten with excitement. She could feel her juices bubbling up inside her sex, and overflowing down her thighs. Something warm and slippery pushed against her nose and mouth. The familiar aroma of liquid sex swamped her senses, and a mushy pulp-like swell of cunt-flesh oozed across her face. Obscene images filled her head. She was at a drunken, Roman orgy, naked and roped to a couch. A man lay under her, fucking her slowly in the arse. His companion straddled her tummy, his toga up around his waist, driving himself into her swollen cunt. A third man, a huge armour-clad soldier, squatted over her face and pushed his big cock past her welcoming lips. Either side of her stood two oiled and naked boys, young men hardly out of their teens, their penises long and erect. Her hands were wrapped around their shafts and she was milking them vigorously. All five cocks erupted at once: five penises giving up their store of cream, filling her body and splattering her skin.

Tamara shut her eyes and surrendered to her orgasm. The earth seemed to be rising up around her, drawing her down. Her body felt as if it were dripping in come; but she knew that couldn't be right. This was all fantasy, make-believe. There was something inside her head; something pulling at her, destroying her. She had to resist; but then her orgasm began to build up again and she knew that resistance was the last thing on her mind.

A woman lay across the Contessa's lap. She was naked and her tiny body shone with sweat. The Contessa stroked her spine, from the base of her neck down to the cleft of her arse. Taking hold of the girl's left buttock, she squeezed it hard, her fingers digging cruelly into white unblemished flesh. Between the girl's sundered cheeks, a Minion's cock moved in and out of her rectum. A second Minion crouched behind the first, his penis buried deep in the woman's cunt, his hips jiggling gently from side to side. Both men were dangerously close to orgasm, now. So, too,

was the woman. But they must all three hold back if the spell were not to be broken. The Contessa smiled. Poor Tamara Knight, she thought, *Did you really think you could hide from me?* She closed her eyes and concentrated hard. The pleasure of her servants passed into her vulva and she felt her own excitement mount. But she, too, must resist. The pleasure was to be passed on, into the mind and body of Tamara Knight. But this pleasure would not please. It would destroy. Her enemy had passed into her domain now. There could be no escape.

She laughed, but it was a cruel laugh as, in her mind's eye, she watched Tamara hasten ecstatically towards certain death.

Max was dreaming. He was floating through a starless, pitch-black night. Spunk flowed from his cock in short, sharp bursts, each surge like a blast from an engine, propelling him backwards across the inky void. A voice called to him from somewhere in the darkness. He twisted and turned. His penis spurted yet again, driving him now towards the source of the fearful cry. Pleasure riddled his body, his every nerve on fire, his every muscle taut with lust. He felt himself begin to spiral helplessly out of control, plunging down through an infinity of time and space. Excitement drove all meaning from his world. A huge vulva opened up around him, drawing him home. He was struggling to break free. Sap leaked into the darkness, long, damp strands of female arousal coiling around his body, holding him fast, sneaking into his every orifice, tugging at his swollen balls, dribbling into the open eye of his cock.

He was mad. He knew that now. Stark, staring mad.

Tamara's body throbbed with need. She felt her clitoris quicken and her labia engorge. How much was real, how much was false, it was impossible to say. In any event, she was unable to clear a space in her brain for long enough to give it any serious thought. This was sex. *She* was sex. There was no longer any divide between herself and the act

itself. Every part of her body was quaking with arousal. She tried to fight back, but it was hopeless. The feelings in her cunt betrayed her at every turn. The earth rose up around her. It was in her hair and in her nose and in her mouth. She was choking. She was coming. She was everywhere and she was nowhere. Madness reigned now. It was wonderful.

A voice whispered into her ear. It was a familiar voice. At least she thought it was. But the pleasure ripping through her vulva clouded everything. There was no point in fighting this. No point at all.

Something was wrong. The Contessa's eyes flared open. The Minion inside the girl's cunt was moving too rapidly. He opened his mouth and yelled, 'Yes! Yes!'

'Do not fuck so hard!' screamed the Contessa. 'You will come!'

'I cannot stop myself, Mistress. I cannot! Please! Help me!' he cried.

'No!' The Contessa reached down and pinched his shaft between her fingers, squeezing hard to stem the flow of seed. Her golden phallus lay beside her on the Living Throne of flesh. Was that a sudden movement she had caught? Surely not. Her head began to burn. If she felt pain then it must mean that Guy was feeling pleasure. And if he felt pleasure . . .

'No!' she screamed a second time, stretched out her arm and took hold of the thick, metal rod. A tortured groan broke from the mouth of the second Minion. He began to ravish the girl's rectum with renewed passion. This was Guy's work, damn him! She had no idea how he had done it, but he must be free of the phallus. Curse him to hell and back!

Suddenly the second Minion was coming. He shrieked with pleasure and emptied himself into the girl's arse. Almost immediately his companion unleashed his seed into her cunt, shaking his hips violently and howling with delight.

Damn them! Damn them all! The Contessa stood up,

pushing the girl from her lap. Both Minions fell to the floor, senseless now that they had reached orgasm. The Contessa's face darkened. She threw back her head and let out a dreadful roar of anger. Vengeance burned within. She turned towards the golden phallus and her eyes tightened. Darné, who had been present throughout, shifted anxiously in the silence that followed. The Contessa's eyes remained fixed on the globe when next she spoke.

'Send Valli to me,' she said. 'I have a task for her . . .'

Tamara sat up and shook her head. It ached terribly. She was so tired, she hardly had the strength to move. She groped around in her pocket, searching for her torch. Locating it, she flicked the switch and gave thanks for the thin beam of light that sliced into the darkness. Whatever had threatened her had gone. But what was it? In her mind's eye she saw Hugo Morgan stretched out on his hospital bed. Was this what had happened to him? She shuddered. What had saved her? She wasn't sure. But it was the voice that had caught her by surprise. It must have been her imagination surely? What else could it be?

She called out into the darkness. 'Max?'

There was no answer. Of course there wasn't. Max wasn't here. Yet it was Max's voice she had heard, telling her not to worry, that he was going to get her out of this. Crazy. But where was Max? She wished she knew the answer to that one.

The telephone rang. Aubrey Manners was in no mood for conversation. The young girl whose head was currently nestling in his lap, her lips tight around his prick, was giving him so much pleasure. These silly young things. What was she, eighteen, nineteen? Hardly a woman at all. But such girls seemed drawn to a man in his position – a man of power. And, of course, a man who knew exactly what to say to them. A man who dabbled in the black arts had a distinct advantage in matters of sex, he had discovered.

Valli bent over. She had a lovely big arse. The Contessa stroked each flank and squeezed the flesh. She let her fingers sink down into the crack and felt for the girl's anus. It was large and elastic; far more so than that of any other woman she had known. The girl could gain no pleasure from being penetrated vaginally. All her fulfilment came from the most profound buggery. Her bumhole was now slick with grease. Kalya had seen to that. Valli steadied herself, aware that the Contessa was about to use her in a way that would bring both pain and pleasure. She was not afraid, though, for she knew that to serve the Contessa was the greatest joy of all.

The Contessa raised the golden rod and pushed it up against the girl's greased sphincter. She had abused Guy in many ways since first imprisoning his soul inside the phallus. But never like this. The milky cloud began to change colour. She had seen this before: pink meant fear. It was pink now; almost red in fact. The Contessa smiled.

'I will bend you to my will, Guy,' she said, easing the glans into Valli's rectum. The girl's arse opened up around the globe. She felt the phallus shudder in her hand and was forced to tighten her grip. Guy was struggling. Good. It would increase the punishment. He had to be taught that he was not to roam; that he was not to interfere. She could smash the globe, of course, but that would merely release Guy's spirit into the ether. He might find rest. That was not what she wanted. She wanted him to suffer.

He was suffering now. She watched with glee as the orb began to vanish into Valli's behind. The woman must have a rubber rectum, mused the Contessa. Already, further games were forming in her head. Valli let out a muted moan of arousal and discomfort, which was hardly surprising. The Contessa doubted whether even her arse could take the full thrust of this phallic monster.

Now the girl was rotating her hips gently, anticipating that sweet moment when the globe would send her into spasm. The Contessa's head was full of strange, unbidden thoughts. Somewhere far away, and yet so very near, Guy screamed. She had not yet fathomed the precise nature of

his existence within the sphere. He appeared to experience pain and pleasure in reverse measure to the normal order of things. When she held the phallus – and sometimes even when she did not – the two of them became linked. His pleasure, her pain; his pain, her pleasure. But what was he feeling now? Was it torture to be inserted into Valli's rump or sweet delight? The phallus gave a series of keen judders. Guy was finding it hard to breathe! Oh exquisite joy! Struggling to breathe brought him pain. But his pain gave the Contessa pleasure and she felt her vulva tighten with excitement. Lowering her head, she watched the sap begin to leak out on to her thigh. She gave the phallus one last push. Valli arched her back, rolled her eyes towards the ceiling and warbled cheerfully.

'Oh, Mistress!' she shrieked. 'I'm coming! I'm coming!'

Yet the Contessa knew that despite her words the girl was holding back, awaiting her permission to spend.

'Unleash yourself, my darling,' she allowed. 'Let him drown in your delight!'

The girl pushed back and incredibly took yet more of the phallus inside her cavernous arse. The shaft shook and jerked in the Contessa's hand; shaken by Guy's despair and by the girl's convulsing rectum as she came. The screams almost tore her head apart. She had never known such joy; nor Guy so much terror. It was divine.

She eased the phallus from the girl's rectum. It emerged, slick with her spendings, like a monstrous ball emerging from the hole of some dark, forbidding cave. The Contessa marvelled at how the girl's stretched anus quickly refashioned itself into a tightened sheath of muscle. She began to have the most obscene thoughts. She wondered if it could take a man's head. Perhaps next time a Minion was to be punished she might see what could be done. An interesting notion. But for now, there were other matters to attend to. There was no movement inside the globe. Guy must be somewhere in limbo; exhausted and impotent. That would teach him to defy her. He would not be so eager to escape again. For the moment at least she had stayed his travels. But he had thwarted her none the less,

she was sure of that. She would just have to hope that her second plan was more successful.

Max was lying on his back, inside a large chalked circle. His arms were stretched above his head and his legs were widely parted. There were hard leather bands around his wrists and ankles, which fed into metal links fixed to the cold, stone floor. He wasn't sure where he was; it no longer seemed to matter. At the back of his mind was a vague recollection. He had been dreaming: a dream that made no sense. But, then, when did they ever? He had lost all track of time. How long had he been a prisoner now? He had no idea. If he ever escaped the clutches of these unusually demanding women, he would have to have words with Tamara. She'd let him down. It really wasn't on.

Four women circled his body. They were naked. He recognised two of them as the Amazons, Darné and Kalya. The other pair were unfamiliar, but they were tall and statuesque, like their sisters, dark-haired and brown-skinned. The Contessa stood nearby, with a deep silver bowl held aloft in her hands. She swirled it round several times, chanting words that meant nothing to him. He watched her lower the bowl to her lips and sip the contents slowly. Darné stepped forward and relieved her Mistress of the container. The Contessa looked down at Max and her eyes blazed like two flaming coals. It was unnatural. She nodded at the women. They bent low and quickly undid the ties that held Max in place, taking hold of his limbs and using their own strength to keep him pinned. He twisted his body in a vain attempt to try and break their grip. It didn't help that he found his restraint something of a turn-on. His prick unfurled against his will and hardened against his tummy.

The Contessa smiled grimly. 'So you enjoy the struggle, Max. You naughty boy.' But her tone was far from friendly. She crouched over his cock and pulled it towards her so that it protruded at a painful right-angle to his body. It should have made him wilt, but instead, with her warm fist tight around him, his penis grew even harder.

'I'm going to fuck you, Max,' she told him. 'Struggle by all means, but resistance is useless.'

Max did struggle, but it was a token effort. He wanted the Contessa to fuck him, and he wanted the girls to hold him down while she was doing it. He couldn't help himself. There had always been something of the submissive in him. He wriggled his hips from side to side as the Contessa guided his penis between her fat cunt lips. As her labia smudged the tip of his cock, his problem wasn't so much trying to resist as trying not to ejaculate. When she engulfed him in one seamless movement, sinking down so that her labia nestled in his pubes and her buttocks against his balls, he wanted to climax there and then. But she held him with her eyes and something deep within him stemmed the urge to come. He had never known such a warm, pulsating vagina. It was as if her muscles were fashioned from snakes, slithering around his penis, squeezing and tickling, holding and caressing.

The Contessa raised her arms high and began to chant again, some unintelligible mantra. Max decided to do some more struggling but he was tiring fast and his heart wasn't really in it. Besides, though his mind still seemed to be his own, he couldn't tear his eyes away from the Contessa's face. She rose and fell over his cock and he climaxed suddenly and strongly. He felt his semen pump through his shaft in long, luxurious surges. Just when it seemed to be over, it began again. It felt as if it would never end. But it did; suddenly and painfully. The Contessa tightened her cunt around his cock until it hurt. Then she rose quickly and stood over him, her eyes closed, for several long minutes. Freed from her mesmeric gaze, he watched her stomach muscles shift and contract, as if she were going through an elaborate series of tummy exercises. He expected to see his spunk begin to leak from her cunt and run down her thighs, but it didn't. He suddenly realised that the Contessa was holding his seed inside her, though he couldn't fathom why.

It was only when she opened her eyes, then moved out of sight behind him that he began to worry.

She knelt down and pressed her huge, muscular thighs either side of his face. Looking up, he saw her massive vulva open and contract above his head. Her labia were like two rippling panels of flesh, fat and swollen, very pink and very wet. He wanted to turn away as she lowered herself but part of him wanted this, too. She had fucked him; now she was going to sit on his face. What more could he wish for, he asked himself as he tested his arms and legs and found that the girls were holding him as fast as ever. Between his thighs, his penis began to fatten as the smell of the Contessa's cunt-flesh filled his nostrils. This was crazy, but he couldn't help himself. He wanted her all over again. He just wished he could fuck her instead of being fucked, but, hey, being on the receiving end wasn't all bad.

He felt her softened sex slide across his face, engulfing him, covering his nose and mouth. The Contessa's pussy was hot and wet, with a fragrance he had never known before: rich and spicy and laced with musk. She began to move more rapidly now, pressing down hard so that he found it difficult to breathe. His balls were filling again; it seemed impossible, but he could feel them stirring. Something was leaking into his mouth; it was sweet, sticky and strangely heady. He wondered if it was her sap, but the consistency was unusual, very thick and viscous. Then it began to flow more easily. He parted his lips and drank willingly; it seemed the least he could do bearing in mind what was happening between his legs.

Then suddenly the Contessa was coming. Her juices began to flow more freely and, despite himself, Max opened his mouth to swallow the flood. A dull, light-headed sensation washed over him. He felt his own excitement boiling up inside his shaft, but with no friction to tip him over the edge he knew he was to be denied his release. But it didn't matter. All that mattered was that the Contessa was spilling her honey into his throat, and filling him with her essence. He wanted nothing more. Somewhere at the back of Max's mind, that little voice began to speak to him again. Not that he was paying it much attention now. He was gobbling away like a starving

man at a banquet, gagging on the Contessa's thick, oily cream. But that didn't bother him either. She could sit there forever if she wanted to, drowning him with her juices and smothering him with her cunt. He was in heaven.

Ten

The young man lifted the edge of the wire netting and signalled to his companion to squeeze through. She glanced up and down the dark, deserted lane.

'Are you sure about this?'

'Of course!' he reassured her. 'Don't worry. No one's going to find us. And even if they do, that's part of the fun, isn't it?'

Suzy shrugged her shoulders and her hard little breasts trembled in the moonlight. 'I suppose so,' she conceded and scrambled beneath the wire. Safely installed on the other side, she held it up so that Colin could slip through. 'What now?' she asked.

Colin grinned, slipped his arms around her waist and held her close. 'We enjoy ourselves.'

Suzy wasn't wearing a bra beneath her tee-shirt and he enjoyed the feel of her small, apple-hard tits against his chest. They were so firm that even when she ran they barely moved at all. Sliding his fingers up under the loose cotton, he cupped her left breast in his hand and squeezed it tightly. Suzy whimpered, squirmed closer and began to lick the side of his neck, just beneath his ear.

Though it was a warm night, he felt her shiver. Her nipples inflated into hard little steeples of flesh. They pressed insistently against his palm and sent shockwaves of excitement down into his balls. His erect cock twisted its way through the gap in his Y-fronts, and the dry knob scraped against the zip in his jeans. Suzy giggled when he deliberately pushed himself up against her tummy. She

stood on tiptoe and jiggled her hips, delighting in the feel of his hardness as it pressed against her through her thin skirt. When he eased one hand up under the short hem and groped her left buttock, she lifted her knee and rubbed the inside of her bare thigh against his leg.

Arousal lent him the courage to squirm his fingers beneath the elastic of her knickers and wriggle them into her crack. She was hot and sticky and he loved the way her cheeks tightened as he probed towards her anus.

'No, you don't!' she protested, pushing him away. Retreating an inch or two, she rearranged her panties through her skirt, tugging the material out from between her buttocks.

'Oh, come on,' he said, reaching out, pulling her back. 'I only want a feel.'

'Not my bumhole,' she told him. 'I don't like it.'

'All right,' conceded Colin, holding her fast, one arm around her shoulders, the other stretching down towards the small of her back. He reminded himself to be careful. They'd only met an hour ago. When he'd suggested they leave the disco and go somewhere a bit more private he thought she'd tell him to get lost. Instead, she'd pressed herself against his crotch and whispered something filthy in his ear. He'd have taken her home, but he couldn't, because his mum was waiting up.

The old dig site was a brainwave. He told Suzy he knew a way in. She said she didn't mind where they went as long as he gave her a good seeing to; she hadn't been laid since she'd chucked her boyfriend the week before. Colin couldn't believe his luck. He hadn't had a fuck for almost a month and he was getting desperate. Magazines were OK, but they were no substitute for the real thing, and Suzy was most definitely the real thing, right down to her cheap gold ankle chain and her black stiletto heels. With a bit of luck he'd get his finger up her arse, too, whatever she said. Once he had her on her back he'd manoeuvre her legs around his waist. Most girls seemed to like that: it let them rub their clits against his cock and usually made them come. She'd be so spaced out, she wouldn't know what he was up to until it was too late.

'Penny?' whispered Suzy.

'Just thinking of fucking you,' he lied. He squeezed her arse through her skirt and felt his balls tighten against his cock. He wanted her badly now; very badly indeed.

Gioseppi da Vinci stared at the couple three places ahead of him in the queue. They were holding hands and giggling. When the girl turned sideways on he saw that she had the most enormous pair of breasts. It was quite obvious, from the way they wobbled so freely, that she was not wearing a bra. He studied them for a moment or two, wondering what it would feel like to hold those large, quivering orbs; to pinch her flesh; to bury his face or suck gently on the teats. Would she be soft and salty after the long flight? He spotted a gleam of sweat in the hollow of her neck and noticed that little beads of moisture had trickled down into her cleavage. Judging from the prominence of her nipples, a casual onlooker who knew nothing of such matters might have been forgiven for supposing that she had attached two large acorns to her areolae. He wondered if it was the cooling effects of the airport air conditioning or excitement that had made them stiffen. He glanced down and watched her companion grope her big denim-clad arse. Had he ever sodomised her, he wondered, or sucked from the ring of her anus?

'Oi!' A rough, coarse-edged voice broke his thoughts. He looked up and found himself staring into two pairs of angry eyes.

'Had enough excitement for the day, have we?' asked the stubble-faced young man. His companion wrinkled her nose in a clear statement of disgust.

'Dirty old sod!' she said contemptuously.

The couple were waved through passport control, saving Gioseppi from further rebuke. He was cognisant, however, of the appalled looks from his fellow passengers.

The criticism had been undeserved. He was not a dirty old sod, nor had he taken any pleasure in examining the girl's body. His interest had been purely academic. He might have wished it otherwise, but he had lived with his

132

indifference long enough. What *had* puzzled him had been the rather crude image his mind had briefly conjured up. It was not the product of a conscious effort. The uncouth young man had been lying on top of his overweight partner, taking her quite vigorously. As for Gioseppi, in his mind's eye he had been kneeling behind the happy couple and had, with equal ardour, been buggering the pair of them one after the other.

It really was quite strange.

'It's a bit stupid, this,' said Colin, booting a heap of carefully sifted soil. 'Load of grown men digging around like kids.'

'What do you think they're looking for? A Mummy or something?' asked Suzy.

'Who cares?' replied Colin. He made a grab for her and she laughed and pulled a face.

'Perhaps we should exorcise the evil spirits,' she giggled.

His hands were hurrying over her body, squeezing and pinching her young, pliant flesh. 'How d'you suggest we do that?' he mumbled, burrowing his face in her neck and biting her roughly.

Suzy squirmed and gave a feeble moan. 'Have a fuck,' she whimpered.

They pulled each other to the ground. Suzy lay on her back, pulled up her skirt and showed him her panties: a tiny white triangle, held in place by a tight, spaghetti-thin band. Colin's greedy eyes devoured the damp patch spreading out from the cotton-covered mouth of her cunt. Unzipping himself quickly, he undressed and kicked his trousers into touch.

Suzy raised her hips, tugged her knickers down and draped them over her discarded handbag. Her pussy was small, with a faint covering of fluffy blonde curls. Colin's stomach churned with excitement when she reached down and began to finger the narrow slit of her sex.

'Oh come on, you bastard,' she crooned. 'Give us a fuck!'

If that was what she wanted, he was happy to oblige. He

lowered himself over her, pushing at her with his prick. He was so excited that he couldn't find the target. It was her fault, he told himself: her cunt wasn't big enough.

'Wait a sec,' she said, reaching down between her legs. 'I'll give you a hand!'

She giggled but Colin couldn't see the joke. If he didn't get into her soon he was going to come. Her warm fingers closed around his shaft and he felt his penis jerk uncontrollably. He threw his head back and howled. 'Oh, no, please! No, noooo!'

But it was too late. His balls overflowed, filling his cock with spunk, sending his cream hurtling along the length of his shaft and out into the warm night. Thick wads of sperm spattered the earth, his belly and the inside of Suzy's turned-up skirt.

'You filthy bastard!' she yelled at him. 'You stupid filthy bastard!'

Colin fell forward on to his face, sobbing as his cock continued to leak semen. Suzy opened her bag and pulled out a tissue. She began to wipe at her skirt, ignoring Colin, who had fallen back on to his haunches, and was trying to catch his breath. His penis was dribbling seed, twitching a little but still very erect. Suzy scrambled to her feet. He looked at her with a blank expression on his face.

'What you doing?' he asked.

'What d'you think I'm doing?' she responded sharply. 'I'm going home. You're no good now, are you?'

He reached up and took hold of her hand. 'No, wait a minute,' he pleaded. 'We can still do it. I haven't gone down. Look!'

'No thanks,' she replied contemptuously. 'I'm not in the mood any more.'

He tightened his grip around her wrist. She might not be in the mood, but he certainly was.

'Leggo!' she shouted. 'I'll scream!'

She tried to pull away, but he held on fast to her hand. A moment later, she was on her back, with Colin wriggling on top of her, his erect cock digging into her stomach.

'Get off me, you bastard!' she screamed and somehow managed to roll sideways on to her tummy.

Her skirt flew up and exposed her bare backside; in her hurry to escape she'd had no time to put her knickers back on. Colin threw himself forward, pinned her flat and began to claw at her hips. She yelled in horror when he drove his hand into her cleft. But it was too late. He found the rubbery knot of her anus and pushed at it with his index finger. Suzy clenched her bottom, arched her back and let out half a scream before Colin's other hand closed over her mouth. She felt his finger wriggling against her unprotected bumhole. Another second and he'd be up her arse. The bastard! The dirty filthy bastard!

And then it happened.

The earth began to open up. A low, shuddering moan came from the entrance to the underground cavern; whispers of blue-grey fog curled up out of the ground, spinning towards them. Colin froze, his eyes staring straight ahead. Suzy took her chance to push him away, jump to her feet and run. She didn't turn round, so she never saw what it was that had so transfixed her attacker.

Neither for that matter did he.

Far away, another young man was fully alive to his plight. He should have known it was too good to be true. It wasn't that he was unlucky with women, but even he had never managed to seduce two at once.

He had bumped into them outside the student pub.

'Hello, Stephen,' one of them had grinned. He had wondered how they had known his name, but after five pints of lager and a vodka chaser, he didn't really care. He had to struggle now to recall theirs. The blonde's, he thought, was Lana and the black girl's Jenny, no, Joni, that was it. They had told him they would open his eyes to pleasures he could not conceive. How could he resist? The tall black girl had a big, hard arse while her friend had small, lemon-shaped breasts, a pink oval mouth and sparkling blue eyes. When she smiled at him and licked the corners of her mouth, he knew his fate was sealed. He had taken them back to his flat and hung their knickers over the bedroom handle. One pair was the standard sign for

'do not disturb; man at work'. Two pairs was simply boasting. But if his room-mate came home unexpectedly (which, sadly, he doubted), then he wanted his triumph announced with a trumpet.

He had begun to undress, but they forestalled his efforts, giggling as they pushed him down on to the bed. He had struggled for a moment, then the black girl had said, quite harshly, 'Don't fight us, boy. We're going to rape you.'

How could he resist them after that? It was all he had ever wanted from a woman; let alone two at once. They had used their bras to tie his hands to the headboard; their stockings to secure his feet. My God, he thought, surrendering cheerfully to his fate, they're into bondage, too. Could it get any better? He closed his eyes and watched in his mind as they began a long, merciless ravishment of his body. Blinking them open again, he saw that the girls had stripped naked. They unzipped his trousers and pulled out his cock. The black girl had taken him into her mouth and sucked him gently for a few minutes, while her friend stood to one side and masturbated. She opened herself up to reveal the heated flesh of her inner labia, and he had watched with growing need as the evidence of her excitement began to dribble down the inside of her thighs.

They had taken it in turns to fuck him. The black girl first, then her friend, then the black girl again and so on until he quite happily lost count. More than once he was sure he would climax, but while one of the girls rode him, the other would pinch the root of his cock and stem the flow of seed each time it threatened to erupt into his shaft. He breathed rapidly through his nose, short, noisy puffs of air. His hips began to twist as if they had assumed a life of their own. At last, when he thought he could take no more, the black girl had begun to buck energetically, and he knew his ordeal was nearly over. He came almost at once. With amazing dexterity, Joni dismounted before his ejaculation was complete, took hold of his cock and squeezed. The blonde girl's fist circled his shaft and she squeezed, too.

'To the Mistress!' they declared, as if it were a toast. He

might have asked himself what the fuck they were talking about, but at that moment his sperm began to issue from his cock in sharp, creamy spurts.

'Oh my God! Oh my God!' he screamed as the full force of his orgasm struck him. Joni reached sideways and pressed her hand across his mouth. Lana placed hers on top of her friend's. He grunted savagely into warm flesh as they continued to draw the sting of his climax, pumping together and repeating over and over again, 'To the Mistress! To the Mistress! To the Mistress!'

After they had milked him dry, Joni held his legs apart while Lana wriggled a long, thin finger into his rectum. She touched something deep inside his bowels and his penis unfurled, engorging with blood. This time, Joni had straddled his upper body and crushed her huge arse to his face, rubbing the pale brown knot of her anus back and forth across his mouth. He lapped at it furiously, stabbing at the hole several times before she shifted position abruptly and anchored the hump of her vulva against his face so that he could hardly breathe. At the same time, Lana sheathed his cock with her pussy and rode him gently like a cantering stallion. Between his legs, his penis had begun to jerk its need into her belly.

But that was then and this was now. After what had seemed a long, long night they had finally slithered from his exhausted body, untied his aching limbs and snuggled either side of him, warming him with their sweat and juices. They had slept for a while, and when they had woken had told him that this was just the beginning. They served a Mistress. He might serve her, too. But the choice was his.

He had chosen. Gazing into the sparkling, blue eyes of the lemon-breasted blonde, he had felt himself grow dizzy. Dark coals had flamed into life and blinded him for a moment. And when his eyes had cleared he was here, in a cold, badly lit room that smelt of damp rock and something else: age, if that was possible. Endless old age.

He was naked; standing on tiptoe on top of a small dais. His feet were pressed together, secured by thick coils of

137

rope, and his arms were stretched above his head. Thin cords had been run around his waist and groin, criss-crossing his balls, separating them one from the other. He had been shaved, too. He could scarcely believe it. When had all this happened? His penis was fully erect, jutting up and out, its circumcised head round and glistening. There was something warm and wet dripping the length of his cock; it felt like oil.

Lana and Joni stood nearby, while directly in front of him was a third woman. She was tall and muscular, with huge breasts, flowing black hair and broad, powerful thighs. Her entire body was encased in a lattice-work of chain and leather. He looked into her eyes and thought he saw something familiar there. He had seen those eyes before.

'I am the Contessa,' she said. 'Do you wish to serve me?'

He should have asked why. He should have asked who. He should have asked a lot of questions at that moment. But there was a growing need between his legs. Excitement tightened his stomach, blotting out the pain. At the back of his mind was the knowledge that service would bring pleasure. He nodded slowly. Yes, he wished to serve. He hardly knew why. Pleasure, that was why.

Lana and Joni stepped forward. They were holding long, evil-looking lengths of leather in their hands.

'Prepare him,' said the Contessa.

Lana stood in front of him, while Joni disappeared behind. A moment later he felt the first cruel lash across his buttocks. Then Lana whipped at his chest. As the blows began to rain down, he threw back his head and screamed his pain and pleasure into the unseen vault of the chamber.

It was the end of one life, but the beginning of another. Between his legs, his cock had turned to stone and his balls began to fill with seed. A hand reached out; fingers sheathed his penis and began to stroke. He was in paradise.

But soon he would be in hell.

Max awoke with a thundering headache. His eyes were heavy and his mind was blank. It must have been some

party, he told himself. He pressed both hands to his aching temples. What party? The mists began to lift from his addled brain. He smelt his breath. It was sweet, but stale: no hint of alcohol. He rubbed his eyes and began to remember. Not that there was much to recall. He was lying on a table at the massage parlour, with a blonde woman lowering herself on to his face. After that, nothing. Now he was sitting on a bench a few feet away from a familiar gilded edifice: the Albert Memorial in Kensington Gardens. Well, it was a start. At least he knew where he was. But how had he got there? He took a deep breath and almost keeled over. If he hadn't been boozing why did he feel so drunk? He felt inside his jacket pockets. Everything seemed present and correct: wallet, credit cards, driving licence. He jangled a pair of keys in his hand. They weren't his and yet they seemed familiar. Another memory stirred into life. It was as if they were stacking up somewhere at the back of his mind, like aeroplanes waiting for landing clearance. He was back at Omega. Funny, that was only this morning and yet already it seemed an age ago. With a start he examined his watch. Odd: according to the digital date today was the fourteenth. That couldn't be right. He'd arrived at Omega on the morning of the tenth. He'd been taken to see Hugo Morgan that afternoon, one of the few memories he would have been happy to shed. The following morning he and Tamara had gone to the British Museum, seen the lunatic Professor Abigail Crayshaw, then followed the Minion to Soho. That was the eleventh. According to his watch, three days had passed since then. So where had he been? And how had he got here? And whose were these keys? Another memory was given permission to land. Max shut his eyes and concentrated. An address. Not his; not Tamara's. Just an address. He remembered. He glanced down at his wrist a second time. It was 11.30 a.m. He wondered how long he'd been sitting here. Not that it mattered. What mattered was finding Tamara. He looked around him. Someone must have brought him here. They might be watching him right now. He considered heading back to Omega HQ. But perhaps

that was what they expected him to do. He shook his head. If only he could remember where he'd been and what had happened. He licked his lips. That taste in his mouth should have told him something. It was odd, like a blend of exotic spices, and something else. It was no use, he couldn't place it. Dropping the keys back into his pocket, he stood up and walked down into Kensington High Street. Occasionally he looked around, but as far as he could tell, he was not being followed. He dodged into the tube station and caught the first train to Wimbledon. He went three stops, then changed; then changed again; then caught a bus, then got off. No one else did. He made his way to another main road and caught a taxi to Chiswick. After two minutes, he informed the driver he'd changed his mind, got out, ran down a side street and caught a bus back into the centre of London. If anyone was still following him after all that, he decided, then they deserved to find out where he was going.

Erica Stanislav looked out across a blur of rain-soaked English countryside. Her plane had been diverted due to bad weather over the French coast. Instead of touching down at Heathrow as planned, she had been forced to disembark in Manchester. Fortunately, she had a telephone contact number for use in emergency. Though her English was not perfect, it was good enough for her to get through to Allessandra Favelli's office at Diablo Worldwide and explain her predicament. Unfortunately, Allessandra was out of the office on urgent business. After apologies and commiserations all round, her secretary, Bethany, suggested that Erica catch the next available Intercity to London. Her ticket would be booked from their end and Erica could collect it at Manchester Piccadilly. She would be met at King's Cross by a private car and taken to her hotel as previously arranged.

Sitting alone in first class, she was aware that she felt terribly randy. It was hardly surprising; after all, she had not fucked for nearly twelve hours. She tugged the lapels of her jacket away from her bosom and admired the swell

140

of her cleavage. The black halter-top outfit she had chosen for the journey set off her figure very nicely. *Sans* bra, she saw that her nipples had hardened into taut peaks of flesh that protruded through the thin fabric of her dress. Slipping her hand beneath the material, she pulled out her left breast and squeezed it gently, fingers fiddling with the teat. She was so engrossed that she failed to hear the whoosh of air as the connecting door to the carriage slid open. Glancing up she saw a tall, wiry young man in a blue, starched jacket, matching trousers and yellow-trimmed peaked cap. He looked ridiculously gauche, thought Erica, and felt a rush of excitement dampen her knickers.

The young man froze at the sight of her exposed breast. Erica held his gaze for several seconds then casually squeezed herself back into her dress, fluttered her eyelashes and grinned. His face, bright red with embarrassment, seemed fixed in stone, his feet rooted to the spot.

'Yes?' she smiled sweetly.

His Adam's apple bobbed up and down. When he spoke, it was with such difficulty that she had a fleeting image of a team of tiny men pushing the words up and out of his throat.

'I ... I need to see your ticket, please, Miss,' he stammered.

Erica made a pretence of searching through her handbag. 'Oh dear,' she sighed. 'I cannot seem to find it. That is so odd. I was sure it was here earlier.' She looked up into the young man's eyes and gave him her naughtiest wink. He visibly wilted before her. How sweet, she thought, he's shy. He was probably a virgin, too, like those awkward, whining boys she'd enjoyed so many times in her classroom back in Budapest.

'I am silly,' she blushed, lowering her voice to a sensuous whisper. She patted the base of her tummy. 'I remember now. I hide it in my – how do you say – knickers, for safekeeping.'

The young man's face flushed deeper red. He backed away when Erica put her handbag on the inside seat and

stood up. She decided to take the bull by the horns, stepped forward and wrapped her fingers lightly around the edge of his lapel. He was at least six inches taller than her, and as she leaned forward she knew he could see straight down the front of her dress.

'You would like to come to the bathroom, yes? And help me search for him?

'What?' There was a shrill edge to the young man's voice.

Oh, this was so delightful, thought Erica. One word from her, one very special word and this poor, helpless boy would do all she commanded. But how much more satisfying to use her own skills to entrap him. She released his jacket and slipped her long fingers around his wrist. Then she turned towards the bathroom, leading him by the hand. He followed obediently, like a lamb to the slaughter. It was an image she rather enjoyed.

Once inside the large washroom, she closed the door and engaged the lock. Then she reached up with both her arms, circled the young man's neck, and pressed herself close. She could hear his heart thumping rapidly. When she plunged her tongue past his lips and into his mouth, she was surprised to discover how dry it was. His big fists began to claw at the back of her dress, but they were unsure, adolescent gropings. She pushed him away, kicked off her heels, then stepped back and crossed her hands in front of her. Taking hold of the hem of her dress she pulled it up and over her head in one fluid movement. The young man's mouth fell open at the sight of her bare breasts. Her nipples were long, pink and erect. Erica brought her palms up and squeezed her flesh, then shook her hands so that both orbs wobbled. Then she let go, rested her fingers on her hips and parted her short legs. Apart from a tiny black G-string, she was naked. The young man seemed transfixed, like a rabbit caught in her headlights. Erica lowered her eyes and pulled lightly at the front of her knickers.

'I cannot see the ticket,' she simpered enticingly, before glancing up. 'You will have to look for him. He must be in here somewhere.'

The conductor licked the corners of his mouth, but remained rooted to the spot. Erica lost patience. She needed satisfaction and she needed it now. 'Down!' she ordered, pointing to the floor.

The young man still hesitated. But only for an instant. Then he dropped to his knees. Erica walked forward until she was standing just in front of him, her pussy almost at the level of his face. She threw his hat to one side and saw that his ears were very large and very red.

'Take down the panties with your teeth,' she told him. The young man leaned forward, until his forehead was resting lightly on her belly.

'Too slow! Too slow!' she admonished. Swinging round, Erica pressed her back up against the wall of the washroom for support. Taking hold of the young man's hair, she tugged him sideways, altering the angle of his face. Then she pulled him sharply forward. His nose pressed through the thin gossamer of her G-string and into her pussy. As the sweet smell of her labia washed over him, he finally sprang into life. It was about time, reflected Erica, as she felt a rush of warmth to her groin. The young man opened his mouth and fastened his lips around her vulva, rubbing his face from side to side.

Erica raised her left leg and swung it over his shoulder, securing her hold on him. He dug his fingers into her hips and made little grunting noises. She felt herself teetering on the edge of her climax. She came quickly and furiously, holding on to the man's head for dear life. Her heart pounding, she pushed him away, yanking her knickers down and kicking them to one side. She wasn't finished with him yet. She dragged him to his feet and began tugging at his belt. The young man was pulling at his zip, now, trying to unfasten himself. As his trousers fell away, Erica ripped at his pants, exposing his penis. It was long, hard and heavily veined. She took it between her fingers and felt it twitch dangerously. She had forgotten that this was an excited young man, one who had not yet learned the art of self-control. His shaft jumped in her hand, and the first of his seed spurted into the air. He closed his eyes

and fell back against the wall, groaning happily. Erica leaned into him, raised her right leg and brought her pussy down over his glans.

'Fuck me! Fuck me!' she yelled, but in truth it was she who was doing the fucking. The young man screamed as if she had stabbed him, his hands holding her close as he emptied the rest of his seed into her. He rubbed his back up and down, wriggling his hips and gurgling.

He slumped to the floor, suddenly spent. Erica replaced her G-string and climbed back into her dress. She bent down and kissed him lightly on the cheek. 'I will let myself out,' she whispered.

Closing the door behind her, she leaned back into it and rested for a few moments. Her immediate lust had been slaked. Yet the encounter had, perversely, excited her all the more. There were still three hours to go and several carriages to explore. She would use the time productively. There must be more victims to be enjoyed before she reached London.

Allessandra Favelli examined the guest list. Preparations for the party were well under way. It had been a while since she had hosted a gathering at Farnham Reach. But this latest entertainment would make the wait worthwhile. She stood on the balcony, looked down at the blue and white waves rolling in from the Atlantic and breathed the warm sea air. It was always nice to escape from London, even for a few hours. The proximity of her coastal retreat to Dorford Haven had proved an unexpected bonus. On the other hand, the house had been chosen primarily because the area was so steeped in occult mystery. It was really no more than a sharp piece of forward planning. She glanced at her watch. She had kept Erskine Santer waiting for well over an hour. He would not be happy, but it would show him who was in charge.

She made her way down into the reception area. Erskine was standing by a rude and unusual painting of *The Three Graces*, examining it closely. Without a word, Allessandra walked past him and towards the main entrance. He

looked round, recognised the back of her head and hurried after her.

'This way,' she said, without turning round to acknowledge him. She strode through a large pair of open double doors and out on to the front grounds. Erskine puffed along behind her. Though he was a tall man, he was not as fit as she had imagined; but tolerably good-looking in a rugged, lived-in sort of way.

'I understand that progress is not as swift as we had hoped,' said Allessandra.

'You can't hurry these things along,' replied Erskine. 'Archaeology is a careful business.'

'My employer does not pay you to be careful,' snapped Allessandra. 'She pays you for results. She grows impatient at your delay.'

'I can assure you, Ms Favelli, I am doing the best I can.'

They were past the pond now and Allessandra continued to stride out. She wore a black sleeveless vest and no bra. Matching dark leggings drew attention to her long, shapely legs and emphasised the tight curves of her arse. She guessed, quite rightly, that Erskine would be unable to keep his eyes from her body. That was, of course, the object of the exercise. In the current discussions, it gave her a clear advantage to have his mind elsewhere.

'My employer fears you may be prolonging this job at her expense. She pays you by the day, after all.'

'Not at all! Never!' protested Erskine.

Allessandra rounded on him. 'I hope not,' she responded sharply. 'I am following you back to the site to see matters at first hand. If I get the slightest hint that you are dragging your feet, heads will roll.'

Erskine looked suddenly very shifty indeed. Allessandra knew she had been right. He *had* been prolonging the work to make more money. It was time to drive home her advantage.

'Might we expect a successful conclusion by the end of the week?' she asked.

'The end of the week!' exclaimed Erskine. 'I – I cannot promise.'

'I *can* promise,' replied Allessandra. She reached out, pushed Erskine up against a tree and took hold of his balls through his baggy pants. 'I can promise that if you do not recover the Chalice by the weekend, you will be parting company with old friends. Do I make myself clear?'

Erskine's reply was immediate. 'Yes!' he squeaked.

Allessandra smiled triumphantly. 'Excellent,' she replied. 'I knew we understood each other.'

Her hand moved to his cock and she began to stroke him gently, still talking as if nothing was amiss. Erskine's eyes bulged and his neck went red.

'You should be back at your camp by five o'clock. I will be there just after six.'

His eyes expanded into huge excited circles. Allessandra tightened her fist and began to masturbate him vigorously.

'I wish to see all your daily reports, and I will inspect the site personally.'

Her hand rose up and down and she could feel his shaft filling with spunk. One more pull should do it.

'If I suspect anything is not as it should be, you will pay for it, my friend, in ways you cannot begin to imagine. Do I make myself clear?'

He was still nodding stupidly as she gave his cock a final twist and he came, flooding his pants with sperm. She felt it soaking into his trousers.

'What was that?' she enquired. 'I didn't hear you.'

'Yes . . . I said yes!' he groaned as she released him.

'Excellent,' she replied. 'Now I really must be going. Please let yourself out.' And without a single backwards glance, Allessandra Favelli walked away and back towards the house.

Max had found the address he'd been searching for. His memories had begun to firm up as he wandered back and forth across London. Though he could recall nothing since the incident in the massage parlour, the rest had come back to him. The keys were to a safe flat in Maida Vale. Tamara had told him he was to go there if he was in trouble and for any reason couldn't make it back to Omega. He hoped

146

he wasn't being trailed, but reasoned that it was better he be followed here than back to HQ. No one would thank him for the latter. He had just tried the key in the lock for the first time when the door was flung open.

'Tamara!'

'Max!'

This was the last thing he had expected.

'Where the hell have you been?' she asked, dragging him inside before he had a chance to reply.

'I've no idea,' he answered honestly. He shook his head and did a double take. 'What have you done to your hair?'

'It's a long story, Max. Though maybe not as long as yours.'

She was wrong on that score and Max quickly put her straight.

'You really remember nothing at all?' she asked him once he'd finished.

He shook his head. 'Nothing,' he repeated.

She pulled back a corner of the curtain and peered down into the empty street. 'Are you sure you weren't followed?'

'Not really,' he admitted.

Tamara frowned. She told him her story. He looked as bewildered as she had on hearing his.

'A building can't just vanish like that,' he protested.

'Well it did.'

'Does the mad professor have any theories?' asked Max, rubbing the side of his head. It was beginning to ache again. His stomach was churning, too. He'd knocked back three cups of coffee and he couldn't get that strange taste out of his mouth.

'She's out of town,' said Tamara. 'I've left messages.'

Max looked up at her and smiled for no particular reason. Tamara smiled back.

'You look tired,' she said.

'Do I?' answered Max. 'I don't feel it. In fact,' he added, standing up and putting his hand on her shoulder, 'I'm feeling less tired every moment I'm in your company.'

Tamara felt her pulse rate quicken. But not with excitement. There was something wrong here. This was

147

Max. No doubt about it. But it wasn't Max. That didn't make sense, but quite frankly very little about anything seemed to make sense just now.

She let herself be carried along for a moment. To be honest, after what she'd been through in the last few days, she was glad to see Max again. It was nice to have his hands on her shoulders, moving down to her breasts, holding her close. But when he kissed her on the lips, she drew back. What was it? Something odd there, something on his breath. Not unpleasant. Just odd in some indefinable way. What was the matter with her? She was being silly now.

Max had unbuttoned her blouse and scooped out her breasts. He was squeezing them gently. It was nice and she felt her sap leaking out between her legs. She had to give it to him, Max knew how to turn a woman on. He undid her bra and it fell away. Now his mouth was over her flesh, sucking and nibbling; his teeth biting gently at the swollen points of her nipples.

They were on the bed and she was tugging at his trousers. He pulled at her skirt, then began to claw at the waistband of her knickers. What was it about him? He was suddenly so rough. She hadn't known Max long, but she had known him long enough to know that this wasn't like him. Tamara pushed back. It was a reflex action, nothing more. She hardly knew why she did it. But it seemed to inflame him. He forced her down and ripped her skirt clear.

'Max!' she yelled. 'What the hell are you doing?'

'What the fuck's it look like?' he responded. It was his voice, but it wasn't his tone. Alarm bells began to ring. Tamara pushed at his shoulders and succeeded in repelling him for a moment. But then he was on her again, pinning her back, pushing his knee between her thighs, opening her up. She looked down and saw his cock. It was erect and nudging at her pussy. She wanted him desperately. This raw animal lust was insidious in the way it crept under her skin. She could feel herself leaking heavily, her oily secretions soaking into her gusset. But then Max was

tearing at her knickers and she knew something was wrong. Too late, she tried to shift sideways. Max's cock entered her, driving up to the hilt. He began to pump his hips, making wild, grunting noises. She both wanted to push him off and she didn't. It was all so confusing.

The Contessa closed her eyes and dreamed of victory. She sat on her Living Throne and felt the exotic play of flesh beneath her buttocks. Two Minions knelt between her open legs, fighting to lick her cunt, scooping up the thick honey that seeped from the mouth of her slit. Pleasure flooded her belly. She delved down between the threshing bodies and found a cock to pump. Another Minion straddled her face and drove his penis into her mouth. She opened wide and sucked at his balls. Darné and Kalya knelt behind her and squeezed one breast each. This was sublime. Far away she watched through another's eyes and saw Max straddle the Knight woman. She felt his thrusts, too, as if they were her own. The fool had no idea what she had done to him; had no idea that she had impregnated him with a deadly poison. She had taken his seed into her vulva, where it had mingled with a magic ointment. Then she had returned it to his body when she had sat on him and smeared him with the deadly essence. Her hold on his mind was tenuous, she knew that. But it would last long enough for him to spunk into his partner. And the moment he did so, she would die. It was such a sweet revenge. She swayed happily as the hands and tongues pleasuring her worked their magic. It would soon be over now. It would soon be all over.

Max was screaming like an animal. Tamara hammered on his shoulders. 'Max, you're going too fast!'
   He ignored her. She let her body go limp and it seemed to take him by surprise. Then she hardened the muscles in her thighs and pushed upwards, throwing him off-balance. His cock fell free and his eyes blazed. No, thought Tamara, they hadn't blazed. They had gone dark and empty. She had seen that look before. It was the look of a Minion. But

Max wasn't a Minion. He had not been erect when he entered the room. But something had happened to him. She pushed him sideways. He recovered quickly and came at her with his penis, pushing it between her legs. Tamara reached down and grabbed his shaft. What she should have done was grab his balls, but she didn't want to hurt him. Whatever was happening, it wasn't his fault.

Max whinnied like a horse and stabbed again, Tamara rolled out from under him and off the bed. Max sat up and lunged out with both his hands. Tamara ducked, took hold of his arms and pulled. Max went flying over her shoulder and hit the carpet with a thump, landing on his back. Tamara threw herself forward, straddling Max's head. Grinding herself down over his face, she locked her thighs together in a desperate bid to subdue him. Max twisted beneath her. She reached out for his cock.

Far away, the Contessa opened her eyes and screamed. 'Yes! Yeeeess!'

Tamara's fingers closed around Max's shaft and she began to pump. He lurched violently and his hands clawed at her buttocks. She knew he was short of air, that she had only seconds to masturbate him into submission before he fought his way free. Once, twice, three times she pulled at his cock. Suddenly it was jerking of its own accord. Tamara heard a voice scream 'Nooooo!' It must have been Max yelling, and yet it seemed unreal and far away. His seed spat into the air, long curving arcs of cream, tracing squiggly patterns in the nothingness, splattering the floor. She forced his penis down so that none of the seed touched either of them. Where it hit the carpet, the fabric sizzled and steamed. She wrenched Max on to his side so that the last spurts missed his tummy. He collapsed in her arms as she hoisted him upright to a sitting position, holding his cock as if he was a small child and she was helping him to pee. She kept pumping until the last of his sperm had been spilt. It was only then that she realised Max had passed out.

* * *

Far away, the Contessa lay on her back, her breasts swaying. Darné and Kalya stroked her huge nipples and smoothed her skin. Sweat ran in tendrils across her flesh. She was exhausted. They had never seen her spend herself so freely; never seen her so drained. Beneath her breath, she sobbed, uttering foul obscenities, words they had never heard before. They wondered what she would do to them when she finally recovered herself, and found themselves hoping against hope that it would be something very, very bad indeed.

When Max woke up he was tied to a chair. He had a vague idea that he'd done a lot of passing out lately. And been tied up a lot, too. He couldn't quite remember when, how or why, but the novelty, he felt, was beginning to wear off.

Tamara gazed at him from the edge of the bed. She had on a blue silk dressing gown which had fallen open to reveal her breasts and legs. He shook his head and felt his cock begin to stir.

'Why have you tied me up?' he asked. 'Is it another initiation ceremony?'

'It seemed the safest option,' replied Tamara. 'In the circumstances.'

'What are you talking about?' Max licked the inside of his mouth. 'God, what have I been drinking?'

Tamara ignored his question and came back with one of her own. 'What do you remember, Max?'

'I've told you. Nothing.'

'Do you remember coming here?'

The word 'yes' began to form on Max's lips, then he stopped. He frowned and shook his head. 'No,' he said slowly. 'I don't. I remember a park bench, and some keys . . .'

'We're at a safe house,' she reminded him. 'You just tried to kill me.'

He let the irony pass. Tamara pointed to the floor. There was a dark hole in the carpet.

'I'd get that looked at if I were you,' suggested Max.

'You did that.'

'What with? A bottle of sulphuric acid?'

'With your cock. Well, to be more precise, with your spunk.'

'Come off it,' responded Max. 'It's hot stuff, but not that frigging hot!'

Tamara walked around in front of him. The dressing gown fell open and displayed her long bare legs and cunt. Max's cock stirred again. His heart began to beat faster. He wanted her. He tugged at the ropes. This was more than simple want. This was urgent, primeval need.

'Come on, Tamara, untie me!' he pleaded.

'Why?' asked Tamara.

'Why do you think?' he yelled. 'I want to fuck you, you stupid bitch!' He froze. 'Did I say that? What the hell's wrong with me?'

'Sorry, Max,' said Tamara. 'I think the Contessa did something to you. I think she took you prisoner, poisoned your semen and sent you here to kill me.'

'Wouldn't a gun have been easier?'

'Perhaps,' said Tamara. 'But not as sexy.'

'So what happens now?' enquired Max. He was still pulling on the ropes, but Tamara had done too good a job. There was no way he could free himself, however hard he tried.

'I'm going to have to make sure you're not still under her influence,' replied Tamara.

'How?' asked Max, shifting nervously.

'I'll have to see what's left in your cock,' said Tamara. 'If it's harmless, then I imagine you are, too.'

'Do I take that as an insult or what?' asked Max.

Tamara smiled. 'Just a friend helping you out, Max.' She took hold of his penis and began to stroke him gently.

'That's nice,' he said.

'Good,' answered Tamara and began to pump more fiercely. 'Let me know when you think you might come.'

Max swallowed hard. 'OK,' he answered. His voice quivered. He was stone hard already.

'Are your balls filling?' asked Tamara.

'Yes,' squeaked Max.

152

'Do you want to fuck me?'

'Yes! Oh God, yes!' Max shook so hard that the chair jumped beneath him. 'I have to fuck you, please, Tamara, please!'

Calmly, Tamara picked up a tall crystal goblet and slipped it over the top of Max's cock. She gave a final tug on his shaft and he began to spit into the glass. Thick dollops of viscous cream splattered the crystal surrounds. For a moment nothing happened. Then the liquid began to sizzle and fume. Tamara waited until Max had stopped coming, then removed the goblet and studied its contents.

'Well, it doesn't crack glass,' she said, 'but it still looks pretty nasty. It must react with the air, otherwise I dread to think what it would do to your guts.'

'Thanks,' said Max. 'That's very reassuring. I hadn't thought of that.'

Tamara wiped Max's cock clean with a damp cloth.

'Now what?' he asked.

'We do it again,' she said, 'until it's all gone.'

'How long will that take?'

'Who knows?' said Tamara. 'Could be all night.'

She looked at him and smiled. It was obvious that he didn't know whether to laugh or cry. She suspected it was probably a little bit of both.

In fact, it took until three in the morning before the liquid in the glass, thin as it now was, no longer sizzled. Tamara examined it closely and sniffed it once or twice. Max, for his part, was past all caring. His balls ached and he desperately wanted to go to sleep.

'Is it OK?' he asked weakly.

'I think so,' said Tamara. 'Only one way to be sure, though.' She raised it to her lips.

'What are you doing?' asked Max. He was now wide awake, a look of horror plastered across his face.

Tamara let the liquid slide into her mouth and ran it around her tongue.

'No!' he cried instinctively.

For a moment there was nothing. Then Tamara grabbed her throat and her knees buckled. She let out a dreadful

retching noise and rolled her eyes. Max stiffened and strained against his bindings. 'Tamara!' he yelled.

She straightened up and poked out her tongue. It glistened. 'Just kidding!' she said.

'You bastard!' he retorted angrily. 'I was worried.'

She patted him on the head. 'It's nice to know you've got my interests at heart.'

'You won't think that when you untie me!' he growled.

She smiled warmly. 'That sounds too good an offer to resist,' she said and began to loosen the ropes.

Max rubbed his arms and legs. They ached like crazy. 'Now what?' he asked sleepily.

'We get some shuteye,' replied Tamara. 'We've got a long day ahead of us tomorrow.'

'Why? Where are we going?'

'The International Symposium.'

'Bit of a needle in a haystack, isn't it?' said Max.

'Not any longer,' replied Tamara. 'While you were out for the count, I had a call from Abigail. It seems that about eighteen months ago, an archaeological dig funded by the Diablo Foundation unearthed the remains of a first-century altarstone near St Albans.'

'Nhaomhé's?'

'Abigail thinks so, yes. It was badly damaged, but there were five significant pieces intact. And with writing on them, too.'

'The Sacred Prayer?'

'Well it wasn't her recipe for currant buns.'

'So what happened to the pieces of altar?'

'They were given to five translators to work on, experts in Edrish, the pagan occult tongue. Two of them died within three months. One from a heart attack, after being found in a brothel.'

'Dirty sod.'

'He was a part-time lay preacher.'

'That makes it worse.'

'The other was a seventy-year-old spinster. She was found dead in the arms of twin eighteen-year-old toyboys.'

'You have to be joking.'

'If only,' replied Tamara.

'And the remaining three?'

'Still alive and well at the last count: Dr Marsilio Quellorozata, Dr Erica Stanislav and Professor Gioseppi da Vinci.' She paused. 'And guess where they're all going to be tomorrow?'

'The International Symposium,' said Max without surprise.

Tamara nodded. 'I've discovered something else, too. The burial site at Dorford Haven is protected by a series of occult charms. Almost as if the Contessa was trying to stop Vanjja breaking out. Which doesn't make sense if the whole purpose is to release her.'

'What does Crayshaw think?'

'She's not sure. It could be that if Vanjja isn't freed according to ritual, she'll run amok. It makes finding the Chalice and deciphering the Prayer even more important. For us *and* the Contessa.'

'Things don't get any easier, do they?'

'No, Max,' replied Tamara thoughtfully, 'they don't.'

Eleven

Allessandra Favelli hurried forward, her arm outstretched, her dark eyes gleaming.

'Chief Inspector!' she smiled, holding his hand for a fraction longer than was necessary. He was quite handsome for a policeman, she considered. She liked men with broad shoulders; men who gave the impression that they took care of themselves. He smiled back.

'It's just Inspector,' he admitted, 'Inspector Daniels.'

'Please won't you sit down,' she suggested, waving him towards a leather chair opposite Erskine Santer's ridiculously large desk. She perched herself on the edge of the table and crossed her legs. Her skirt fell open, exposing the top of her left thigh up to her hip. She was pleasantly reassured to see a band of red suffuse the Inspector's neck. It was essential she gain the upper hand as quickly as possible. Thank heavens she had decided to remain overnight and not return immediately to London as planned. If Santer had not been able to get hold of her this morning, all hell would have broken loose. As it was the Contessa would be furious when she heard. There had been enough setbacks lately.

'I understand that a young man has gone missing?' she began, pre-empting her visitor, whose eyes, she was happy to note, were fighting a losing battle with the attractions of her leg.

He tore himself away for a moment. 'That's right, madam.'

'Allessandra, please, Inspector.'

The policeman struggled to retain some semblance of professional detachment. 'His name is Colin Ginton. Nineteen. Local lad.'

Allessandra smiled. She allowed the fingers of her right hand to brush lightly against one breast, then openly squeezed the circle of flesh beneath her black cotton T-shirt.

'I'm sorry, Inspector, but I don't see what this has to do with me?'

She knew perfectly well what it had to do with her, of course. She wasn't stupid. Something had gone wrong. For the second time, forces had been unleashed, forces they had mistakenly believed to be under their control. She knew what had happened. Santer had told her when he phoned this morning. The police wanted to speak to her, as his employer. It was all she needed, but what could she do except remove her bra and knickers, put on her shortest skirt and calf-length boots, and set out to do what a woman like her could always do best.

'The young man's girlfriend said they came here last night for a, well, let's just say for a bit of slap and tickle.'

Allessandra laughed openly. 'Oh, how quaint!' she declared. 'My dear Inspector, you mean they were here for a fuck!'

He blushed. It was clear that her direct approach was not what he had bargained for. Allessandra scratched her right leg, clawing back the silk hem to deliberately expose the dark plane of her cunt. The Inspector sat back in his chair, blushed but did not immediately avert his eyes.

'We all have needs, Inspector. I certainly do.' She paused. It was time. She reached for a clip at the side of her dress, unhooked it cleanly and peeled back the flimsy material from around her hips.

She stood up: a woman in a T-shirt and boots and nothing else.

'Mrs – madam –' The Inspector was totally adrift. Allessandra knew he was fighting a lost cause. On the one hand he was here as a policeman to conduct an official inquiry; on the other, he was face to face – no, correct that

– at the moment, face to cunt with a beautiful and, quite evidently, available woman. She leaned forward and kissed him on the mouth. Her right hand pushed into his lap and she felt the hardened ridge of his penis as it rose to meet her. She brushed her lips against his ear.

'Please fuck me,' she whispered. 'Across the table. Now.'

She had won. His hands were at the waistband of his trousers, tugging down his pants. Allessandra turned round, leaned across the desk and tilted her hips to raise her buttocks in the air. She felt the hard circle of his glans nudge against her outer labia, push forward and pierce her downed defences. She bent her fingers into claws and dragged her nails across the wooden surface of the desk.

'Harder!' she urged him. 'Harder, you bastard!

Behind her she was aware of the Inspector grunting with each furious thrust of his hips. His breath was laboured now, and there were strange, animal-like noises coming from his throat. She tightened the muscles of her cunt and held him fast. Rapid milking movements rippled through her vulva, drawing the semen from his imprisoned cock. She heard another sound, too, the one she had been waiting for. The door to the bedroom opened and Darné entered. The Inspector screamed as the first of his seed surged along his penis and into Allessandra's cunt. Then he was struggling, his hands clawing at his face as Darné held the sodden swathe of silk around his nose and mouth. Allessandra reached back and took hold of the policeman's hips, holding him fast. He was trapped between the pleasures of her cunt and the chloroform-soaked threat presented by the pair of knickers clamped to his face. Both woman held on grimly as the man's body rattled between them. Allessandra enjoyed the struggle; she always did. Her clitoris knotted with excitement then gasped its release into her belly. She pushed back hard and gave herself up to bliss at the very moment that Inspector Daniels of Dorford Haven CID gave up the battle and surrendered to his own fate.

Aubrey had been able to combine business with pleasure. His luck appeared to be in at the moment. Perhaps he

should have tried his hand at the casino. Then again, perhaps not. It would not have been proper for the British Home Secretary to be seen in such surroundings. Still – first the capture of the new Omega agent, Max Creed; now this. The Contessa would be pleased. It would make up, in some small measure, for the tirade of abuse he had suffered when she had learned of his enforced foreign sojourn. She had fashioned a plan which required his presence at the Brimstone Club. Even members of The Order did not escape her wrath when her schemes were thwarted. But he had met up with his old friend, the Minister for Trade and Telecommunications. They had sat up into the early hours, deflowering two virgins. Well, the deflowering had not taken all night, of course, far from it. But what had followed had been quite sublime. The virgins had been young men, flown in on the Minister's private jet. Eighteen, nineteen years old, Aubrey couldn't quite remember now. It had been a while since he had enjoyed such paederastic pleasures. He had particularly enjoyed the troilistic finale when, sandwiched between the two young boys, he had both pleasured and been pleasured until all three of them could scarcely stand.

But that was by the by. The Minister's news was all that he had wished for. Permission had been granted for Diablo Worldwide to begin transmission. All the Minister had requested in return was an invitation to the Brimstone Club when next in town. It had been a painless arrangement.

Aubrey settled back in his seat and closed his eyes. He was tired. He needed to rest. It was a long flight and he had always hated flying at the best of times. Still, he would soon be home, with news to delight his Mistress. And then there were the delights of the Brimstone Club to look forward to. He wondered how Joni and Lana had fared. He had recommended them to the Contessa. She had set them a task. He hoped they had succeeded. He really would be flavour of the month. Things were moving rapidly, faster than any of them had imagined. The call from Allessandra had surprised him. Those forces again. It

was a race against time, but one they must win. The day of The Order was fast approaching. He smiled: Order and Chaos, a delightfully incongruous mixture. He began to drift off into a pleasant sleep. Girls. He wanted girls now. He could not wait to get back to the club and enjoy a few.

The Favelli Foundation Centre was an impressive building, just over a mile down-river from the South Bank complex. Aggressively *avant garde* in style, it sprawled over several acres: all gleaming mirrors and slender towers, set behind screens of tall trees, landscaped gardens and man-made waterfalls.

Max and Tamara were mingling politely with a hundred or so archaeological experts, experts' assistants, experts' partners and, scattered freely throughout, a number of curiously indefinable individuals who looked suspiciously like the experts' bits on the side: male and female. It had been their first chance to socialise. There was a break in the proceedings, the sun was out, and they were drinking, nibbling and generally whiling away a pleasant afternoon.

They had decided it was best to keep their story simple, passing themselves off as Crayshaw's assistants: David Trent and Linda Warren. In the circumstances, they reasoned, it was a subterfuge not so far removed from the truth.

They had sat through a brace of dull lectures in the morning, lunched lightly on chicken salad, then attended a short slide-show given by an elderly gentleman with a polysyllabic name and an irritating cough. It was now three o'clock and Max was desperately bored. But at least he was beginning to make some headway. In the rush for the outside world, he had briefly lost contact with Tamara. It was then he had spotted the tall, tanned and well-built gentleman with whom he was now chatting: a man who looked as if he were more at home in his local gym than his local library. He had recognised Dr Quellorozata at once from the photos Tamara had obtained from Omega that morning. To date, Gioseppi da Vinci and Dr Stanislav had been conspicuous by their absence. Gioseppi, however,

was scheduled to deliver the next lecture. Stanislav would have to wait. The original plan had been for Tamara to pair off with one of the men and Max with the diminutive Hungarian. Though Tamara had quickly spotted Max and hurried over, she had been ambushed at the death by a portly Frenchman with a goatee beard and handlebar moustache. Max, for the moment, was forced to soldier on alone. Doctor Quellorozata, however, had proved an engaging, if somewhat distracted, companion. Having said that, Max, too, found it difficult to give his full attention to their conversation. Like the Brazilian, his eyes continually strayed towards Tamara's long, stocking-covered legs. Other eyes, too, snatched cautious glimpses. Though her navy-blue skirt was not particularly short, the slit down one side drew the eye with every deliberate twirl of her hips. Tamara had honed the knack of teasing into a fine art. She was very good, observed Max lustfully. Or very bad, depending on your point of view. On several, tummy-tingling occasions he had caught sight of her frilly black suspenders. Earlier that morning, he had warned her to be a little more careful – a sudden gust of breeze and everyone would know the colour of her knickers.

'What makes you think I'm wearing any?' she had replied, winked crudely and minced away, a dozen or more heads (male *and* female) turning to pursue her firm, retreating rear.

'So where can I get a woman?' asked Dr Q abruptly. (Max had long ago abandoned any attempt to get his mind round all those syllables.)

'I'm sorry?' Max did a quick double take. He was pretty sure he'd heard correctly, but his companion was sipping a tall glass of G & T and it was possible, though only just, that what he'd, in fact, asked for was a lemon.

'A woman!' repeated the tall Brazilian loudly, putting an end to all doubt. He clenched his spare fist and pumped the air. 'You know. Good shag. Rumpy-pumpy.'

Max looked startled, and looked around hurriedly. No one seemed to have overheard the doctor's outburst, or if they had, they had tactfully chosen to ignore it.

'Erm, I'm not sure,' he replied. 'Soho, I suppose. If you're really desperate.' He was baffled. This was not how doctors of archaeology were supposed to act. Surely it was part and parcel of their job description?

The Brazilian nodded his head in Tamara's general direction. 'This one. You know her? She is very attractive.'

'Ta– Linda?' said Max, correcting himself quickly. 'Yes. She is, isn't she?'

'You have fucked her? Is she good? She looks good. My God, I'd like to give her one.'

Max was stunned. The good doctor was doing little to hide his interest. He wondered if Tamara had overheard. 'She's not that sort of woman,' he protested lamely, more for Tamara's benefit than anything else.

The doctor snorted in disbelief. 'Any woman who dresses like that is no nun, my friend.'

Max felt a shiver of unease begin to form in the pit of his stomach. By now he should have asked the Brazilian several pertinent questions about Erdish, or Edrish or whatever it was. Tamara wouldn't be very happy. Perhaps it was time to introduce the two of them; strike while the iron, or at least the Brazilian's ardour, was still hot. Max glanced at his watch. 'We'll have to be going in soon,' he said. 'Another lecture.'

The doctor threw back his drink, temporarily abandoning his mental pursuit of Tamara. 'Ah, yes, Professor da Vinci. Pagan architecture. Not my cup of tea. Too dull.'

'So what is your cup of tea?' asked Max, spotting a chance to lead their talk in the required direction.

'Pagan hymns and incantations. Yourself?'

'Nothing so interesting,' answered Max quickly. 'So you're an expert on pagan ceremonies? Rituals, that sort of thing?' He was determined to steer this conversation along the narrowest of channels. Fortunately Dr Q appeared more than happy to paddle alongside.

'Indeed. I have done a lot of work on Helmi. She was the pagan goddess of lust, also known as Gho'van, or Vanjja. Sometimes . . .'

Max was no longer listening. He should have been, but

he wasn't. Instead, he was looking over the doctor's shoulder to a small huddle of figures some twenty or thirty yards away. A woman and three men were engaged in somewhat animated chat. The woman was small with a bun of blonde hair, pale skin and firm, prominent breasts. Her arms moved rapidly, each point she made reinforced by the squeeze of a wrist or the stroke of an arm. It was clear from the contented smiles on the faces of her companions that they took no offence to her hands-on approach, quite the reverse in fact. Max recognised her at once from those photos, again. It was Dr Erica Stanislav. She was not pretty as such, not in a conventional sense. But there was something about her, a raw animal magnetism that gnawed at his guts. It made no immediate sense, even to him. He felt his stomach muscles tighten and his penis stir inside his pants. An image came uninvited into his head. Erica Stanislav was fully clothed but straddling him, her knickers pulled to one side. She was bouncing up and down, screaming and tearing at her long, blonde unfastened hair. Dribble ran down her chin and she shook her head from side to side. She swore, but they were crazy words, words he'd never heard before. A second image pushed out the first. It was quite obscene. Even Max felt shocked that he could conjure up such a thought. Across the way, she turned her head, caught his eye for an instant and smiled. He felt his tummy do a somersault. He turned abruptly, took his companion by the arm and began to steer him towards Tamara.

'Let me introduce you to Linda,' he said. Max suddenly wanted to get away and talk to the small Hungarian. It was ridiculous; he felt like a horny teenager, wanting to screw the prettiest girl in the room. What was it all about? It didn't matter. Tamara could handle Dr Q better than him any day. Besides, she was showing too much attention to the Frenchman, and Max didn't like the French very much. Not since a Parisian called Henri du Pois had pinched his first girlfriend.

Well that was the plan at any rate. Unfortunately, Max was forced to put it on hold, because when he turned to

introduce his new companion, Tamara was nowhere to be seen. Nor for that matter was the short Frenchman to whom she had been speaking just a few moments earlier.

Allessandra Favelli knelt in front of the ornately gilded mirror. It seemed to be alive with movement. Serpents squirmed around its edges, animated slitherings of gold and silver. Smaller, darker, worm-like creatures scurried left and right. Disembodied faces, gnarled and twisted, snapped greedily at the wriggling passers-by, until they in turn were swallowed whole, devoured by the snake-infested, living frame.

There was a thick black phallus screwed into the floor between Allessandra's legs, its bloated head just nudging the delicate folds of her open cunt. She was naked apart from a mesh of thin golden chains linking her hands, her breasts and her vulva. Her arms were half-raised, so that her palms were at shoulder height and turned towards her nude reflection. There were small metal clamps around her nipples. She had taken great care when attaching them, making sure that they were screwed tightly enough to cause maximum discomfort but without tearing the sensitive skin of her areolae. There were two more clips attached to her labia, firmly fastened to each of her thick, ruby-red lips. When she moved her arms above her head, as she now did, the network of metal linking wrists, cunt and nipples drew taut, so that every upward movement, however gentle, caused her excruciating pain.

Behind her a clock chimed three. At the third stroke, she pulled her arms out and upwards, so that the chains tightened further still and yanked fiercely at the clips fastened to her flesh. The mouth of her cunt distended crudely, the membrane of her labia stretched wide, revealing the glistening pink maw of her sex. Her nipples throbbed horribly, pulled into long stinging streaks of flesh. Tears welled up out of her eyes and rolled down her face as the pain struck her. But then a familiar pleasure began to kick in. Juice welled up inside her vulva and leaked from her open cunt, dribbling along the insides of her firm brown thighs. Carefully, Allessandra lowered her

big hips, impaling herself on the huge phallus, sheathing it completely. She began to rise and fall, until the huge rubber shaft grew slick with her juices, slurping in and out of her with every dip and buck of her body.

Allessandra stared at her reflection in the mirror, her breathing loud and rapid now in tune with the pleasure gnawing at her belly. 'Oh fuck me,' she moaned. 'Oh fuck me, Mistress. Fuck me, please . . .'

Mouthing hushed obscenities, she began to move her hips up and down, varying the force of her thrusts so that at times the phallus would vanish inside her rapacious cunt, while at others she would hold its very tip between her engorged labia.

The mirror misted over and her reflection began to slowly change. All at once, she was no longer staring at herself but at the Contessa. The latter was seated on her Living Throne, bodies moving crudely all around her. Allessandra watched through eyes blurred with tears and pain as somewhere far away the Contessa's servants rocked against each other's flesh; hands, cunts and penises dancing to the tune of a beloved Mistress. It was beautiful.

A man lay spreadeagled across the Contessa's lap. She was holding his erect penis in her hand and slowly masturbating him. His cream was in the process of spilling out over her long dark fingers. His pelvis jerked awkwardly and his small buttocks twitched against her thighs. The Contessa continued to milk him long after he had spilt the last of his seed. Soon he would begin to cry with pain, but he would not resist because his pain would give his Mistress pleasure and that was all that mattered. He was a good and faithful servant, Allessandra told herself, as were they all.

The Contessa spoke. 'Allessandra?'

'Mistress?' Allessandra's voice shuddered as she swayed between the pleasures of the phallus and the torments of the cunt and nipple clamps.

'What progress at Dorford Haven?'

'I have spoken with the fool Santer. I am assured results will follow soon.'

'I cannot countenance further delay. There is danger.'

'Mistress . . .' Allessandra's voice faltered for a moment.

Even through the cloud of pleasure that swamped her every conscious thought, she knew the Contessa had caught the fear that laced her voice.

'Speak!' thundered the Contessa.

'There has been another incident.'

'Explain!'

'A boy is missing. A young man. I believe the powers we have unleashed . . .'

'No! It cannot be! Not again! Not now! We are so close!'

'It is dealt with, Mistress!'

'How?'

'They sent a policeman. Darné and I subdued him. I used my powers. His mind is ours now. He will report to his superiors that nothing is amiss.'

'The site was not investigated?'

'No, Mistress. There has been no breach of security.'

'It is a sign, Allessandra. The forces move against us. There is little time.' She paused and for a moment clouds blurred the translucent surface of the mirror. Then as if shunted away by a sudden wind, they vanished. 'The Prayer, Allessandra! I must have the Sacred Prayer! What progress?'

'None, Mistress. Not yet. Not yet . . .' Allessandra raised her arms to intensify the pain she felt and squealed horribly as its full force hit her.

'The Three are gathered. I must know the results of their work. Gioseppi da Vinci. Begin with him!'

'Mistress . . . shall . . . shall I bring him to you?'

'No. Deal with him yourself.'

Allessandra swayed her hips from side to side, riding the inflated dildo, smearing it with her essence. Butting her clitoris hard with every downward stroke, she knew she was taking herself close to the limits of endurance. And as her pleasure grew, so the image in the mirror came into even sharper focus. Her ears were locked to every word that fell from the Contessa's lips, her eyes fixed on the small penis still jerking with unnatural vigour inside her Mistress's huge, closed fist. She was suddenly aware of how long it was since she had last fucked a man. Two days at least. Two days too long.

166

'What – what would you have me do?' asked Allessandra feebly, her senses muddled with excitement.

'Gioseppi interests me. He resists the call. I must know why.'

'May I abuse him, Mistress?'

'Enjoy him in whatever way you choose.'

The Contessa paused for a moment, then added, 'But ...' She allowed the word to hang with tantalising threat in the ether.

'Yes, Mistress?' breathed Allessandra.

'. . . be cruel,' whispered the Contessa.

Her words were music to Allessandra's ears. She drove herself down on to the phallus and felt herself teeter on the brink of sweet oblivion. The vision in the mirror began to fade. No! She must not climax yet. Not yet. If she did, she would lose contact with the Contessa. That would be unforgivable.

'The time approaches, Allessandra. Things move faster than I dared hope.'

'*Si*, Mistress.' Allessandra's words struggled to escape her throat. Her head was spinning with excitement, her belly alive with lust.

In the mirror, the Contessa smiled and waved one hand imperiously. With her other she squeezed the penis between her fingers, furiously clenching and unclenching her fist. And then the impossible happened. Gobbets of clear liquid spat from the eye of the man's cock. Allessandra heard a high-pitched scream of distress that far outstripped her own and then the mirror went blank. Immediately, she thrust down hard, tugging on the chains, sheathing the phallus one last time as she came.

Extending her tongue, she lapped at the tears of pain and pleasure that ran down her face. Then she closed her eyes and thought of Gioseppi da Vinci. She hoped he would continue to resist the call. It would be a pleasure to interrogate him; and then to enjoy him until her cunt ached from the torture she would put him through.

Oh pleasure. Such sweet, sweet pleasure.

* * *

It had not taken Max long to discover Tamara's whereabouts. As the rest of the delegates shuffled back to the lecture hall, some clutching their drinks, some clutching each other, he reluctantly parted company with Dr Quellorozata. When he looked around, he saw that Dr Stanislav had vanished, too. He made his way against the flow of human traffic towards the large man-made lake at the centre of the grounds. It had not been a deliberate decision on his part, nor was it, he reflected ruefully, the consequence of some psychic premonition: it was just that he knew Tamara hadn't gone past him and, given the layout of the grounds, there didn't seem anywhere else she could have vanished to.

It was the faint murmurings of pleasure that first caught his ears; a series of broken grunts emanating from the far side of a gentle incline. When he looked over the top of the brae, he saw Tamara and her companion by the edge of the lake. The Frenchman was staring down into the water, his pants and trousers gathered in a heap around his feet. Tamara stood close behind, her arms looped around his waist. She was holding his erect cock in her right hand, and cuddling his balls with her left. Tamara's arm was moving smoothly up and down and from the noises the Frenchman was making he was apparently in seventh heaven. From the way he wriggled his hips and moaned, it seemed likely that he was nearing his climax.

'*Merde*! *Merde*!' he muttered as Tamara jiggled her fist up and down. Almost immediately, his knees buckled and he emitted a loud mewl of delight.

'*Mon Dieu*! *Mon Dieu*!' he squealed as his cream spat in all directions, long milky threads of spunk peppering the air like mini vapour trails. Then, splattering downwards, they hit the water like summer rain, congealing into short globular strands which swam away like creamy tadpoles.

Watching Tamara masturbate the Frenchman had given Max an incredible erection. He felt jealous. More than that, he felt vindictive. A sudden vision came to him: a laughing, bearded, one-eyed Henri du Pois, cycling off with the love of his life. That did it. He took a few steps back and called out, 'Tamara! Are you there?'

A muffled curse came from the far side of the hill, followed by the sound of a zip being wrenched up in record time. Out of some vague consideration for the man's feelings, Max remained where he was and waited till Tamara strode into view. There was no sign of the Frenchman who, Max assumed, was scurrying back to the lecture hall by as circuitous a route as possible.

Tamara looked totally nonplussed. She grinned and said, 'You're a cheeky bastard, Max!'

'What do you mean?' he asked, affecting his most innocent expression.

'You know exactly what I mean. Poor François. If it wasn't for his stiffy, he'd have wet himself.'

'Well, I was jealous. Can you blame me?'

Tamara reached out and felt his groin. 'My, my, Max, we are up and about early today, aren't we?'

He made a sudden grab for Tamara's waist. She retreated like an agile kitten and poked out her tongue. 'Who's a randy little boy, then?' she chuckled, wriggling her hips and sending her skirt flouncing up into the air, revealing the top of one wide, creamy thigh.

'You're a terrible flirt!' he complained.

'Of course I am,' she replied, pushing out her breasts. 'The question is: what are you going to do about it?'

'Are you really not wearing any knickers?' he asked.

Tamara pursed her lips and swayed her hips provocatively. 'Why don't you try and find out?'

Max was in just the mood to do that. He made a second grab and this time didn't miss, tugging Tamara to the ground and rolling over so that he was on top of her. Her skirt flew up and his hand flew down.

She wasn't wearing any knickers.

He palmed her pussy, his fingers tickling the hot wet mouth of her sex. Tamara gave up any pretence of struggle, and anchored her mouth to his lips, kissing him hard.

There were hands at his trouser zip now. At least one of them was his, but it was Tamara's that were doing all the real work. She quickly undid him, tugged down his pants, and exposed his erect prick.

He entered her smoothly, groaning all his pent-up frustration into the damp heat of her mouth. His cock felt as if it was pushing through warm treacle: damp and sticky and pleasurably tight. He began to buck his hips, jerking into her so fast that for a moment he almost lost control. Tamara must have sensed the urgency of his need because she plunged her fingers down between their bodies and squeezed the base of his shaft. Though he yelped with discomfort, his seed remained trapped in his hard, rolling balls.

Now Tamara began to move her body, twisting her hips from side to side, grinding her cunt against the ridge of his pubis. She pushed her tongue into his ear, whispered crude nothings and was rewarded by a renewed round of thrusts into her pussy.

'Oh, yes!' she squealed. 'Oh, yes! Now, Max! Now!'

Max hardly needed the encouragement. He couldn't have held back if he'd wanted to, and surrendered willingly. With a deep, primeval grunt of triumph he drove his hips forward one last time. His entire body suffused with pleasure as his spunk began its inexorable rise out of his balls and into his shaft. Tamara wrapped her long legs around Max's waist and held him fast as her orgasm shuddered away, squirming on his cock until every last drop of his seed had been spilled inside her.

'That was lovely,' she said, after they had rolled apart and begun to tidy themselves up. She grinned. 'You really needed it, didn't you?'

'What do you think?' he asked. 'Watching you wank that French guy was a real turn on.'

'He certainly seemed to think so,' replied Tamara.

'Why did you do it?'

'Why not?'

'Don't get all philosophical on me,' he complained.

'I felt like it,' admitted Tamara truthfully. 'He seemed like a nice fellow, so when he asked me if I'd give him a spot of hand relief –'

Max was stunned. 'He asked you?' he yelped. 'He actually had the cheek to ask you?'

'He's French, Max,' said Tamara, as if that somehow explained everything. 'They don't have the same hang-ups.'

'Bugger me,' said Max and shook his head.

Tamara poked out her tongue and smiled. 'He probably would if you asked him nicely.'

'Very funny,' he responded. 'Anyway, I've been chatting to Dr Q.'

'I know. I heard what the randy old goat had to say.'

'I did wonder,' said Max, slightly embarrassed at the memory.

'What did you find out?'

'Apart from the fact that he wants to fuck you, not a lot.'

Tamara pouted coyly. 'He wants to fuck innocent little me? Oh, I don't know about that. Mind you,' she paused as if to consider the prospect for a moment or two.

Max cut in. 'I saw Dr Stanislav.'

'Good. Did you fancy her?'

'No. Well, yes, that is to say . . .' Max wondered if he should mention the curious images that had come to him: of first being fucked by the good doctor, and then . . . no, perhaps not. That second vision was not something he really wanted to dwell on. He wasn't sure if it was physically possible. He was sure it wasn't legal.

'Any sign of Gioseppi?' asked Tamara.

'No. But then he's probably inside preparing for his lecture.'

'We'll wait till this evening, when we get back to the hotel. Then we'll move in on them. Remember, Max, this is just reconnaissance.'

Max felt his penis stir again. He reached forward and cupped his hand around Tamara's groin. 'That's what you call it, is it?' He smiled.

She smiled back. 'You're insatiable, Max!'

'I know,' he murmured, unzipping himself and extracting his penis.

'We'll have to be quick, or we'll miss the start of the lecture.'

'Who cares?' replied Max. But as her fist closed around his aching shaft, he struggled to keep an image at bay.

Then his balls rolled, and he felt his penis begin to fill with seed.

Twelve

The Chamber of Utter Devotion lay some distance beneath the lower dungeons. Access was via a dark, labyrinthine network of tunnels: narrow twisting pathways hewn from the dank brown rock. Devoid of lighting, natural or otherwise, it posed deadly perils for the unwary. There were countless bores to left and right where the careless might plummet to certain death. And even if this particular fate were avoided, of the many other tracks the uninitiated might stumble across, all without fail led only deeper and deeper into the bowels of an unforgiving earth.

Not that anyone dared venture along these corridors alone, for this was the Contessa's special domain. Minions, Faithful, even members of The Order itself were forbidden from entering the Chamber without express permission. The penalty for disobedience, unlike most other transgressions, was not incarceration in the Darkness. It was death: slow, protracted and hideous. What that might actually entail remained a mystery because to date the penalty had never been exacted; no one had been foolish enough to defy their Mistress's edict.

The flames from several dozen torches lit her path as the Contessa strode along the cold, tortuous route. Minions danced attendance all around her, scuttling forward to light the way ahead, running behind to warm her broad, bare back. It was unnecessary. Although she wore no cloak down here, she remained, as always, impervious to the chill. Her leather harness groaned with every step she took, and her boots drew sparks from the brittle granite floor.

There were chains around her arms and legs, cinched tight across the bulging muscles of her thighs. Spiked leather bracelets adorned her neck, her upper arms and calves. Long, black hair cascaded about her hard shoulders, gathering in thick clusters over her back and around her large gourd-like breasts.

A single massive doorway barred the entrance to the Chamber. It opened not sideways but upwards, the mechanism operated by pulleys left and right. Six Faithful hurried forward, careful to have lagged behind until this moment and only now moving to outstrip their Mistress. They unravelled several coils of cleated rope and then, three to each side of the narrow tunnel, began to draw down hard, raising the big, weighted mass. It moved slowly, the ancient structure creaking on unoiled hinges, tiny fragments of wood splintering free. The door was clearly a dreadful weight, the extent of the women's task reflected in their swollen biceps, their tightly muscled thighs and the sweat that ran down their backs and between their legs.

The Contessa came to an abrupt halt as the structure reached its apex, sending several of her Minions scattering. The door locked into place for a moment, enabling two of the women to tie off four lengths of rope into a series of taut coils, while their companions held the huge wooden framework in place. Their work complete, the six then knelt with their heads bowed as the Contessa strode past them and into the vast and silent gloom beyond.

Minions scuttled left and right, touching their flaming brands to hundreds of staves that covered the craggy cavern walls. As each flambeau scorched into life, the blackness began to retreat until very soon the entire Chamber was bathed in a warm, flickering light. The surrounding walls dripped with oily slime and thick, fetid water. Mottled rock soared cathedral-like towards the flickering emptiness of a huge domed ceiling, its upper limits masked in darkness. Hundreds of unseen fissures linked the Chamber with the lower dungeons somewhere far above. The natural acoustics were such that every

sound generated in those distant cells would normally resonate around these dark, festering walls. Tonight, however, the Chamber was unnaturally quiet, with only the occasional muffled keen to break the cold, stinking silence. And it was not, as so often, the cry of a prisoner in distress. Rather, it was the torment of an Angel, bereft of that which gave her life its dark, unholy meaning; a captive prey to feed on. The Contessa did not like the silence and made a mental note to despatch a dozen slaves on whom her girls might feast before morning. It was only right. She was a just and fair Mistress, after all.

Now that the cavern was fully lit, a single splendid structure dominated the emptiness. At the centre of the Chamber stood the Pillar of Mádrofh: Destroyer of Virtue, Scourge of the Pure; the Mistress of Lust to whom they all, even the Contessa herself, bowed in reverence. It was almost eight-feet high, a classical stone-built rendering of a naked hermaphrodite warrior: long, flowing hair, huge breasts, powerful muscular arms and legs. Its knees were bent and its arms outstretched as if on the point of grappling with an unseen foe. This was a warrior prepared for combat, and as she contemplated the huge marble façade, the Contessa felt a rush of juices sear her naked sex.

The most magnificent part of the Pillar was its penis: a massive trunk of marbled manhood, bursting out of hard, artificial loins. The cockhead was shiny smooth and exquisitely carved, a hint of veins etched into the long, rounded shaft. The glans itself was shaped like a female vulva, swollen labia open at the tip. It seemed hardly possible that any normal woman could mount it and live. As she closed her eyes for a moment and dwelt on the thought of such a monstrous violation, the Contessa felt something warm and wet dribble down the insides of her heavily muscled thighs.

It was time to prepare herself for communion with Mádrofh.

It had been a long and rather dull afternoon. Gioseppi da Vinci was doubtless an acknowledged expert on pagan

architecture, but an accomplished speaker he was not. When he had walked on to the stage at the start of his lecture, Tamara had been somewhat disappointed. Though tall, he was a rather nondescript man. Which was odd because he dressed well; designer clothes that sat oddly on his lean, slightly gangling frame. Tamara found herself wondering what he looked like beneath his loose, well-cut Italian trousers. She closed her eyes for a few moments and gave herself up to a brief, and very crude daydream. The illusion was shattered when he opened his mouth. There was a dull nasal quality to his voice that touched several raw nerves at once. Oh, well, Tamara told herself, if she could keep him quiet in bed, all might not be lost. She'd just have to give him something to nibble on, that was all. And if that didn't work, well, there was always the brooding Dr Q from Brazil.

Outside the conference hall, a fleet of cabs was lined up, waiting to ferry the delegates back to their overnight accommodation: the Diablo Hotel in the Strand. Judging from their lack of luggage, most of the guests had already checked in, but Max and Tamara were not alone in being marked as late arrivals. The receptionist, Max was pleased to note, was a tall, cheerful blonde with a light Australian accent. She had big, friendly breasts that moved like warm oil beneath her starched white blouse. The top three buttons of her shirt were undone, so that when she leaned forward Max was able to enjoy an unhindered view of her tanned and indisputably bra-less cleavage. She handed over their keys, caught Max's roving eye and responded with a big smile. Max, expecting a stern glare of disapproval, smiled back. If he had nothing better to do later on, he considered, he might pop down and make her better acquaintance. He was always happy to do his bit for Anglo–Antipodean relations.

'Laura will escort you to your room,' said the young woman.

Max's eyes widened when a young girl stepped up and took their small overnight bags. This was definitely his kind of hotel, he told himself. Looking around, he was

surprised to see several other uniformed women moving efficiently to and fro, carrying cases or chatting to customers. Like the other female porters, Laura wore a starched white shirt over breasts that looked as if they yearned to be set free. Her blouse, like that of the friendly receptionist, was unbuttoned at the top, and because she was on the short side, Max had a bird's-eye view of her small, apple-shaped tits. A bright red waistcoat stretched around her young, well-formed bosom. Her lower half was squeezed into a pair of black, skin-tight leggings that emphasised every curve of her youthful body.

'Down boy,' whispered Tamara into his ear.

'Too late for that,' he replied, following Laura to the lift. The globes of her buttocks pushed against each other as she walked. If he'd been a dog, decided Max, they'd have had to chisel his nose out from between her sweet little arse-cheeks.

The lift-ride to their floor was torture for Max. If he'd been on his own he might have tried to take things further. Mind you, given Tamara's appetites he told himself, perhaps it was worth a try. On the other hand, maybe not.

Their room was large, bright and airy. A complimentary bottle of iced champagne sat on a table in the corner; alongside two glasses and a small bowl of fruit. A large wide-screen TV was set into the far wall. Nearby was a combined fax machine and computer which Laura explained could be used to send email. Certainly no expense had been spared for their comfort.

'If there's anything else we can do for you, you only need to ask,' smiled Laura.

'Don't mind me,' said Tamara lightly, heading towards the bathroom. 'I need a pee and a shower.'

The door closed behind her, leaving Max alone with the pocket-sized porter. She smiled sweetly and Max felt his penis strain to be unleashed. It caught him completely by surprise when she reached out and pressed her hand into his groin.

'You seem tense,' she said. 'Perhaps you need to unwind.'

This was unbelievable. This couldn't be happening. She unzipped him and pulled out his cock, which was already erect and hard against his belly. Then she pushed him back so that he fell into a chair, removed her black leggings and placed them on the table. She wore a minuscule black G-string to which his eyes were now glued. Without pausing to remove it, she stepped up and sat on his lap, pressed herself close and kissed him softly on the mouth.

When she pulled back, he found himself staring into two warm, turquoise pools of youthful excitement.

'We shouldn't – I mean, we – what if . . .?'

Max was making no sense and he knew it. What the hell! So what if Tamara did come back? No. What was he thinking about? Tamara wouldn't come back. She'd left them alone deliberately. Laura raised herself from his lap, reached down and circled his cock with her surprisingly tiny fingers. She pushed her other hand up against the gusset of her panties. It was then, for the first time, that Max realised why she hadn't taken them off. Her little labia poked through the open crotch, pink and puffy and glistening with her sap. Max held his breath when she positioned the mouth of her sex over his cock-head and pushed down. He had never known such a tight cunt. It felt more like an arse than a vulva and she seemed to take an eternity to fully sheathe him. He wondered for a moment or two if the task was beyond her, but he needn't have worried. She settled back and began to ride him gently. Max looked down and saw that her gusset appeared to have sprouted curls, then realised belatedly that they were his. The walls of her vagina felt warm, hot and sticky, as if his cock were being dipped in treacle. He brought his arms around her waist and fanned his fingers across her bottom, squeezing each buttock in turn. They were cold, like her hands. It seemed odd for an aroused woman to be so cool. He could feel the sweat already leaching from his skin, soaking his shirt. But she seemed ice-cold, almost as if she were unmoved, almost as if she were not really there.

Max put such stupid thoughts out of his head. He

177

pushed his fingers under Laura's rump. His fingers probed into her crack. Again it was cold and dry. Her bumhole, however, was damp enough for him to push the tip of his finger inside. He was almost at the end of his tether now. Suddenly her hands were at her blouse, unbuttoning herself. She pulled down her bra-cups and exposed her tits. They were smaller than he'd expected, but then her bra, he realised, was underwired. Her breasts smelt young and fresh as if she'd dabbed them with talcum powder. She fed first one, then the other into his mouth and he chewed on her small, olive-soft nipples.

Suddenly she clamped her mouth against the top of his head and groaned something that sounded like 'Nggh! Nghh!' into his hair. She rose and fell rapidly as her orgasm ripped through her and that was enough to send Max into orbit, too. He felt his spunk explode along his shaft and into the girl's hard little cunt. At the same moment, her arse contracted around his probing finger, pulsing in time to the vibrations in her pussy. He mouthed his pleasure on to her breasts, grateful for the fact that they muffled his screams.

Suddenly it was over. Laura rose from his lap, more easily than she had descended, brushed herself down, pulled up her leggings and rebuttoned her blouse.

'I hope that's helped to bring the swelling down,' she said dryly. Max looked into her eyes, searching her face for a hint of sarcasm. If it was there he was unable to find it.

'If there's anything else sir requires, he only has to ring for room service,' she said demurely, smiled and was gone.

Max was still pondering the entire, bizarre incident when Tamara walked out of the bathroom. The water was still running and it caught him by surprise. She had on a short, pink bathrobe, presumably courtesy of the management.

Max hastily tried to do himself up.

'Did we enjoy ourselves?' Tamara enquired, draping herself lazily across the bed. She pulled her legs up so that the bathrobe fell open and exposed one of her thighs.

Max saw little point in subterfuge. 'You shouldn't have been listening.' He glanced across at the door and saw that

it had a large keyhole and no key. 'Or watching,' he added indignantly.

'Oh come on now, Max, you wouldn't deprive me of a little voyeuristic fun, would you?'

'You were supposed to be taking a shower,' he complained.

'It slipped my mind,' she responded. 'I think you could do with one, though.'

'Well you certainly don't care about conserving water, do you?' he scolded her.

Tamara stood up and let the bathrobe fall open so that her breasts spilled out. 'Come on,' she said, 'I'll join you.'

Max followed Tamara into the bathroom. It was full of steam. He quickly stripped off and joined her in the shower. She wrapped her arms around his neck and kissed him on the side of the face.

'So what was she like?' she asked.

'Not bad,' he replied.

'It's quite a service they offer here, isn't it?'

'I suppose it is, rather,' he admitted, enjoying the play of water on his body, streaming down his back.

Tamara laughed. 'You really are a dope, aren't you, Max?'

'What do you mean?'

'This place is owned and run by the Diablo conglomerate.'

'So?'

'So.' She let the word float in the air for a second or two, like a hook on which to hang her next sentence. 'That woman who just fell for you is one of the Contessa's so-called Faithful.'

'You're kidding me?'

'Of course I'm not. I mean, I know you're a randy bugger with an irresistible animal magnetism, but didn't you think it was all a bit too easy?'

'Well if you knew what was going to happen, why didn't you stop me?'

'I didn't want to spoil your fun. Besides, I should think every other delegate is getting much the same treatment. If you'd turned her down, it might have looked suspicious.'

'Doctor Q will be happy,' said Max.

Tamara handed him a loofah and some soap. 'Wash my back,' she told him, turning round. Max wrapped his arms around her top instead, squeezing her breasts.

Tamara giggled. 'Predictable as ever, Max.' She leaned back into him. 'My, my, we are a big boy. And so soon again. I'll take that as a compliment. Oh, well, shame to waste it . . .'

The Contessa knelt on the cold stone floor. She was naked, her head bowed, her bare arms raised towards the Pillar of Mádrofh. Seven Minions gathered around their Mistress, embracing her in a crescent of jutting cocks. The balls of each servant hung between parted legs like plump fruit, heavy and swollen with seed. They had been prepared for this moment. Permanently erect, those chosen for the honour had undergone further hardship: long hours of masturbation and unfulfilled arousal at the hands of Darné and Kalya. At least two men had surrendered to pleasure and spent themselves shamelessly. They had been thrown to the Angels, screaming for their worthless lives. They were not screaming now, for they were long gone; sacrificed to the Darkness and the needs of the women they had all too briefly served. Now their companions stood ready to serve their Mistress; even unto death, though for them at least, that fate was not today.

Behind each Minion stood the tall, imposing figure of a Faithful; and to the rear of each Faithful, one behind the other, stood those remaining Minions, twenty-one in all, who had accompanied the procession to the Chamber.

The Contessa raised her head towards the Pillar. Her eyes blazed like dark jewels. The tendons in her neck stood out like thin wire cords.

'Let the Sacred Spending begin!' she commanded. Immediately, her Faithful reached out with both arms. Fingers tightened around long, hard cocks, and hands pinched at balls that bulged with unnatural fullness.

'Bathe me in their essence!' cried the Contessa. Fists pumped up and down; the men howled, wept and

shuddered as the semen was squeezed from their shafts. Seven cocks erupted as one. As each man emptied himself across the Contessa's naked flesh, he was thrown to the floor, dragged away by either Darné or Kalya and another Minion forced into his stead. A storm of semen rained down on to her body, splashing across her breasts, her arms and her legs. It soaked her face and soiled her long, sable-black hair. She rubbed it into her skin until it coated her completely. Occasionally, she would reach out and draw a penis into her mouth, sucking the last drops of its seed into her throat before pushing its owner away and taking another between her lips. As each man collapsed, and fell senseless, it was as if their life-force flowed into the Contessa. She grew stronger and more insatiable. Tearing at her flesh like a maddened beast, she thrust one hand into her capacious cunt, pumping herself as if astride a giant cock. As her vulva expanded around her wrist, she drove her second hand down into the cleft of her huge arse and reamed herself with her long, powerful fingers.

'Enough!' she screamed. The last of the men fell to the floor, collapsing across the senseless heap of his fallen companions. There were bodies strewn everywhere. Not a single Minion remained standing. Her Faithful dropped to their knees, now, heads bowed. The aroma of freshly spilled semen filled the air.

The Contessa raised her arms high and cried aloud, 'R'aa'vé!'

None but the Contessa witnessed the statue begin to move, its huge arms lowering towards her. It scooped her up and lifted her high into the air, holding her above its huge, exquisitely fashioned shaft. Then, slowly, it drew her down until the mouth of her cunt brushed the head of the magnificent vulva-tipped phallus. Incredibly, the Contessa's vagina began to stretch around the head, swelling obscenely as it ate away at the stone girth, subsuming it within her body, sliding along its length until it filled her completely. Now the cock began to move: up and down. The Contessa bellowed in pain and pleasure. Beneath her, not a soul looked up; all eyes averted from the awesome sight.

A voice came from the heart of the Pillar: a voice which only the Contessa heard. It was beautiful and it was evil, a voice that could kill with words alone. It was the voice of Mádrofh. And it spoke to the Contessa's heart. Her pleasure overflowed and she began to climax. The Minions' seed dribbled down her arms and legs, covering the statue in a dull, slimy sheen. It ran over her lips and she sucked it greedily into her mouth. Somewhere far beyond this earthly sphere, Mádrofh tasted it, too; tasted the Contessa's pleasure in a world in which all pleasure was denied her.

Flames began to lick the outside of the statue. They appeared from nowhere, engulfing the Contessa's body. Again, she screamed in pain and pleasure, drawing the tongues of heat into her, until they faded and were gone.

And when she had endured all, and the last shivers of pleasure had fled her trembling flesh, she knew what must be done.

Allessandra Favelli mused on how so much of a man's life was dictated by the needs of his cock. Very few could resist the lure of an attractive female. They would leap to open doors, give up their seats on crowded trains, carry the heaviest of parcels up the longest flights of stairs. And for what? Not the certainty of a fuck, for that was rarely on the cards. No, simply for the pleasure of believing that the woman in question might – just might – fancy them; might wish to take them to bed and do incredibly wicked things. She knew that if she had been an ugly old harridan, Gioseppi would not have wasted a moment of his precious time on her. But because she was Allessandra Favelli, he would have been happy to sit here and discuss wallpaper patterns if she'd asked him to.

She glanced over at the bed and gave an affected yawn. 'It looks so inviting, does it not?' she said.

Gioseppi went a deep, deep red. How sweet, thought Allessandra, he's shy. Hardly surprising, she told herself. He was a rather nondescript little man. This was probably the most exciting thing that had ever happened to him. She

decided to be bold, stood up, took him by the hand and led him towards the bed. He resisted only for a moment, and that she assumed was because he could hardly believe his luck.

He seemed happy enough at first for her to take control, allowing her to guide him on to the mattress, then making him lie on his back. It was only when she reached into her shoulderbag and extracted four small cuffs that he appeared to have second thoughts.

'You don't mind?' she breathed huskily.

'I – I'm not sure,' he replied. It was clear that the idea of being restrained had not entered into Gioseppi's considerations. Allessandra decided that a robust approach was best in the circumstances, held his left hand down and fastened his wrist to the bedstead. When he offered only a token resistance, she took this as acceptance and quickly cuffed his other hand. It was only when she began to restrain his legs that he seemed to have another change of heart.

'I'm not sure,' he murmured. 'We don't have to do it like this, do we? Not really?'

'Of course we do,' grinned Allessandra, overriding his feeble protests. 'I don't want you fighting back, do I? This way, when I start to fuck you, you won't be able to stop me.'

Her provocation was deliberate. She had found on previous occasions that most men seemed to like it: talking dirty, taking control. They might seem to object, but deep down none really did. She snapped the last restraint into place, looked at Gioseppi and smiled. Reaching forward she unbuckled his belt, undid the top of his zip and pulled his trousers down. Beneath his long, blue boxer shorts, she was surprised to see that his penis was still limp. She arched her eyebrows and shook her head sadly. 'Don't you know to stand up when a lady enters the room?'

She stretched out her hand. Her fingers sheathed him tightly, a warm fist around his shaft. He remained limp. She turned and stared at him. An awful thought struck her. 'Do you like women, Gioseppi?' she asked.

'Yes,' he answered, a nervous edge to his voice. Allessandra wondered if it was because she was holding his penis and he feared the wrong reply might elicit retribution.

'Perhaps you prefer boys? Yes?'

His dark eyes clouded over. 'No!' he responded.

There was a strength of feeling in his reply that seemed genuine enough, but she had to be certain. She began to stroke his cock gently, then leaned forward and kissed him on the glans, tickling the eye of his urethra with the very tip of her tongue. Nothing. She frowned.

'You are impotent!' she declared.

'No!' he protested.

'Yes!' she countered. 'Of course. That is why.'

Now it was his turn to look puzzled. 'That is why – what?' he asked.

Allessandra smiled. At least she could allay her Mistress's fears. This explained why Gioseppi had not responded as they had imagined he would. The Doctors Stanislav and Quellorozata had run true to form. No problem there. But Gioseppi had spoilt the party. He had thrown the project into doubt. No longer. And yet . . . Another thought occurred to her. She turned to face him; looked deep into his eyes and searched his soul. He did not look away. She knew she was a beautiful woman. This was no conceit on her part. Perhaps even Gioseppi, for all his lack of libido, could long for her embrace.

'I serve a Mistress,' she said quietly. His eyes narrowed. He did not understand her. 'The one who funds your work, Gioseppi.'

'I do not know who funds my work,' he replied. It was true enough. Amounts were simply paid into his account each month. Three times what might have been expected. The aim was to buy both loyalty and results.

'My Mistress funds you,' explained Allessandra. She stroked his penis. 'How long since you have enjoyed the pleasures of the body?'

He tried to look away, but she held his gaze. She knew that he did not want to look away. It was, for him, a difficult moment; a moment of awful truth.

'I have never known them,' he admitted quietly.

She had guessed as much. 'Do you wish to know them?' she asked.

He shrugged. 'I am not sure. Once, no. But now . . .'

'Why?' She was probing now.

'Recently, I have had feelings. Thoughts. Dreams.' He looked away. It was not a conscious decision, he was simply lost in reflection; adrift in his own, rather sad world.

'Tell me your dreams,' urged Allessandra.

He closed his eyes and shook his head. 'I cannot,' he said quietly.

'Are they obscene?' she enquired. 'Do they disgust you?'

He nodded. 'Yes.' A pause. 'But worse than that.'

'How so?' she asked, still stroking his cock, the fingers of her other hand moving in to tickle the hairs of his balls.

'They excite me, too.'

'But that is good, Gioseppi,' she told him. 'It is good to know the pleasures of the flesh.'

He looked up at her with wide, imploring eyes. 'But I do not know them!' he declared forlornly. 'I can never know them!'

Allessandra squeezed his cock and smiled. 'You will know them, Gioseppi. I swear it. Before this day is out, you will know them . . .'

Dinner was to be served at 7.30 p.m. It was now a quarter past seven and the bar adjacent to the main dining area was packed. Gioseppi da Vinci was nowhere to be seen. Not that it mattered for the moment. Tamara could only handle one man at a time. Well, so far as small talk went at any rate. She was currently chatting to the effulgent Dr Q. Taking into account his natural proclivities, she had decided to wear a plunging halter-neck to emphasise her cleavage, and a tight black skirt to draw attention to her bum. It seemed to have done the trick. If the light in his eyes was anything to go by, his defences were already well and truly down. A little more softening up and she would be ready to move in for the kill.

Max, for his part, was standing on his own, by the door,

sipping a coke and feeling bored. He had briefly considered slipping outside and chancing his arm with the big-busted receptionist. Unfortunately, she appeared to have gone off duty. Her place had been taken by a large bearded man who he didn't really fancy at all.

Erica Stanislav had vanished again. Or was at least conspicuous by her absence. Not the same thing, perhaps, but, semantics apart, the practical consequence was that he was at a loose end. Watching his partner chatting up the randy Dr Quellorozata was not designed to lift his spirits. If necessary, Max knew that Tamara would be happy to fuck the good doctor until the early hours, if it would get him to reveal what he knew about the Sacred Prayer. He doubted he would see much of her before morning.

There might be a free meal on offer, but Max wasn't hungry. What he was, however, was decidedly randy and erect. He couldn't understand it. It wasn't as if he'd exactly restrained himself today. Maybe Tamara was right. Maybe he *was* insatiable. His attention began to wander. A young waitress skipped past, balancing a tray of drinks. Max watched her backside shuffle seductively for an instant as she squeezed herself between two men. Then she was gone. Which was just as well. Another second and he would have hurried after her, lifted up her short black skirt, wrenched down her tights and taken her across the nearest table. He shook his head and finished his drink. What was he thinking? He had to get out of here; get some fresh air; clear his head.

Gioseppi was standing on tiptoe, his wrists cuffed, his arms chained to hooks in the ceiling. The expression on his face was quite pathetic. Allessandra's eyes narrowed.

'Do you wish to serve my Mistress?' she asked him, stroking the back of his head. It seemed an oddly affectionate gesture and one which took him by surprise.

'I – I don't know,' he replied hesitantly.

Allessandra smiled sweetly. 'I think you do,' she whispered, one hand still around his penis, the fingers of the other bunching up and tugging at his hair. She pulled

his face towards her and covered his mouth with her dark, wet lips. She squeezed his shaft gently, and he whimpered like a sleepy child.

'The Mistress rewards all those who serve her,' whispered Allessandra, though it was clear to her that Gioseppi was beyond caring. She was stoking a need in his loins that had to be satisfied. But she must awaken that need first.

Allessandra released his cock and ran her finger down the ridge of his back. His skin felt impossibly soft and smooth.

'Have you ever been whipped?' she enquired flatly, as if the matter were of no great interest to her.

She felt his body tighten and knew the answer before he had given it; knew, too, the fear that her words had engendered.

'No!' he declared. 'Never!'

Allessandra stood up and crossed to a bureau. She opened a drawer and extracted a short black tawse. She lashed out with it, striking the edge of the table with such force that the sound reverberated around the room.

'Well, we must all learn new experiences,' she said quietly.

'Dear Lord, no!' he answered back and began to tug hard at his restraints.

'Please, Gioseppi, don't be such a baby. You'll enjoy it. You know you will.'

The Italian began to wriggle furiously. 'Never!' he cried.

'Where shall we begin?' Allessandra asked herself absent-mindedly. She pressed her hand between his cheeks. 'Maybe the bum. You've got some padding there, so it won't hurt as much. It will build up your ability to withstand pain.'

Gioseppi wriggled and yelled some more, but Allessandra ignored his protests. Deep down, she sensed acceptance, even hope. He wanted this. He just didn't know it yet. Moving to the front of him she stood with her legs apart so that he could feast on her body. She pressed the handle of the tawse up against her pussy and began to

twirl it round very gently. She was already excited at the prospect of using Gioseppi and her sap oozed out through the thin satin, a dark patch discolouring her starched white panties. Pushing harder, she forced the end of the tawse into her pussy, driving the material into her cunt. Gioseppi could only watch in silent wonder as she began to masturbate herself, using the tawse as a dildo. True, she was achieving only minimal penetration, but it was enough to stimulate her clitoris and carry her to the brink of release. She pushed her hips back, screwed up her face and bit her lip. Gioseppi said nothing, his eyes glued to her cunt, watching the smudge of darkness spread as Allessandra's cream leaked from her vagina.

'I'm wanking myself, Gioseppi,' she moaned feebly through clenched teeth. 'I'm w– w– wanking myself . . .' The words were forced from the back of her throat now as she drove herself towards inevitable release. One last, hard thrust of the whip handle and her orgasm broke. Her hips sawed back and forth. She pushed her tongue out of her mouth and chewed it fiercely, emitting bizarre mewing noises, her face contorted as if she were in the most dreadful torment.

As the eddies of pleasure ebbed away, Allessandra drew herself up to her full height and plucked the tawse-handle from her vagina. The material of her panties remained wedged inside her pussy. She was pleased to see the lustful look on Gioseppi's face as she carefully eased the satin free. The gusset was now sodden with her juices. Putting the tawse to one side, she eased her knickers down over her broad hips and stepped out of them. Then, moving forward with them in her hand, she dangled them over the Italian's face.

'Can you smell me, Gioseppi?' she asked him. 'This is what I smell like when I'm excited. Taste me, Gioseppi. Taste me . . .'

She extended her arm so that her knickers brushed against his nose and mouth. She wanted to see if he would recoil in horror, but instead he took a deep sniff and pushed his head forward so that his parched lips made

188

contact with the soiled crotch of her panties. A sudden thought struck her and she stepped behind him. Rummaging in a drawer she took out a long, silk scarf. Reaching around his head she crumpled the knickers into a ball and pressed them against his nose. Then she passed the scarf around his face, secured her panties in place and knotted the scarf behind his head. Lifting the phone, she made a quick call to reception. Within a few minutes, there was a double-knock at the door. Allessandra opened it to admit one of the female porters, Mandy, a buxom black girl.

'Who have you serviced?' asked Allessandra bluntly.

'Professor Julie Laver, madam,' answered the girl, 'and a Dr Quellorozata.'

'Ah yes,' remarked Allessandra. 'The lesbian from Canada, and the madman from Brazil. I trust you gave them both satisfaction?'

'I believe so, madam. Professor Laver has asked me to join her for drinks once my shift ends. I believe she wishes to spend the night with me.'

'Excellent,' replied Allessandra. 'But not the doctor?'

'No, madam. Though he did ask me if I knew of any interesting nightspots where women could be procured.'

Allessandra snorted. 'You offer them steak and still they hanker after burger and chips. Still, the good doctor is one of us, though he does not know it yet.' She shook her head sadly, then said, 'You have not changed your underwear?'

'No, madam.'

'Good, then please remove your knickers.'

Mandy bunched up her short skirt, pulled down her panties and handed them over.

'Thank you,' said Allessandra, sniffing the crotch and smiling dreamily. The smell of semen and vaginal sap was strong and heady. 'You may leave us now.'

The girl bowed curtly and left the room without another word. Allessandra crossed back to Gioseppi, scrunching up the knickers in her hand.

'We must gag you, Gioseppi, so that you do not wake the other guests.'

He looked down at the roll of black material in Allessandra's hands. Even at this distance he could smell the mingling of male and female essence.

'*Per piacere*! *Please*! *No*!' he breathed.

Allessandra stared deep into his dark brown eyes. 'Do you really mean that?' she asked him.

'*Si*!' he muttered, but without any real conviction.

Allessandra smiled. 'You are lying,' she said. 'You want this more than you dare admit.'

He shook his head as if to deny it, but Allessandra knew better. A man like Gioseppi had led such a cloistered life: school, university, and the private world of dull old books and ancient artefacts. She was offering the chance for something else. Something far beyond his wildest dreams. His head said no, but his cock would say yes.

'Open your mouth,' she ordered. This was the moment of truth. Whatever he decided, there would be no going back. If he chose to resist her then she would take him anyway, but the Contessa always preferred her victims to willingly embrace her cause. Only willing lust was sure to last and give Mádrofh the world she longed for.

Gioseppi opened his mouth. Allessandra smiled, and gently stroked the side of his face. 'Good boy,' she said. 'Welcome to paradise.'

She pushed the soiled knickers past his lips. They were not large enough to restrict his breathing, that would be stupid. But they would give him something to bite on and to chew should the pain become too much to bear. As it certainly would.

She picked up the tawse and struck him lightly across the buttocks. He swung awkwardly and grunted into the gag. She struck again, harder this time, and then harder still. Tears began to roll down Gioseppi's face.

The next time she struck him she felt the first of her freshly revived juices well up in her pussy and leak out on to her thigh.

Between Gioseppi's legs, blood began to flow into his penis.

Allessandra smiled. Lust was at large in the world. And even Gioseppi could not resist its siren call to arms.

And soon there would be more. Soon there would be so much more.

And then there would be Chaos.

Her Mistress would be pleased. So pleased.

Max strolled down the Strand towards Trafalgar Square. It was a busy night, as always, with hordes of tourists milling around. There seemed to be some sort of commotion near the fountains as he approached. It came as a surprise when he saw what it was. A young couple were frolicking in the water. They were stark naked and running around after each other. What was crazy, however, was that no one seemed remotely interested. People wandered past as if nothing unusual was happening. Perhaps they were embarrassed, mused Max, moving in closer because he wasn't embarrassed in the least. The woman was tall and statuesque, with big breasts, broad hips and long dark hair. She looked vaguely familiar. The man, too, he seemed to know, though his face was obscured by spray. Suddenly the woman leaned forward and growled threateningly. Her cry was so loud that Max looked round to see if one of the lions had come to life. But no, everything seemed normal, if watching two naked people grappling in the fountains in broad daylight passed for normal these days. A change came over the man's demeanour. Suddenly out of the water behind him, rose a second woman. She was as tall and big-breasted as her companion but with short blonde hair. Again, she looked familiar. The duo fell on their victim and the three of them vanished for a moment into the foam. Then the blonde goddess hoisted the man into the air and swung him in her arms. His cock was upright and very big. He wriggled uselessly and his captor laughed. The second woman reached out, took hold of the man's prick and pulled him towards her. He kicked and squirmed, struggling to escape the inevitable. Max could hardly believe his eyes. What he was watching was a man being held fast by one woman while her friend prepared to rape him. He looked around for some reaction. Maybe he'd got

191

it wrong, maybe he was mistaken. Maybe he'd come in late to a film shoot. He spotted two policemen – sanity at last! They were staring directly into the fountain, so they could hardly miss what was happening. Yet that was exactly what they seemed to be doing. They were looking straight through the scene as if it wasn't there. Max closed his eyes sharply, took a deep breath and opened them again. If he had hoped that the brief pause might somehow right his topsy-turvy world he was sadly mistaken. The second woman lunged forward. Her victim writhed and threw back his head, his arms flailing uselessly. Suddenly his eyes met Max's. They were wide and imploring. Inside his head, Max heard the words, 'Tamara! No!'

Something snapped. He took a step towards the fountain. At that moment, the woman holding the man around his waist turned her face and stared straight at Max. He drew up short, as if a thunderbolt had hit him between the eyes. He careered into a Japanese tourist, busy filming a pigeon defecating on to his girlfriend's shoulder. The tourist yelled and everyone turned in their direction, including the two policemen who now approached rapidly. Terrific, thought Max. Then, equally surprisingly, he felt a woman's arm snake round his waist. A pair of lips clamped themselves against his mouth for an instant, then pulled away.

'Darling,' said an unfamiliar voice, tinged with accent, 'where have you been? I look for you everywhere!' The two policeman stopped in their tracks, recognised the incident for what it was and moved on. The Japanese tourist bowed as if the entire business was his fault and politely backed away, holding his camcorder tight against his chest.

Max looked back towards the fountain. The naked trio had vanished. Everything was as it should be. Then he turned to face his assailant. Or his saviour? Either way, this was a turn-up for the book. He was staring into the sparkling, and distinctly lustful blue eyes of the diminutive Dr Erica Stanislav.

Thirteen

It was crazy. They had scrambled over the gates into Green Park, like a couple of excited kids. Now they were huddled in the bushes, the light from a single street lamp coating their naked bodies in a dull, flaxen sheen.

They had fucked three times already. On the first occasion very quickly, on the second with more finesse, and on the third with a vigour that had taken them both by surprise. Erica nuzzled her head into Max's chest and stroked his penis. It still felt good, even after three successive orgasms.

'You English,' she murmured. 'So upright!' She laughed as his penis began to twitch against her coaxing fingers. Max frowned. He knew he shouldn't feel like this. He had hardly spoken a word since the diminutive Hungarian had saved his bacon at Trafalgar Square, then hailed a passing taxi and dragged him off to Piccadilly Circus. Confusion still clouded his senses. But it was more than that. There was something at the back of his head. He knew something. But whatever it was he knew, he didn't know. Crazy.

Erica's fingers were feathering his balls. She took hold of one of his hands and placed it around her left breast. 'Squeeze me, English,' she said, in a voice so stylised it might have been an act.

He pinched her nipple. 'Is good,' she told him and he pinched again. She turned her head and looked up into his eyes. 'Something strange,' she said.

'What do you mean?' he asked, though he had the same feeling.

'You know, I think,' she replied. 'You saw. In the fountain.'

'What did I see?' he asked.

'What I see. And no one else.'

Max was at a loss. If they had both seen what he knew he had seen, then it still made no sense. Why had no one else seen it? Another memory pushed its way through the crowds. He recalled the way their eyes had met at the Favelli Centre: his and Erica's. They had seen something then: something in each other; something they had recognised. And that made no sense either.

All that made any sense was the fact that his penis was hard again.

'Stand!' said Erica. The abruptness of her command caught him by surprise. 'Quick!' she urged him, releasing his penis for a moment and jumping up.

'There is a ceremony,' she began. 'In pagan time. To fertilise soil. Pagan priestess would masturbate man so that his seed spill on the land. This is thought to give land the special nourishment. Make crops grow big.'

Max frowned. 'Really?' he said. He found the notion of the Hungarian doctor spilling his seed on the ground rather exciting. She took hold of his shaft and began to stroke. Max felt his balls roll gently in their sacs. It was scarcely possible that they could be filling with seed. Not already.

'Is beautiful,' murmured Erica, tightening her grip, drawing his foreskin up and down as she spoke. 'A shame to waste the fruit.' She took hold of his hand and led it down to the delta of tight brown curls that adorned her vagina.

'Lift me, please,' she asked, but in a tone that made it sound like an order. Max took hold of her legs and hoisted her up so that her cunt slipped on to his cock, sheathing it. He leaned back against the rough bark of a tree.

'Do the fucking, English!' she gasped. 'Do the fucking. Now! Please!'

Max needed no encouragement. He bucked his hips so that his cock pushed up into her cunt. He felt the swollen

lozenge of her clitoris press against the top of his shaft, as it had on the three previous occasions they had made love. Erica began to squirm with excitement, aroused as quickly as him. Suddenly her body tightened.

'I'm having the come!' she groaned. 'English, I'm having the come!'

Her pussy began to squeeze around his shaft and Max knew that he was, amazingly – and to use her delightful little expression – about to have the come, too. Suddenly she raised herself on the saddle of his lap, sliding up, so that his cock began to emerge.

'Not in my cunt!' she gasped. 'On ground! On ground!'

And suddenly he was spurting free, his seed spilling on to the green turf around their feet. He put her down as gently as he could, but his strength was almost gone. When he looked down, he saw that his semen had vanished into the earth.

Erica smiled. 'We shall come back in ten years' time, English,' she smiled, 'and see if there is a forest here, yes?'

Max smiled. He covered her cunt with his hand and eased two fingers into her.

Stanislav swooned. 'Oh damn you, English. Again? No? Not again, please!' She was protesting, but Max knew it was a sham. He felt a gush of oily warmth over his palm and held the doctor close as she gave herself up to her second spasm. He stroked her hair gently and kissed her on top of the head. He didn't know why. It just seemed a nice thing to do. She took hold of his hand and pressed his fingers to his nose.

'Do I smell nice, English?' she asked him. In truth her smell was intoxicating. It made him want to have her all over again. He should be asking her questions: discovering what she knew about the Contessa and the Sacred Prayer. But he didn't care. All he wanted to do was fuck her. And then fuck her again.

And again.

'Where the hell have you been?'

Tamara was furious. It was not the welcome home he had expected. No, wait a minute, on second thoughts it

195

was just the welcome home he had expected. After all, it was three in the morning.

'I didn't want to disturb you and Dr Q,' said Max defensively. It was the best excuse he could conjure up on the spur of the moment.

'Some chance,' replied Tamara. 'He disappeared with two of the chambermaids the moment my back was turned.'

'Oops,' said Max, unable to hide a grin.

'You haven't answered my question,' Tamara reminded him.

The smile vanished from Max's face. 'I've been with Erica Stanislav,' he said. 'And that's not all.'

Tamara flicked a wall switch. 'I'll make us some coffee,' she said. 'Then you can tell me everything that's happened.'

Doctor Quellorozata was lying on his back, his arms and legs secured to the four corners of the ornate brass bedstead. There was a woman sitting on his face and he was finding it difficult to breathe. A second woman knelt on the mattress, milking his penis. In reality, she had long since drawn the last drops of his seed, sucking them into her mouth and letting the sharp creamy liquid trickle down her throat. Occasionally, the woman astride his face would shift forward, allowing him to draw a breath of air. She did so now, lifting her bottom just a fraction.

'Dear God, have pity!' he screamed, or might have done had the woman not sat back at once and cut off his strangled attempt at a plea. He grunted into her bare behind and twisted his hips.

The girl tightened her hold on his cock and continued to milk his empty, aching shaft.

Two floors above him, Erica Stanislav lay on her bed, too, her body similarly secured. A black chambermaid rose and fell over her face, enjoying the play of the doctor's tongue as it strobed against her vulva. A second woman tickled the thick pink lozenge of Erica's clitoris, while a third

pushed a large rubber phallus in and out of the doctor's cunt. Erica's body heaved with pleasure, then twisted with pain. Like Dr Quellorozata, she had lost count of the number of times she had been made to orgasm. Like him she both cared and did not care. She wanted this and she did not want it. But like him, she wanted it more than she did not.

She came again, her vagina contracting around the dildo twisting inside her.

Allessandra sat astride her victim's face. He had not come. Not yet. She had not let him. His penis stood like a hardened rod between his legs. He wept as the thrill of arousal engulfed his every nerve and muscle. She had stroked him to the edge of climax so many times now, only to release him at the last and wriggle her own excitement across the hard edge of his nose or tongue. Time and again she had unleashed herself into his mouth, smearing him with her essence, soaking him with the warm juices that spilled from deep within her belly. The first time she had climaxed, he had screamed for mercy, twisting his head madly in a futile attempt to avoid the oils that spilled into his throat. Only on the fourth occasion had she detected a lessening of protest; whether from fatigue or resignation it was hard to say.

She knew she must judge the moment to perfection. If he came too soon he might never come again. She must train his body to long for the ecstasy of release. Rising from his face, she reached forward and felt for his balls. They were large and hard, like stones on a beach. He wept in pain when she squeezed the sacs.

'It is time, Gioseppi,' she whispered softly.

'Dear Lord,' she heard him murmur pathetically between her thighs.

'Do you swear fealty to my Mistress and to the Darkness?' she asked him gently.

'I do . . . I do . . .' he answered weakly.

'And shall pleasure be your Mistress, too? All the days of your unworthy life?'

'It shall . . . it shall . . .' he replied in a voice that seemed to fade in strength with each word spoken.

'Then breathe deeply, my friend,' she told him, tightening the muscles of her hard, damp thighs. 'And enter into paradise . . .'

Allessandra heard Gioseppi draw a massive breath into his tired, aching lungs. Then, sitting back, she lowered her full weight on to his upturned face. For a full two minutes she straddled him in silence, waiting for the air to grow stale in his chest. His body began to twitch, and then to squirm and then to struggle. His penis jumped between his legs, bobbing up and down as he wriggled in fear. She felt his lips widen around her vulva; felt the maw of her cunt bloom within his mouth. She reached down with one hand and pressed the nub of her clitoris. With the other she circled the hard surround of his shaft. As she emptied herself into his throat for the last time, she felt the shudder of his cock as it leapt in her hand. Cream spurted from the eye, splattering her hand and her face and her belly.

Far away, deep within her Lair, the Contessa closed her eyes and felt Gioseppi's pleasure and his pain. She thrust the golden phallus deep into her cunt and felt another's pain and pleasure, too.

The end time was almost upon them.

Nothing could stop her now. Nothing at all.

It was 5.30 in the morning. Still time to be in bed, thought Max. Definitely time to be in bed if you hadn't yet been to bed. Which he hadn't. And not likely to at this rate. Maybe never again. Oh well.

He had told Tamara everything: the obscene images; Trafalgar Square; Erica Stanislav; the feeling he had that something was not quite right. Something he couldn't quite put his finger on. He was so exhausted that he didn't even try to put a finger on Tamara. Perhaps he was going down with something.

Tamara had listened in silence, nodding every now and then to show him she was still awake. Several cups of

strong black coffee had helped. Then, when he had finished his own story, she had told him hers. Not that there was much to tell. Doctor Quellorozata had vanished in the company of two other women. Tamara had little doubt they were Faithful. The entire staff was in the pay of the Contessa in one way or another. She had decided not to follow. She was hopelessly outgunned. Better, she decided, to wait for back-up in the shape of Max. But that had been a waste of time. Still, at least she had got some sleep, which was more than he had. And there had been another plus. A phone call had come through from Omega. Erskine had been trying to get in touch. She had left him the number of her fictitious publishers – a special number patched straight through to HQ. They'd told him she was in a meeting. It was late, but that was the mad and wonderful world of literature for you. He wanted her back at once. There had been a development. He could say no more. They promised to pass on the message, which they had. Tamara could guess what it was all about. Things were moving at last and he wanted her there at the kill. There was just one thing puzzling her. Why? While Max snatched forty winks, Tamara had made another call – to Crayshaw.

Which was why they were driving across London at such a ridiculous hour.

Max yawned and rubbed his eyes. 'I need to kip,' he moaned. 'I'm knackered!'

'Then do it on your own time,' replied Tamara unsympathetically.

She was a hard woman, he told himself. Which was, if he was honest, the side of her that appealed to him most.

There were others who couldn't sleep. Gioseppi, Marsilio and Erica for three. Even now their torture continued. All part of a plan. All part of a diabolical plan.

All part of the plan for Chaos.

The Contessa did not sleep. She lay on her Living Throne, the golden phallus deep within her cunt. Guy's screams of pleasure and despair fed the flames that burned so

beautifully into the engorged hump of her clitoris. She fed, too, on the pleasures of her servants: Allessandra, Aubrey and the other members of The Order. All were preparing themselves now. All knew the moment of truth would soon be upon them. Another step along the road towards the Great Darkness. Perhaps the final step of all.

And then there were the torments of the Three: those whose work had hastened this moment of sublime endeavour. Their reward would be great. As would their joy.

And their death, of course, would be exquisite.

A few yards away the young student, Stephen, lay on his back, chained to a broad metal frame. The black girl Joni straddled his midriff, moving rapidly, her large breasts shaking from side to side. She was an eager hussy who would need to be taught the pleasures of restraint. Lana was sitting on Stephen's face, grinding the ridge of her pubis over his mouth, her sap dribbling across his chin. Their victim heaved for a moment, but Lana's vulva deadened any cry he might have tried to make.

The Contessa felt a sudden rush of pleasure into her cunt. She twisted the phallus full circle and let out a shrill warble of delight.

Somewhere far away and yet so near, Guy screamed.

Desperately short of air, his balls empty, his cock shuddering with the pain of repeated orgasm, so did Stephen.

It was, reflected the Contessa, quite, quite beautiful.

Crayshaw's house was out in Hampstead. It was a big, early Victorian building, with large windows and gloomy towers. Just the sort of place a weirdo like Crayshaw would live, thought Max. The cool morning air did something to revive his senses. What did more, however, was the sight of the dark-skinned girl who opened the door to them: a pocket Venus of a beauty, with long black hair, big brown eyes and a fluttering emerald green sarong.

'Crayshaw keeps an interesting entourage,' explained Tamara as they followed the girl across the hallway and

into a big study. The walls were lined with books; carpets cluttered with furniture and ancient, scattered *bric-a-brac*. A space had been cleared in the centre, and a pentagram chalked on to a black, wooden floor. Tall, perfumed candles guttered and filled the room with the smell of incense.

Crayshaw tumbled out of her chair and rolled towards them, hands outstretched. Max couldn't help but notice that she too wore a sarong, only red. From the way it flowed around her body, he suspected she wore little if anything underneath.

'Everything is ready,' she announced. 'We haven't got much time. Take your clothes off, lad, there's a good fellow.'

'What?' yelped Max.

'We have to root around inside that head of yours,' explained Crayshaw, poking him with a big podgy hand. 'Clothes just get in the way.'

Max turned to Tamara, and she gave a resigned shrug. He began to unbuckle his belt, then stopped because he realised the girl in the green sarong was still present, watching him intently.

'Don't mind Sha'ni,' said Crayshaw. 'She's one of the family.'

Max pulled down his trousers. He couldn't help it. Undressing in front of three women had aroused him. As he took off his boxers, his penis stood out proudly and unashamed against his tummy. All his fatigue seemed to vanish as the red blood of arousal coursed through his veins.

'Right,' said Crayshaw. 'Let's see what our boyo knows, shall we? Or doesn't know he knows!' She gave a loud laugh and her flesh undulated fiercely. Max wondered why she didn't collapse through the floorboards.

'You'll have to lie down here,' she explained, pointing to a spot on the floor. Max did as she asked. Out of the corner of his eye he watched Sha'ni disrobe. She was naked beneath her green sarong, her brown breasts small and hard, her tanned legs short and slender. When she stepped forward, he saw that her vulva was dark, plump and shaven.

'I should have explained,' said Crayshaw. 'Sha'ni is a white witch – a Hedwynne.'

That makes a lot of sense, thought Max dryly. But at the back of his mind something stirred. Vanjja had been thwarted by the Hedwynne. He was too tired to ask if there was a connection. They probably wouldn't tell him anyway.

'She has mystical powers. One of which is the ability to draw out the inner psyche. I don't think simple hypnosis will work on this occasion. We need something much stronger.'

Max was lying on his back, staring up at an erotic painting on the ceiling. A man and woman were fucking, doggy-style. A second girl was standing on the first woman's back, her pussy pressed over the man's face. A third woman stood at his rear. She wore a dildo and was vigorously buggering him. Max felt his cock harden, which puzzled him as he thought it was already hard enough.

Sha'ni straddled his midriff. She poured warm scented oils over first her body, then his. It brought to mind the Double Delight at the massage parlour. But that had been sex. This was something else, something more sensual. Sha'ni took hold of his penis and drew it towards her cunt.

'Sha'ni will enter your subconscious through your sexual drive,' explained Crayshaw. 'It's a very ancient art. Not practised much these days.'

Max didn't care, so long as it was about to be practised now. He sighed as he felt his shaft sink into Sha'ni's deliciously tight pussy.

She looked up. 'Please hold him,' she said. Max was puzzled. He couldn't see why they needed to hold him. He was going nowhere. That was, if you excluded paradise. Tamara took hold of his feet, while Crayshaw's big meaty fists engulfed his wrists. Sha'ni began to bounce. Slowly at first, then faster and faster. She leaned forward and slid her breasts across his tummy. Max squirmed and began to push up with his hips to increase the friction between their bodies. He groaned as he felt the seed fill his balls and trickle into the root of his shaft. Sha'ni tensed and

tightened the muscles in her cunt. An incredible tickling sensation gripped his cock, then spread up into his belly. He began to fidget awkwardly. Pleasure radiated out into every corner of his being. It was like an orgasm which built up, then overflowed, yet never really happened. Some Far-Eastern love ritual, he assumed. Wild.

The pleasure turned to pain, then back to even greater pleasure. Something hot seared the inside of his groin and he screamed. He imagined someone would shove something into his mouth to shut him up, but they didn't. Sha'ni continued to slither about, tensing and untensing her cunt muscles, wiping her breasts across his mouth. He tried to clamp his mouth over her dinky little tits but they kept moving out of reach. This was teasing taken to a new level.

'No more! No more!' he found himself yelling. He cursed himself. Why no more? He hoped they wouldn't listen to him. They didn't. But deep down he hoped they would and squirmed some more. He shut his eyes in pleasure, not pain. No way was this pain. But it had also gone beyond pleasure.

He tried to open his eyes but they were no longer responding. Darkness swirled. Black clouds formed, broke and reformed in the inky world behind his lids. And then he saw Sha'ni. And someone else, too. It was Erica Stanislav. There were other shadows: people, people he knew. Or at least he thought he knew. Then one face cleared and he realised it was his own. Only it wasn't him. He looked different. It didn't make sense. Nothing made sense. Sha'ni swam into view again. She was floating over his head. He was floating, too. Then sinking. He watched, fascinated, as his cock twitched in the blackness of his dream-world. Sperm shot into the air, silvery-white against the black night. His seed splattered and broke and danced like so many raindrops. It continued to spurt long after it should have. It was as if there was a never-ending supply. It filled the darkness, bringing light where there had been gloom. He knew he was climaxing in his head, but not in his body. In his body the torture went on. He was exhausted, stretched this way and that. It was as if he were

being torn apart. Then everything went well and truly black.

'How long?' asked Erskine. He was standing in the main excavation chamber. A fresh series of holes had been dug, and ultra-sound equipment set in place.

A young bearded man frowned and bit his lip. 'Another five or six hours, I should think.'

'We have to be right,' said Erskine. 'Our backers won't like it if we're wrong again.'

The earnest young man chewed his lip and sniffed with all the certainty of someone who knew what he was doing even if those around him did not.

'We won't be wrong,' he said. 'We're almost there.'

Max listened in silence to the story of his kidnap, interrogation and torture. Apparently he had not passed out again, which was some consolation. He had gone into a trance and talked at length, telling them everything that had happened.

He was dressed now and drinking a generous brandy, which was just what the doctor ordered. He sat in front of an open fire and shivered.

'After-effect of the mind-link,' explained Crayshaw. 'You'll feel groggy for a while.'

'There's something else,' said Tamara. 'Something we haven't told you.'

'Oh, good,' said Max, though he doubted very much that it was.

'The Contessa planted a command in your head. If you were successful in killing me, you were to meet up with Aubrey Manners at his private club.'

'Well that's stuffed,' replied Max.

'No, it isn't,' said Tamara. 'He had to deputise for the PM at some overseas do. It must have happened before the Contessa set you up. You're to meet Aubrey this morning.'

'Oh, terrific,' groaned Max. 'Can't a man get any sleep around here?'

Tamara glanced at her watch. 'Maybe a little,' she smiled.

'Where the hell does she think I've been for the past couple of days?'

'Who cares?'

'I care!' responded Max. 'She's no fool.'

'Max, she's a megalomaniac. She won't dream that you failed. She'll just assume you laid low.'

Max snorted. 'So let's get this straight. What you're suggesting is that I turn up at this club of his and tell Manners that I've bumped you off.'

'Something like that,' said Tamara.

'Why?' asked Max. It seemed a fair question.

'To see what you can discover. If the Contessa wants you there, it must be because she's got something planned.'

'I've been on the receiving end of things she's had planned for me already,' said Max. 'I didn't like most of it, thank you very much.'

'Sha'ni has planted a post-hypnotic suggestion in your mind. If Aubrey Manners asks what happened to me you can tell him. It's all there. How you succeeded in your mission.'

'You think that'll protect me, then?' asked Max. He was not convinced that her argument was sound.

'Have I ever lied to you, Max?' asked Tamara.

Max thought for a minute, then said, 'I don't know. Have you?'

Tamara ignored his question.

'How should I behave?' asked Max.

'With impeccable good manners,' replied Tamara. 'Remember to keep up the good name of the department.'

'Very funny,' replied Max. 'You know what I mean.'

'We can't be sure,' said Crayshaw. 'But Sha'ni thinks she knows what the potion was and how your mind would react.'

The young girl nodded. 'You must be yourself. Do not try to hide anything. Do not pretend that you have discovered your dark side and are happy for it. Be normal, be confused.'

'I am confused,' said Max. He frowned. 'I don't even know where the wretched place is.'

'Yes, you do,' said Tamara. She tapped him on the head. 'It's all in there. Trouble is, because you didn't do what you were supposed to, most of it's locked away. But you told us while you were under. I'll draw you a map.'

She looked at her watch. 'In the meantime, get some sleep. There's a bed made up in the next room. You've got about four hours.'

'And what will you be doing while I'm getting my arse kicked?'

'I'm going back to Dorford Haven. I think something is about to happen. I need to be on the spot.'

'Good,' said Max. 'At least I won't be the only one likely to get a red-hot poker up the bum.'

Tamara smiled. 'Whatever turns you on, Max.'

After Max had left the room, Tamara turned to Sha'ni and said, 'Are you sure about this?'

Sha'ni nodded. 'I saw into his mind. There is no doubt.'

Tamara looked suddenly very serious. 'I suppose I knew all along.'

'Of course you did,' said Crayshaw.

'But it's dangerous now. More dangerous than before.'

'Yes,' agreed Crayshaw. 'But it would be more dangerous still if we told him what we know.'

'Will you be able to keep track of Max's movements?'

'Sha'ni has established a mind-link. He can't get away from us.'

'I hope we know what we're doing,' said Tamara.

'I doubt that very much,' responded Crayshaw. 'If we did, I doubt we'd do it.'

Tamara glanced at her watch. 'I'd better be going.'

'Good luck,' said Crayshaw.

'Thanks,' said Tamara.

Good luck. She was going to need plenty of that where she was going. They all were.

Fourteen

Aubrey Manners regarded him with suspicion. Even Max could see that. He tried his best to look relaxed.

'So Tamara Knight is dead?'

Max frowned. He was following Tamara's advice. Act dumb. Act confused. Act whatever. Just act. And hope for the best. In case he was a lousy actor.

'I did what I was told,' answered Max indifferently.

The look on his inquisitor's face gave nothing away. Max tried to remember where the door was. He might yet need it in a hurry.

'So what did you do with the body?' asked Aubrey.

'Weighed it down, dumped it in the sea. I can tell you where, if you want to look.'

'That won't be necessary,' replied Aubrey.

Thank God for that, thought Max.

'One moment.' Aubrey sat back in the chair and closed his eyes. When he opened them again, they were strangely different. The blue-grey hue of his pupils had given way to black. Max tried to look away but the eyes flared, like a pair of dark, shimmering coals, holding his gaze. The Home Secretary leaned forward with outstretched arms, clasped his fingers around Max's neck and began to squeeze. Max didn't move. He couldn't. Every muscle in his body was locked solid. Aubrey moved closer and kissed him on the mouth. That was an even bigger shock. Immediately, the light faded and the fingers relaxed. The Home Secretary sat back in his chair, his breathing slightly laboured.

Max wasn't sure what to say. He wiped his lips. At least he could move again. Aubrey noticed the gesture, frowned for a moment then smiled. 'My, my,' he said softly. 'We *are* in the Contessa's good books, aren't we?'

Max kept silent. He was at a loss for words.

'Did you enjoy killing her?' asked Aubrey abruptly.

Max had been ready for this. 'No, of course I didn't!' he responded angrily. 'She was my friend!'

'So why did you do it?'

'I did it for the Contessa.' Another prepared answer. He hoped it was the right one. It was hard to tell.

'So you are happy to surrender to your dark side?'

'No,' replied Max, now warming to his role. 'I'm just happy to surrender to the Contessa.'

'You can't help yourself can you, you poor fool?' said Aubrey. His words rang with undisguised contempt.

'There are worse things,' said Max.

Aubrey shook his head lightly. 'Oh no, there aren't,' he replied, and laughed. His teeth bared like those of a wild animal, and for a moment Max could feel those hands around his throat again. Only this time, it felt as if it were his mind being squeezed.

The other man stood up. He extended his arm and they shook. 'Welcome to the Brimstone Club,' he said. 'Now, if you follow me, I think I can show you something of interest.'

The Home Secretary led him out of the room, then down a labyrinthine network of corridors until Max lost all sense of direction. They went through a blue-panelled door and into a spacious, glass-fronted booth. The Home Secretary ushered Max into a chair, then sat down beside him. Max looked through the window into another room. He saw two men and a woman. They were naked, and he recognised them at once: Dr Marsilio Quellorozata, Gioseppi da Vinci and Erica Stanislav.

Erica was on her knees, sucking Dr Q's cock while Gioseppi buggered her. After a while, the Brazilian began to jerk and white froth bubbled around the woman's mouth. Gioseppi pumped his hips and screamed obsceni-

ties into the air. The room was presumably wired for sound. Max's Italian was rusty, but he knew a swear word when he heard it. As for the sound of sex, of warm, excited bodies attacking each other with uninhibited relish – that required no translating. The trio separated, and Gioseppi went down on all fours. The tall Brazilian knelt behind him, his limp penis up against the Italian's arse. Erica squirmed beneath Gioseppi's body, pushed her head up between his legs and began to gnaw at his balls. He lowered his head and sucked at her cunt, peeling her labia wide and lapping at the swollen lozenge of her clitoris. At the same time, she stretched out with one hand and clawed at Dr Q's buttocks. Forcing her palm between his cheeks, she extended her fingers and probed for his anus. The Brazilian's cock jerked into life, unfurling and filling with blood. Erica sucked Gioseppi's balls into her mouth and a thin column of flesh rose between his legs. Soon all three were writhing into another round of orgasms.

Uncoupling, Erica forced Gioseppi on to his back and straddled his head, rubbing her oozing sex against his face. He drove his tongue into the damp, sparkling groove and gobbled at the swollen bulge of her cunt. Dr Q stood over her and presented his cock to her open mouth. Erica's lips closed around his shaft and she began to suck. At the same time, she dug one long finger into his anus and tickled his balls with the fingers of her other hand. Dr Q reached down and squeezed her breasts, teasing her nipples into proud points of flesh which he then pulled until they became long, painful stalks. Erica began to bounce, grinding herself on to the Italian's face, depriving him of air. She reached down and squeezed his cock, stroking rapidly until he ejaculated a thin fluid on to his belly.

Back in the glass-fronted booth, Aubrey pulled out his penis and began to stroke himself. As if on cue, the door opened and two young girls entered the room. They wore short white dresses, bunched at one shoulder and drawn down on the left side to expose the breast. Each girl carried a silver tray, set with carafes of wine, tall crystal glasses, and small bowls. Max crossed his legs instinctively as their

bare feet padded across the room. Now what? he asked himself.

'I thought you might be hungry,' said Aubrey. Though his words were addressed to Max, his eyes remained focused on the glass panel. One of the girls poured him a glass of claret. He took a deep swallow, then claimed a large fistful of stuffed olives.

Max gestured towards the white. This was all rather bizarre. Still, he decided, when in Rome and all that.

Aubrey put down his drink and said, 'Help yourself to whatever you like.'

Max straightened in his seat. The implication was clear. The girls smiled sweetly, and he felt his penis push up towards his belly. Aubrey must have taken his surprise for hesitation, made a grab for the nearest girl and tugged up her dress. She wore no knickers and her pussy was small and shaven. He pulled her across his lap and squeezed each of her buttocks in turn. Then he raised his hand high and brought it down with a loud clap. He looked across at Max and said, 'Have you ever chastised a woman?'

Max returned his gaze with a blank stare. Aubrey shook his head sadly. 'No, I can see not. A good spanking, Max. It's what they all need!' He brought his hand down several more times as if to emphasise the point.

'Would you like to smack me, sir?'

Belatedly, Max realised the other girl was addressing him. He looked up and shook his head. 'No,' he said. 'No, thank you.'

'So just a fuck, then?'

Max felt his tummy hollow. This was surreal. The girl pulled her skirt up over her head and climbed on to his lap. He didn't resist. How the hell could he? He felt her small hands undo his belt, push into his trousers and withdraw his cock. Without a word, she pulled him into her, wriggling her little buttocks against his thighs.

'I'll race you!' challenged Aubrey. He dragged the first girl upright, positioned her over his cock and pulled her down, burying his shaft in her cunt.

'First one to come!' he yelled, like a schoolboy out to

win a bet. Max hardly knew how to respond. The girl helped him by riding up and down, and soon his sperm was welling into his shaft. By then, Aubrey was already gasping his release into the other girl's neck and hugging her close. Abruptly sated, he pushed her away with callous disregard and resumed his watch on the adjoining room. Max let the other girl sit on his lap long after he had climaxed. She was warm and soft and smelled nice. It was strangely comforting. Watching events unfold through the glass, however, had its inevitable effect and soon he was hard a second time.

On the far side of the screen, Dr Q was fucking Erica in an upright position, her arms around his neck, her legs around his waist. Gioseppi stood behind her, his cock once again lodged in her arse. All three were speaking. They were cursing, and they were weeping, but there was something else, too. They were using words Max had never heard before; no language with which he was familiar.

Aubrey was murmuring under his breath, repeating the same unusual phrases. Max's cock began to harden inside the girl's cunt for a third time. He closed his eyes and surrendered to an image so obscene he could scarcely believe it had been dredged from his imagination.

Aubrey's voice cut across his thoughts. He was waving his arms, like a demented conductor. 'Oh, how evil!' he insisted. 'How obscene! I didn't catch that but I'm sure . . . Oh! Exquisite! Divine! No! Diabolical!'

Max's mind began to clear, but only for a moment. Suddenly he was coming. He held the girl close and felt his penis jerk inside her.

'Oh, fuck!' he said, without meaning to.

'Yes,' she whispered back sweetly. 'Fuck. Lovely, lovely fuck . . .'

Max pulled himself together. He hardened the muscles in his arms and lifted her from his body. She did not resist but stood to one side as if awaiting further instructions.

Aubrey turned to him and smiled. It was not a pleasant smile. 'You know, don't you?' he said.

Max shook his head. No, he didn't. Not everything. But

what he did know, he decided, it was best to keep to himself. Or perhaps it was too late for that. Aubrey had the look of a man who had been fooled for so long, but no longer.

'We are all after the same thing, no need to deny it,' said Aubrey, adding quietly, 'if for different reasons. Nhaomhé's Chalice – Vanjja's doorway to this world. But the Prayer, too. One no good without the other.' He paused, muttered something beneath his breath, squeezed his shaft and wriggled his hips. Almonds of seed spat from his cock. Max shook his head in disbelief as Aubrey continued to rub his trembling erection.

The Home Secretary gestured towards the panel. 'Three of the greatest minds in the archaeological world: the good doctors Quellorozata, da Vinci and Stanislav.'

Max tried his best to look still puzzled.

'Like all academics, dull as ditchwater,' said Aubrey dismissively. In the circumstances, reflected Max, the description seemed inapposite.

'Eighteen months ago, we unearthed what we believed to be Nhaomhé's altar. Etched around its base were markings – the wording of the Sacred Prayer, though sadly incomplete. We enlisted the services of five experts in Edrish, the ancient pagan tongue. What they uncovered, as you can see, changed them. Two, alas, shall we say, met with little accidents. But these three stayed the course.'

Aubrey sighed and began to move his hips again. The man was insatiable, Max reflected, but you had to admire him, however reluctantly.

'Incredible,' said Aubrey. 'Last night, we had them thoroughly worked over, subjected to every perversion. Yet look! This is what the Prayer has done to them!'

A thought stirred at the back of Max's mind. There was something wrong. It was something Aubrey had said. He tried to concentrate, but it was difficult. A part of him wanted to fuck the girl again. But a part of him knew he must think. If what Aubrey said was true, then . . .

The Home Secretary stood up and cut across his thoughts. His penis jutted out between his open flies. It was

a ridiculous sight. 'You've seen enough,' he said. 'And so have I. Now we have other business to attend to.'

Tamara was back at Dorford Haven, overlooking the central excavation site. It was abuzz with activity. Earnest-looking figures scurried around, grabbing each other by the arms, whispering and shaking their heads. She had arrived only within the last few minutes and it was obvious that something was up.

But there was something else, too.

There had been something wrong from the start. Her every instinct told her so. She'd guessed Max's secret ages since, but this was different. She had misunderstood something; looked at something the wrong way round. But what?

Or maybe she was just tired.

No, it was there; something really so very obvious that if she just gave it another moment's deliberation . . .

A cry from the main bore-hole wrecked her train of thought. Someone called for Erskine. Suddenly there he was, running from his office. He spotted her at once. It was hard not to, in her short red skirt and white cotton top, all long, brown legs and firm, protruding breasts.

'What is it?' she asked.

'Could be the jackpot!' he replied, his eyes round with excitement.

She followed him down into the trench. No one moved to stop her as she clung to Erskine's sleeve. She meant to be in at the death. Wrong thought, she told herself.

There was a lot of activity in the main chamber. One of the younger archaeologists, a balding, moustachioed bear of a man, licked his lips and shook his big, red face.

'Well?' asked Erskine.

'We've found it,' said the bear.

Erskine clapped his hands together. 'Yes!' he cried, like a child who has just discovered Christmas.

They made their way into the cavern. It was bright with electric lighting. A fresh series of holes had been dug since Tamara was last here; the small, protective urns remained in place.

A hush fell as they stared into the gloom. A large hole had been gouged out of a pock-marked wall. Straight ahead of them, on a broken ledge, perched the lopsided outline of the Chalice. It sat in a delicate wooden tabernacle, the frame splintered and dull with age.

Erskine looked around. His dark eyes narrowed. 'You didn't touch it?' he asked. The question appeared to be addressed to no one in particular. There was a collective shaking of heads.

'Good,' he said. 'Excellent. We must cordon off the area until Ms Favelli arrives.'

Tamara felt a raw chill enter her stomach. Once Allessandra Favelli got her hands on the Chalice, the Contessa was home and dry. She had to get there first. She just wasn't sure how. Problems, she muttered to herself. Always problems.

Problems were something Max was getting rather used to.

Aubrey opened the door and ushered Max into a small, dimly lit room. His attention was immediately drawn to a tall, gilded mirror in one corner. There was something vaguely familiar about it. Four naked women stood to one side of the glass: tall, big-busted, broad-hipped, long-legged. They stepped forward, two to each man and began to remove his clothes. Max didn't try to stop them; it seemed rude to object. Besides, he'd never been undressed by two women before. He was all for widening his horizons.

When both men were naked, Aubrey knelt in front of the mirror. One girl produced a thin cord and fastened his hands behind his back. Another did the same to Max. He should have resisted, but if they were doing this to Aubrey, he reasoned, there couldn't be any danger.

Big mistake.

Two women knelt either side of the Home Secretary, took hold of his cock and balls and began to stroke him gently. A third stood behind him with a whip, raised it high in the air and brought it down sharply across his back. Aubrey's body kicked with excitement and Max watched

his huge balls roll in the girl's hands. The whip came down several times: a torrent of blows criss-crossing his bare flesh.

The mirror began to mist over. The light played tricks with Max's eyes and he imagined that snakes were sliding up and down the edges of the carved wooden frame. He suddenly remembered where he had seen this mirror before; or one just like it. It was in the dungeon at the massage parlour.

Another piece of the jigsaw had fallen into place.

The clouds swirling across the surface of the glass began to clear. Max took a deep breath and felt his stomach tighten. As the fog thinned, he saw the outline of a mass of heaving bodies. A naked woman of Amazonian proportions straddled the trembling human edifice. Memories began to crowd in on him. He knew this place. He knew the woman. He felt suddenly very cold. And very afraid.

'What word?' asked the Contessa.

'As you suspected,' answered Aubrey.

The Contessa was holding something in her hand. It was a large golden phallus. Max shuddered. A series of muddled images chased each other across his mind's eye: Trafalgar Square; a man struggling; Erica astride him and screaming. He was pumping so hard that his seed was pouring from her nose, her mouth and ears. A voice called to him, and he could swear it came from inside the phallus. He was going mad. No doubt about it. The Contessa was speaking but he was no longer listening.

'Have him brought before me.'

Max was seized by the shoulders and shoved to his knees in front of the mirror. This was not good, he told himself. This was not good at all.

'You failed me, Max,' said the Contessa. 'Tamara Knight lives.'

Max's first thought was to deny everything. His second was that it was probably a waste of time. He had been rumbled. Probably had been from the moment he'd arrived.

'I wanted to give you a chance, Max. You would have been a useful – and worthy – addition to my stable. But there is not enough of the dark within you. It could be worked on, but the End Time approaches. Chaos will soon be upon us. I am sorry, Max. But now you must die.'

Max wondered if it was worth begging for his life. There seemed little point. If he was going out, he might as well go out with dignity. If little sense. He should never have let them tie him up. Bugger.

The Contessa was speaking again, to Aubrey now. Max was clearly history.

'Allessandra has arranged the gathering. The others will be there. It is time to usher in the Great Darkness.'

The girl with the whip attacked Aubrey with renewed fervour. His body jerked and his back arched. Between his legs the two women continued to manipulate his cock and balls. Drops of spunk seeped from the eye of his penis and dribbled down his shaft. Max wondered at his ability to concentrate on the Contessa's words. Realisation dawned. It was all so obvious, if just a touch bizarre. They were communicating through the force of sexual energy, just as Sha'ni had communed with him. It beat the phone.

The vision in the mirror began to fade. A final, savage blow struck Aubrey across his red-raw shoulders. He straightened his spine and let loose a string of short expletives. The girls squeezed his cock and balls one last time and he came, his seed spurting high into the air. They leaned close so that it spattered their faces and bodies, then licked it off themselves and each other like cats devouring cream.

Max saw his reflection in the mirror. The Contessa had gone. Aubrey stood up, a little shaky on his feet, his face glowing, his arms and legs scored with sweat.

'I have to leave now,' he said. 'Pressing business. My girls will see to it that you enjoy your last few hours. Goodbye.'

Aubrey turned his back. Max winced to see the lattice-work of cord-like streaks and weals that had been gouged into his flesh. The phone suddenly took on a fresh attraction.

He had no further time to consider the matter. Two of the women took hold of his arms, dragged him from the room and along a corridor. Shallow steps led down, then merged into a short passageway beyond. They threw him into a small, stone cell and closed the door behind them. There were three girls already in attendance. Like their sisters, they were tall, dark-skinned and naked. Max looked up at five unsmiling faces and wondered what hell-tortures they had dreamt up for him this time.

Tamara and Erskine drew up outside Farnham Reach. It was a huge gothic mansion on the outskirts of Dorford Haven. There were several cars already there, an extravagant parade of stretch limos, Mercedes and BMWs. A gathering of the great and gruesome, Tamara told herself, and shuddered. She was really on her own now.

'We're going to a party,' Erskine had informed her. 'It's a Roman theme. Togas, that sort of thing. You don't mind?'

No, she didn't mind. Anything to get into Farnham Reach. Anything to get close to the Chalice. Her chance to grab it first had come and gone. Events were marching out of her control. Now all she could do was play it by ear and hope for the best.

There was a drum-beat sounding at the back of her head. A thought pushing its way through to the front. The something that was bugging her. Not yet on the tip of her tongue, but getting there. Definitely getting there.

Now they were disengorging from cars: small groups of people, dressed in overcoats, a shield against prying eyes and the cool breeze that was blowing in from the Atlantic. Tamara took a deep breath. The chill that gnawed at her stomach had nothing to do with the weather.

Max was in trouble. Which, he reflected, was par for the course. His ankles had been strapped together and his wrists secured behind his back. The girls had produced what appeared to be a large black velvet sack. He had been pushed to his knees and the material drawn up past his

head. Rather bizarrely, four of the women had climbed into the sack with him, while the fifth had pulled the string close and trapped them all inside. In the darkness, he felt the girls clambering over him. A damp, hairless pussy pushed itself into his mouth. He twisted free, only to feel a pair of warm breasts close around his head. A fist circled his cock, hands groped for his balls and a long, hard finger probed into his anus. There were tongues licking at his face, poking into his ears, across his tummy, down into the small of his back. He tried to kick himself free, but he was drowning in a sea of firm, sticky flesh. Soon his skin was slick with sweat and spittle. His balls hurt and his penis ached, passed from fist to fist in the dark, velvet confines. One of the girls closed her thighs around his neck and squeezed. He could hardly breathe. His world was hot, fetid and short of air. The women were using their bodies to suffocate him. His entire world was black; his body shot through with thwarted lust. They were tearing at his skin now, fighting over his balls. A damp, satin-soft heat engulfed his penis and he realised that one of the women was attempting to ride him. His head began to spin. There was a cunt around his cock, a finger in his rectum, thighs around his neck and buttocks clamped over his face. This was it. There was no escape now.

Somewhere far away, he was aware of movement; of shouting and commotion. Sperm pumped along his shaft and his body jack-knifed sharply. He would have shrieked with pleasure but he was choking on a woman's arse. Then suddenly the cover was wrenched from his face. He opened his eyes and the light stung them. There were screams; sounds of a struggle; metal clacking, handcuffs being secured. Something like that. It was hard to say and he didn't really care.

Blinking rapidly, Max was aware that he was no longer being sat on; no longer being smothered or, for that matter, pleasured. His body was sopping wet, covered in saliva and oily, female sap. He looked down at his cock. It lay across his thigh, still dribbling seed. Strong arms raised him, and hands untied his wrists and ankles.

218

He found himself staring into three familiar faces: Crayshaw, her secretary Emma and the dark girl, Sha'ni. The cell-door was open and there was a raised slab in the floor outside.

'Undercor!' chortled Crayshaw, extending a big meaty hand to help Max to his feet. 'Always knew the buggers would come in handy one day!'

Max wasn't bothered. He had only one thought on his mind just now: what the hell was he going to have to do to repay her for this one?

Inside the house, Tamara and Erskine Santer made their way to the Grand Hall. Two tall, muscular women, one blonde, one brunette, stood guard outside the main entrance. They were naked, with shaven labia; their legs open, their arms casually folded. Just in front of them stood a low stone rectangle. A scrawny, dark-haired man lay on his back, securely tethered to the block.

'Tonight is ladies' night,' announced the blonde, and watched Tamara's brow crease with curiosity. 'It means,' she explained, 'that the ladies are in charge. If any man attempts to service us without permission, he will be ejected.'

Erskine fidgeted. Tamara could see the image aroused him. He was more than happy to spend an evening under the female thumb.

'However, to show they are suitable,' added the brunette, 'all ladies must pay the admission.'

'Which is?' asked Tamara.

'You must masturbate yourself into the mouth of this worthless wretch.'

Tamara looked down and saw that the prisoner's face shone with sweat and sap. How many times had he been used already, she wondered. The blonde reached out, took hold of his hair and yanked back his head. A pair of red, watery eyes stared up at them.

'Carlos exists to serve women. He is happy to do our bidding. Is that not so?'

He nodded rapidly and grunted.

'Of course, he is a mute, so we can never be sure!' she laughed and let his head fall back on to the stone. 'Please,' she said, waving Tamara over, 'enjoy him.'

Tamara took a deep breath. If this was the only way in, then so be it. Squatting over his head, she pulled up her toga. Then, reaching down, she drew two fingers through the matt of her pubes, opened herself up and rubbed at the lozenge of her clit. Carlos's lips parted to receive her. She dropped on to his face and felt the warm salt of his tears sting her vulva. Shifting back a fraction, she forced her anus against his nostrils, then drove down with her hips and impaled herself over his nose. The muscles in her rectum went into spasm and she felt a ball of nerves explode inside her tummy. Carlos's body shook as if gripped by fever. Tamara hardened her arse and pressed with all her weight. Resting her fingers on his chest, she felt his heart thunder beneath her hands. Warm air beat against the nub of her clitoris. She threw back her head and howled as the dam within her burst. She felt herself flood his mouth with oily sap and enjoyed the wriggle of his face against her engorged sex.

'Very impressive,' observed an unfamiliar voice as Tamara dismounted. She felt giddy with excitement. What on earth had happened to her? It was as if, for a few short blissful moments, she had been taken over by some outside force.

'My name is Allessandra Favelli,' said the speaker stretching out her hand. It was warm and firm to the touch.

'Laine,' lied Tamara, recovering herself. 'Frankie Laine.'

Allessandra's dark brown eyes pierced her heart and she wondered if she had seen through her charade. She felt suddenly alone and vulnerable. Allessandra smiled and ushered her into the room. Erskine followed, open-mouthed with longing.

Inside, all was Bacchanalian frenzy, the Hall awash with writhing flesh. There were several men, stranded on their backs with their togas up around their necks, being ridden hard. Nearby, a small group of women stood chatting and sipping wine. A man knelt in front of each lady, licking at her pussy and stroking her thighs. One eager party was

being devoured by two men, one at the front and one at the rear. Tamara wondered how she was able to concentrate on the conversation.

She moved on, with Erskine trailing behind like an obedient puppy. In one corner, an unusual game was being played. An empty wine glass had been set up on a table. Three men stood side by side. The women took it in turns to masturbate each man until he came, directing his sperm towards the lip of the glass. There was a shriek of female glee when one man's seed finally struck its target.

Tamara felt spoilt for choice. So many men, so many things she could do with them. As she walked across the sperm-soaked parquet floor, however, she reasoned that she would have to move fast if any male was to be in a fit state to serve her.

What was she thinking about? She stopped and shook her head. There was definitely something in the air. Then she saw it, standing on a plinth in the distance: the Nhaomhé Chalice. A thin muslin veil obscured its finer details.

She stopped suddenly and Erskine barged into her back. He wore such a pathetic look that for a moment she considered putting him out of his misery. But no, why should she? Not yet at any rate.

A good-looking man walked past her. 'You!' she summoned him loudly.

The man stopped and turned to face her. He bowed. 'Yes, Mistress?'

Tamara glowed. She could become accustomed to such deference. An alarm bell rang at the back of her head, but she chose to ignore it.

'Let me see your cock.'

The man pulled up his toga and presented his manhood. It was long and thick, but not yet erect.

'Make yourself big for me,' she told him. Beside her, she heard Erskine's sharp intake of breath.

The man took hold of his penis and began to masturbate. Very quickly, the shaft engorged and fattened until it was plump and erect.

'Has anyone used you this evening?' Tamara asked. Her bluntness surprised even her. It must be something in the air. She really should be concentrating on getting out of here with the Chalice. But what the hell, she wasn't going to look a gift-horse in the mouth. This man could give her pleasure, and pleasure was all that mattered now.

'No, Mistress.'

Tamara smiled. 'So your balls are full?'

'Yes,' he replied.

'Let me feel them,' said Tamara.

He stepped forward and she cupped his testicles in her hands. Oh, yes, they were certainly full, nice and warm and heavy like stones. It was a miracle he could walk upright, she giggled to herself. She looked around and spotted an empty couch.

'Lie down!' she ordered. He settled himself on his back, his cock sticking up in the air. Tamara straddled his midriff, then had another idea, turned to Erskine and presented him with her cunt.

'I want to fuck this man,' she said, 'but I want you to lick me first so that I'll be nice and ready.'

He hesitated for a fraction and Tamara glared. 'Do it!' she commanded, in a voice that brooked no dissent.

Erskine knelt and extended his tongue. He began to lap at her pussy until it was sopping wet. Tamara had to restrain herself. It would have been so easy to have reached orgasm there and then. She pushed him away, and saw that his penis was upright, poking against the underside of his gown.

'Hold up my toga,' she told Erskine. There was a look of desperate longing in his eyes as he picked up the hem of her skirt and watched her lower herself on to another man.

Tamara rode up and down, enjoying the spill of juices washing from her cunt and dribbling down her thighs. 'Oh, fuck, this is so good,' she whimpered, gazing into Erskine's pleading eyes. What was happening? This was not like her at all. She was an active, sexual creature, but she had never been deliberately cruel. Yet not only was she enjoying a man who had no say in the matter, she was teasing another with total contempt for his feelings.

Tamara stretched out her hand and felt for Erskine's cock. His body shifted towards her. Out of the corner of one eye she caught sight of Allessandra watching them. There was a dark, thoughtful look on her face. But Tamara didn't care. All she cared about now was sex. She began to ride her man in earnest, allowing his shaft to rub against the engorged lozenge of her clit.

'Rub me,' she told Erskine. 'Rub my cunt!'

She felt his cock jump in her hand. She had little doubt that unless she told him to climax he was not supposed to. But she decided to remind him, just in case.

'You mustn't come, Erskine,' she told him. 'Not unless I tell you. Do you understand?'

He nodded his head and grunted. It was obvious that he was close to breaking-point. He breathed heavily and his cock pulsed with need. It was more than flesh and blood could stand, imagined Tamara, and felt her tummy twist with pleasure.

She looked down at the man beneath her. 'What's your name?' she asked, tightening the muscles of her cunt and feeling him jerk inside her.

'Thomas,' he managed to reply, biting his lip, his body threatening to lurch completely out of his control. Tamara began to ride him even faster.

'You're giving me pleasure, Thomas,' she said. 'You're giving me so much pleasure. I don't think I can hold back. I'm going to come in a moment. Would you like to come with me?'

The man gave a sharp nod of his head. 'Please,' he whispered through tight lips.

Tamara smiled. 'All right, I'll tell you when.' She turned to Erskine. 'Thomas and I are going to come. I want you to keep rubbing my clitty, Erskine, but – but –' She was fighting for breath now. 'Use your other hand. Now. Put –' Tamara shuddered as a ball of nerves tightened in her belly. 'Put your other hand between – between my buttocks. Stick a finger in my bumhole. You can feel my rectum squeeze when I climax. Go on, do it! Now!' she shouted at him.

He pressed his other hand up between Tamara's open arse-cheeks, his finger probing for her anus. It was so wet that he was able to enter her without resistance. Tamara tightened her grip on his cock. His body buckled at her touch. Suddenly she was coming, exploding over Thomas's midriff. She felt her rectal muscles clamp around Erskine's probing digit. He drove it in and out like a tiny penis. Strictly speaking that was against the rules because she hadn't told him to, and she guessed it was for his own pleasure more than hers. But she let it pass. After all, she was being so dreadfully cruel to him.

She felt her victim's balls roll against her buttocks and his seed splatter her womb. He seemed to spurt into her for ages, then he let out a final yelp and his body went limp. As Tamara dismounted, a fresh wave of euphoria overtook her. Her hand was still clamped around poor Erskine's cock, as it had been throughout her orgasm. She could only begin to imagine the torments he was suffering. She looked across and saw Allessandra smile. All around her the smell of sex and female hormones filled the air.

Tamara wandered around some more, leading Erskine by his shaft. She passed a girl lying on her back, with a man between her thighs, ploughing her cunt. Another two women stood either side, spanking him on the buttocks with their bare hands. At the moment of climax, one of them sat on his bottom so that he was no longer able to pump, while the other ran her long, talon-sharp nails down his back. He screamed as he unleashed himself, wriggling furiously between his captors.

Tamara began a slow circuit of the Chalice. The nearer she got, the randier she realised she was becoming. It was noticeable, too, that the physical activity here was more frantic, as though the Chalice exerted a sexual pull over those closest to it. She began to understand, more than ever, the nature of its power and why the Contessa was desperate to possess it.

At the back of her mind a voice was telling her what she had to do. She had to destroy it, that was what she had to do. But here? That was out of the question. She would

never get out alive. She must bide her time and see what happened. Perhaps an opportunity would arise. Besides, how could she destroy something so beautiful? It was wrong. She shook her head. What was happening to her? She was becoming more excited and loving every minute of it. She didn't want it to end.

Allessandra was standing by the Chalice, her arms outstretched. Two loud gongs sounded and immediately the room fell silent. It was all rather surreal, thought Tamara as she looked around. There were women astride men's cocks; women on all fours being buggered, women with balls in their mouths. There were women being licked; women doing everything imaginable. But just at this moment they stood stock-still, like some monstrous human tableau frozen in time.

Allessandra addressed the gathering with the voice of authority. 'Greetings, friends,' she began. 'I trust you have all enjoyed the evening. Now, it is time for the main event. The moment that defines our togetherness. Please prepare to welcome our Dark Mistress, the Contessa di Diablo!'

The huge double-doors swung open and the Hall was plunged into sudden darkness. Then, as if from nowhere, flames lit up the dark, and the Contessa strode through the centre of the chamber. Tamara felt cold, damp air rushing around her shoulders. Her toga flew up. She squeezed Erskine's cock in fright. It was too much for him. He squealed furiously and she felt his seed spurt over her hand.

There was a loud crack, followed by another. The earth split in several places, huge chasms opened up in the ground, and flames shot towards the ceiling. Winds ripped through the room, flinging bodies into the air, tearing togas; people were running and screaming. Tamara felt Erskine press himself up to her as if for protection, cuddling her like a child. There were demons in her head; wild, obscene images that turned her cunt to liquid and filled her heart with a cold, black fear. A couple rolled around in front of her, still locked together fucking. Tamara felt sperm splatter her face and wondered where it had come from.

Then all fell silent. The air tasted damp and fetid. The lights came up again; but this time they were not bright electric lights but guttering firebrands. They were no longer in the Hall, they were in a huge cathedral-like cavern. Tamara looked around and saw that everyone, herself included, was now naked. In the centre of the chamber heaved an undulating mass of flesh on which the Contessa now sat. She raised one arm and snapped her fingers. Fresh holes shattered the earth, and a living hell of sulphurous fumes rose up and filled the air. Men and women plunged from sight, screaming into the darkness. Tamara felt the ground break beneath her feet and she ran, a dreadful laughing in her ears. Then, she was no longer running. Large, powerful hands took hold of her shoulders and forced her to her knees, twisting back her head. A tall stone statue stood in front of her: half man; half woman.

'Pay homage to Mádrofh!' cried a voice in the darkness. Tamara's face was wrenched around, in the direction of the speaker. The Contessa rose and strode towards her, a huge, golden phallus balanced in her hands. Their eyes met and Tamara knew that the game was up.

'Welcome, Miss Knight,' said the Contessa. 'Welcome to the end of the world.'

Fifteen

'We haven't got much time.'

Crayshaw's countenance was dark with concern. Max was standing in front of the gilded mirror in Aubrey Manners' private room. But the glass was shattered, the framework bent and twisted. Max felt seriously confused. Being naked in the presence of three women didn't exactly concentrate his mind on matters cerebral.

'It is the doorway to the inner darkness,' explained Sha'ni unhelpfully.

'Right,' said Max, paused then added, 'And in English?'

Crayshaw's jowls trembled violently. 'It's how members of The Order communicate with the Contessa. Sha'ni believes they also use it as a means of transport – and that includes into the Lair.'

Max's face lit up. 'There was one in the massage parlour!'

Crayshaw nodded. 'Tamara saw another in Erskine Santer's Dorford Haven office.'

'This one's out of commission,' said Max miserably. 'They weren't taking any chances. So what do we do now?'

'We find another way in.'

'Do we have to?' Though his memories of the Lair remained second-hand, the idea unsettled him.

The professor's jowls wobbled again. 'I had a call from Tam. They've unearthed the Chalice. Knowing her, she'll be right behind it – wherever that leads.'

'You mean into the Contessa's Lair?'

'She is there already,' interrupted Sha'ni softly.

Max turned round. 'How do you know?'

Sha'ni did not reply. She looked Max in the eyes and a sudden image struck him. It was sensual and dark and felt very, very old.

'I think it's time we told him,' said Crayshaw.

'Told me what?' asked Max.

'Sha'ni is a Hedwynne. A white witch.'

'I know. Like the ones who stopped Vanjja. You told me. Back at your house.'

'No,' elaborated Crayshaw. 'Not *like* the ones who stopped Vanjja. She *is* one of those who stopped Vanjja.' She paused, then dropped her bombshell. 'And so are you.'

'What?' This, he decided, was ridiculous.

'It is true,' said Sha'ni. 'Tamara felt as much when she chose you. She has a gift. Guy, too, was one of us.'

'It didn't do him much good,' said Max. He frowned. 'Wait a minute. I thought they were all women.'

Sha'ni shook her head. 'In every age we are reborn. Our spirits remain constant, though our bodies change. Your own powers are not yet developed, yet they protected you from the Sacred Prayer. Did you not feel it?'

Max thought back to the glass-fronted booth. The strange chanting he had heard had enraptured the three archaeologists and aroused Aubrey. Yet they had barely touched him. It was what had puzzled him at the time.

'You sense things,' said Sha'ni. 'Images come to you. We Hedwynne can touch each other.'

He should have told them it was the craziest idea he'd ever heard. But he didn't. He recalled the images that had come to him, at the Conference Centre and Trafalgar Square; and the dream he had had at the Lair, when, without knowing Tamara was in danger, he had imagined himself travelling across time and space to help her. He didn't understand any of this, but it didn't make it any the less true. Bugger. What a week!

'So where are the others?'

Sha'ni shrugged. 'We two and Guy, that is all I know.'

'Can you use your powers to get us into the Lair?'

'No. Alone I am not strong enough. But there is a

chance. You have been there. If another doorway exists, you may be able to enter.'

'Great,' said Max, 'and where are we going to find another doorway at this time of night?'

Crayshaw wobbled. 'It's funny you should ask that.'

'You never meant to summon Vanjja, did you?'

The Contessa's eyes flared for a moment, then narrowed. 'Full marks, Miss Knight. I underestimated you. Forgive me. I won't do it again.'

Tamara was stretched out on a large wooden wheel, her arms and legs secured by leather bands sewn into the frame. Ropes had been threaded into holes drilled around the edges of the structure. The ends were knotted together above her head, and from there a single thick cord had been drawn through a metal link attached to a hook in the vaulted ceiling.

Sulphur fumes still issued from dark fissures in the ground, but the initial bedlam had long since ceased. Now the only sounds that filled the air were those of sex. The Living Throne continued to heave and groan. Several of the Faithful were taking their pleasure – sometimes two or three at a time – with those Minions who remained conscious, and even some who did not. There were men with men and women with women. Somewhere in the maelstrom she spotted Erskine. He was being held upside down by two women, his face crammed between the legs of a third who was busy sucking his cock.

Out of the blackness, several figures moved towards her. They wore long, grey gowns, and their faces were hidden beneath dark cowls. She counted six, no, seven in all and felt her stomach flood with ice. She had no need to be told who these new arrivals were. If The Order was gathering, something special must be taking place.

The seven figures came to a halt. Flames licked around the chamber floor, fashioned into a sudden, familiar shape: a seven-pointed star, strung out around the wheel on which she lay. Gowns were discarded and the seven Select of Mádrofh stood naked before their leader. Each held something vaguely tube-like in their hands.

'So what made you suspect?' asked the Contessa.

Tamara's head twisted back to face her inquisitor. 'All those charms you set in place to guard the excavation site. It didn't make sense. You were worried Vanjja and her daughters might escape. The way they almost did the night Hugo Morgan was attacked.'

The Contessa patted the tip of the golden phallus and smiled. 'That was my first warning. Vanjja was stronger than I had expected. Unleashing the Sacred Prayer didn't help, of course.' She turned and snapped her fingers. More shapes drifted out of the gloom, and Tamara recognised the three archaeologists. They, too, were naked. Doctor Q's penis jutted up against his belly, while Gioseppi's cock stuck out at an unusual right-angle to his groin. Erica Stanislav's cunt bulged like a ripe fruit, and fresh semen ran down the insides of her thighs.

'These three are finished,' said the Contessa dismissively. 'The Prayer has destroyed their minds as it has ravished their bodies. They live only for the pleasure which I concede to them.'

'You're sick!' retorted Tamara angrily.

The Contessa ignored her. She was into her stride now. 'I wanted the Prayer for its own sake, not to summon up a force to challenge my authority. Vanjja would have been a rival. But now that I have the Prayer and the Chalice, the danger is almost past.'

'So what are you going to do?' asked Tamara, though she already had a shrewd idea.

The Contessa turned her head towards the plinth. 'Even covered, the Chalice exerts its force. You felt it yourself, don't pretend you didn't.'

Tamara didn't have to: the memories remained vivid. Her body still tingled with arousal.

'In recent months, I have been consolidating my hold on the global telecommunications market. The final piece fell into place a few days ago.' The Contessa stood over Tamara and her eyes blazed with renewed fervour. 'I control the airwaves of the world. And now I will send a message to my people. A message of lust.'

'You'll never get away with it!' said Tamara, aware that she was hardly in a position to stop her.

'Oh, I think I will,' replied the Contessa. 'When Mádrofh returns, all the world will tremble beneath my heel. My mission cannot be thwarted. It is written in the *Ghis'kra*. Chaos is dawning. And with Chaos will come the thousand years that have been prophesied. No one can stop me.' She looked at the phallus and her face darkened. 'Can they, Guy?'

'Guy?' Tamara repeated. She was lost now.

The Contessa smiled. 'Oh didn't I say? Your former partner and I have become close friends.' She passed the tip of the phallus down between her big, oily breasts and shuddered. The golden globe of the phallus jerked in her hands.

'Isn't it sweet?' said the Contessa. 'When I feel pleasure, Guy feels pain. And vice versa. Though he doesn't often get the chance to show it. Just once or twice recently.' She slammed the phallus against her thigh. 'But I was able to show him the error of his ways.'

Tamara shook her head. 'No. I don't believe you. It's not true.'

'Oh, it's true, Miss Knight. You know as well I. These wretched Hedwynne are almost indestructible. Like your friend Max. Oh, yes, don't look so surprised. I've known that for some time. Still, no matter. Our game is almost over now.'

She snapped her fingers and Darné and Kalya strode forward, took hold of the loose ends of rope and pulled. The wheel began to rise. When it reached waist height, the Contessa lifted one arm and the ascent was stayed.

The seven members of The Order unfurled the tubes they were holding in their hands. Tamara belatedly realised that they were scrolls. They began to read. The words made no sense to Tamara, but she felt her clitoris fill with blood and throb between her legs.

'Oh fuck,' she groaned and threw back her head.

As the words of the Sacred Prayer filtered around the chamber, men and women began to claw at one another's

bodies, mounting each other with renewed gusto. The Living Throne began to shudder dangerously. Tamara felt her vulva melt and flood with sap. The Contessa pushed the head of the phallus up against her cunt. Tamara's labia opened up around the golden glans, and her flesh sucked at the monstrous intruder. She gazed with undisguised lust as the Contessa fed the phallus into her body until it was lodged impossibly deep. Tamara winced with discomfort and with need.

The Contessa stood back and snapped her fingers. Darné and Kalya, who, alone of the Faithful, seemed unmoved by surrounding events, began to pull on the ropes. The wheel continued its slow, upward journey. At its apex, a second rope was tugged hard and the wheel spun round 180 degrees. Tamara closed her eyes and tried to empty her head of all the longing gathered there. She didn't see the ground sunder anew, until flames shot high and singed the leather strap around her right hand. She opened her eyes. A boiling chasm lay directly beneath her, and she felt the heat from the broken earth scorch her skin. Flames began to lick at the ropes securing the wheel in place.

The Contessa laughed contemptuously. 'Do you feel the lust, Miss Knight? Gnawing at your insides? Is it not delicious?'

Tamara grimaced. The words of the Prayer filled her head, and her every nerve burned with arousal. The phallus began to slide from her slippy sex. 'No!' she screamed and tightened the muscles in her cunt.

'It is a bottomless pit, ' said the Contessa. 'Will you fall together, I wonder? Or will Guy perish first?'

Tamara squeezed her pussy tight, clinging on to the phallus. It was difficult. Her mind was seething with crude, obscene images. She wanted to clamp her legs together, to apply the merest friction on her clitoris. Then she would climax. But if she did, then Guy would slide out of her cunt and plunge to his death. But it was academic. She couldn't reach climax. Her bondage prevented that. All she could do was suffer.

Below her, Darné and Kalya dragged a young man

forward. He was naked, his penis erect, his hands fastened behind his back so that he was unable to touch himself. The Contessa reached out and stroked the side of his face.

'Stephen,' she breathed, gazing fondly at her recent recruit, the young man brought to her by the new girls, Joni and Lana.

'Mistress, please!' he screamed. 'Help me, please! I am in torment!'

'You wish to spend yourself?' she asked.

His head thudded up and down. 'Please, Mistress, please!'

'Do you swear allegiance, even unto death?'

He bowed his head low. 'Yes, Mistress! Yes! Only please! Let me spend!'

The Contessa took hold of his erect penis and pulled it towards her, drawing it into her cunt. Her hands circled his buttocks and she held him fast, pushing herself hard against him.

'Fuck me!' she ordered.

His hips began to move. So did hers, though it was clear to Tamara which one of them was doing the fucking. The man was like a dwarf before his Mistress. And he was in heaven, too, his little buttocks jerking in her hands.

He grunted furiously. 'Mistress! Mistress! I'm coming! I'm coming! Help me!'

With a snarl, she tugged at his hips, pulling his cock from her body. In one swift movement, she held him aloft. His penis jerked and the sperm issued from his urethra as she threw him high into the air. Tamara watched as he tumbled into the chasm below. Down and down, until his cries and his flailing arms were lost forever.

'Are you prepared to die?' asked the Contessa.

Tamara turned her head. 'How can I?' she sneered. 'It's a bottomless pit. I won't die. I'll just keep falling. Or is the idea that I starve to death? You really are a sadist, aren't you?'

Then Tamara shut her eyes and moaned softly as images of lust began to swamp what was left of her mind.

* * *

Max was staring at a familiar sight – the fountains at Trafalgar Square.

'Are you sure about this?' he asked.

'Yes,' replied Sha'ni, with surprising certainty. 'It is a gateway to the Lair. You saw things here. It was your power as a Hedwynne.'

Something stirred at the back of Max's mind. He put it on hold. It was important. But so was this.

'How do I get in?' he asked.

'Belief,' replied Sha'ni. 'And the force of your sexual energy.'

'Oh, that again,' said Max doubtfully. 'Right.'

'You must be prepared,' declared Sha'ni, looking about her. Trafalgar Square was crowded enough even at this time of night. A policeman strolled up and down some thirty yards away. Crayshaw blocked his view as Emma and Sha'ni took up a position either side of Max. He was wearing a ridiculously long overcoat, the reason being that underneath it he was completely naked. The pockets had been cut away so that the girls could reach him without it being obvious. A warm hand circled his cock. A second felt for his balls. Behind him he felt fingers press into his crack, probing for his anus. Incredibly, a second finger joined the first. Sha'ni leaned forward and whispered in his ear.

'Do not resist us, Max. Your pleasure must be great before you can breach the Lair.'

'Oh God,' murmured Max and felt his knees bend. There was no chance of his resisting. His biggest problem was delaying his orgasm. Suddenly, Sha'ni's hand tightened. Max sensed that something was wrong. Sha'ni shook her head as if to shake a stray hair from her face. She continued to stroke him gently, but it was obvious that she was troubled. Two long, thin fingers burrowed into his rectum, opening him up. He felt the sperm well up inside his balls. Not long now.

'Tamara is in danger,' said Sha'ni quietly. 'I do not understand. I see . . . I see. No, of course, Max, listen . . .' Now Sha'ni's voice was broken, her words gasped out on the edge of sharp breaths. 'There is a force fighting us. We will lose you. It is dangerous. Too dangerous . . .'

Seed spluttered into his cock. He was coming. It was now or never. Fingers thrust deep and he felt his insides explode with pleasure. Summoning up all his willpower, he tore himself away from the two women who were the source of his excitement. Sha'ni's words rang in his ear as he leapt towards the fountain.

'No, Max! No!' she was crying, but it was too late. Cold water drenched his body and his spunk arced high into the air.

And then he was somewhere else altogether.

The ground was trembling beneath their feet. The Contessa wheeled around, her face contorted with anger and confusion.

'No!' she screamed. There was something wrong, something dreadfully wrong. She could feel it in the coldness of her dark heart. On the altar, the Chalice began to move, caught by the vibrations that rocked the chamber. Vanjja was fighting back. How? It was not possible! The Prayer and the Chalice were combining to summon their Mistress from Vhalgoor!

She hurried forward, then froze in her tracks. It was like running into a brick wall. Her body pulsed with unforeseen pleasure.

Between Tamara's legs, the phallus twisted, and Guy screamed.

Max was spinning through time and space, a cold and dark abyss. Then suddenly he came to. There were cords around his arms and legs and he couldn't move. He didn't know where he was, but what he did know was that something was very wrong. He was naked, lying on his back in a body that wasn't his. A woman was sitting on his cock, and it hurt like hell. Then he looked up and his blood froze. A naked woman stood over him. Her arms were raised high, which served to accentuate and tighten the moons of her massive brown breasts. The V of her cunt was fat and rounded, the labia pink, open and crowned with dark, luxuriant hair. She was chanting something, words without

meaning, yet words which burrowed into his soul and made his tortured penis stiffen.

Max suddenly knew where he was. Somehow he had been transported not just across space, but across time, too. He was staring up at Nhaomhé as she saluted the dark moon, a chalice raised aloft in her hands.

He was able to snatch one deep breath before she lowered her bottom over his face and blotted out all sight and sound. Something warm and wet pressed against his nose. The smell of arse was unmistakable. It filled his nostrils, wafting into the back of his throat so that he could taste it on his tongue. He was unable to open his mouth around her cunt because her backside was everywhere. Soft, warm flesh pooled across his face, cutting off the air supply completely. He tried to shift his lower half, but the woman on his cock had him pinned securely. A swirling lightness in his head gave way to pain and fear began to gnaw at his belly.

Max had no idea how long he lay there, shifting uselessly, grunting his pain into Nhaomhé's arse. All at once she leaned forward and he saw daylight. The chalice scraped across his wet and sticky skin, scooping up the essence of the women who had ridden this body long before he had arrived. His chest heaved; once, twice, before she covered his face a second time. Max clawed the air; his stomach lurched and for one moment he thought he was going to be sick. Then he shrieked and the last of his breath left his lungs. The girl astride his belly was bouncing and somewhere, far away it seemed, he could hear the strains of chanting. His balls rolled and semen pumped into his shaft. His heart was banging in his chest; one more thump and it would surely rupture and explode. He tensed his fear-hardened fists, arched his spine and bucked his hips. He suddenly knew the true meaning of fear: a fear that filled his balls, hardened his cock and sent showers of ice into his stomach. Nhaomhé's cunt was hot and slippery: it seemed to explode over him like warm fruit, covering his nose and mouth. Something hard and wet pressed against his nose and he heard her moan.

Someone called to him out of the darkness. It was

Sha'ni, her voice soft and unhurried. 'Fly, Max,' she told him. 'Fly.'

Instinct took over and he knew at once what he had to do. He must think himself into another body. This one was nearly done for, its life force almost gone.

'Concentrate on your prick,' she told him quietly.

That was easy, it was what he did best. Suddenly he was sitting over a cock, his hands tugging nipples on his big, inflated breasts. Nhaomhé's large brown eyes smiled back at him and he could feel pleasure boiling up in his cunt. He had a cunt! A cold wind whipped around his mind and shunted him on again. Now he saw the world through Nhaomhé's eyes. A man's face twisted horribly between his buttocks, and he felt his clitoris swell with arousal. There was evil here. Too much evil. He had to get away. Max concentrated hard and suddenly he was flying again, back through time and space.

There was a loud bang and a blinding flash of light. A wild, fear-drenched hell-fire erupted all around him and he covered his face against the fumes and sounds that filled his head. Raising his eyes and squinting into the sulphurous gloom, Max had a fleeting image of leaping from saucepans into fires.

He was back in the Contessa's Lair.

Tamara screamed and the wheel tottered awkwardly. Flames licked their way along the rope holding the fragile structure in place. Terror and excitement mingled in her belly. The Contessa and her followers were tapping into an atavistic power that had existed since the dawn of creation: sex itself. It was a potent force and it was destroying her. Her cunt leaked sap and she felt the phallus begin to slide from her body.

The Contessa was on her knees, crawling towards the Chalice. Tamara's eyes locked on to the woman's broad, muscular buttocks and she felt her groin tighten with arousal. My God, she wanted her. It was crazy! The world was crazy! Where the hell was Max? Where the hell was the cavalry?

* * *

Max stood up. He was naked and himself again, but all around was madness. Bodies heaved against each other, men and women rolled and wrestled, fucking one another furiously. The Living Throne tottered and collapsed, and a tidal wave of copulating flesh unleashed itself across the chamber floor. There were figures waving scrolls, yelling strange words into the ether. He knew who they were at once. Then the ground beneath him trembled and he fell. He heard another scream and looked up. Tamara was strapped to a wooden wheel, suspended over a blazing pit, with a huge golden phallus poking out of her cunt. Could things get any madder?

Flames were licking at the rope that held the wheel in place. Any second now and it would snap. He ran across the chamber. Eyes turned towards him; eyes that knew him. Darné and Kalya flung themselves across his path, dragged him to the ground, and pinned him flat. He lifted his head and watched helplessly as the rope begin to splinter.

'Tamara!' he screamed.

She turned her head towards the sound of his voice. 'About bloody time, Max!' she yelled, then shrieked as the wheel gave a downwards lurch.

Reaching the plinth, the Contessa made a final effort, and her hands closed around the Chalice. 'You cannot best me, Vanjja!' she cried. 'I am the Chosen One, not you!'

The Chalice clutched in her hands, she lurched towards the blazing pit. Fresh fissures continued to open up all around her. Max pushed and pulled, but Darné and Kalya were too strong. They dragged him to his feet. Kalya held him fast, while Darné took hold of his cock and pulled it towards her. He had a sudden sense of *déjà vu*, and his blood ran cold. This was the image he had seen in the fountains at Trafalgar Square. Sha'ni might have told him that a Hedwynne could sometimes see the fucking future!

There was a horrible crack to his right. He tore his head around and watched as the rope finally severed. 'Tamara! No!'

Déjà vu again.

Tamara screamed. But the wheel had not fallen. An arm shot out and grabbed the burning cord. Max knew whose hand it was without even looking. All those images he'd had; that special closeness he had felt. Sha'ni had said it herself, 'We Hedwynne can touch each other.'

'Darling,' whispered a voice in his head, a voice tinged with accent, 'where have you been? I look for you everywhere!' Well, now she'd found him, and not a moment too soon. He lowered his eyes a fraction and saw Erica Stanislav pulling hard, drawing the wheel down. She was a Hedwynne, just like him. The something that had niggled at the back of his mind was finally out in the open.

Darné and Kalya's grip slackened for a moment, distracted by the sudden turn of events. Max kicked his way free and ran to where Erica was leaning over Tamara's blackened body.

The Contessa stumbled towards the edge of the pit, the Chalice in her hands. She raised it high above her head. Tamara gazed up at her, hardly aware that Max was tugging her free. Once the Contessa had disposed of Vanjja, there would be nothing in her way.

'No, Max,' she yelled. 'The Contessa! Stop her!'

Max froze. They were too far away. Even he realised that once the Chalice had been jettisoned, they were done for. He and Erica might be Hedwynne, but no way were they yet strong enough to fight the Contessa.

Tamara stared down at the phallus still lodged between her legs, then sideways at the flames burning across the rope.

'Of course . . .' she muttered, took a deep breath and reached out. Max saw her from the corner of his eye.

'No!' he yelled. But it was too late. Tamara closed her hand around the burning rope and screamed. The phallus lurched inside her vulva.

The Contessa roared as the full force of Guy's pleasure – her pain – tore through her body. She was on fire! Twisting madly, she lost her footing, tottered and fell, plunging headfirst into the chasm. Her screams reverberated around the chamber for several, nerve-rending seconds and then there was silence.

Max took hold of Tamara's arm. 'Are you all right?' he asked.

She eased the phallus from her cunt. 'Of course I'm not all right, you idiot! My hand's on fire!'

'We must leave.' It was Erica who spoke.

Tamara looked puzzled. 'When did *she* join the good guys?'

'Erica's a Hedwynne,' said Max. 'You know, those people you have a gift for spotting.'

'No one's perfect,' retorted Tamara, holding her wrist and wincing. Faithful, Minions and scattered members of The Order gathered about them now, hatred burning in their eyes.

'I think this mission may have peaked too soon,' said Max.

White clouds began to form around the walls, and a fresh wind, laced with ice, howled through the chamber.

Tamara shivered. 'What's happening?'

'I don't know,' said Max. 'But I don't think it's good.'

Rocks were falling now, from the dark, vaulted ceiling; black rocks that became white. Where they fell, the blackness was ripped open and clouds of white nothing oozed into the cavern.

'The Lair, it collapses,' muttered Erica. 'Everything ends.'

'I don't understand,' said Tamara. 'Unless . . .'

Max was there already. 'It's like the massage parlour. A place that's there and not there. A place that can't be there. Not really.' Understanding came to him, knowledge from a far-off time and place. 'The Lair *is* the Contessa. It's her mind. Everything. Now she's gone, there's nothing to hold it together. It's crumbling out of existence!'

Tamara frowned. It all sounded a bit too neat. That was the trouble with the Hedwynne: they were a bunch of bloody know-it-alls. Guy had been just the same. She jumped up and grabbed Max's arm.

'We can discuss it later, Sherlock!' she said, picking up the phallus. 'Right now I suggest we bugger off!'

All around them, sulphurous jets ripped through the earth. White steam shot up and seared surrounding walls,

scalding those on whom its hot rains fell. There was only one way out, and they took it: a stone staircase to the rear of the chamber. The winding, circuitous route took them higher and higher, but as fast as they ran the white trail of emptiness followed, eating up the ground behind until it blew at their heels.

They burst through into a long, narrow walkway. A locked door barred their exit. Max's face lit up. 'I know this place!' he said. 'It's the massage parlour!' He looked around him. 'I knew it was too good to be true. Too many rooms, you see. But if it was part of the Lair . . .'

No one was listening. Tamara hammered on the thick wooden frame. Erica screamed. It brought him back to earth with a bump. A cloud of white nothing flew up the stairs behind and erupted into the corridor. Max wheeled about, his mind racing.

'There should be doors! Doors all the way along. I don't understand!'

He shut his eyes and concentrated. He was on auto-pilot now, delving into a past he still wasn't fully aware of, summoning up powers he didn't know he had.

Everything here was a lie. It was all in the Contessa's head. Now it had to be in his. The doors had gone. He had to get them back. Think, Max! Think! he yelled to himself.

Tamara's voice was soft and unafraid as the white nothing poured into the corridor. 'Too late,' she sighed.

An opening appeared in the wall opposite. Yes!

Max grabbed Erica and Tamara and pulled them through. They were in Zelda's dungeon.

'How the hell did you do that?' asked Tamara.

'No idea,' replied Max. The gilded mirror stood where he had first seen it. And it was intact. He positioned Tamara between himself and Erica.

'What now, English?' asked the diminutive Hungarian.

'We have to go through the mirror,' said Max. 'It's the only way.'

'I can't do it,' said Tamara. 'I'm not like you.'

Max's arm tightened around her shoulder. 'Well, let's face it,' he said, 'I wouldn't fancy you if you were.'

There was a sudden rush of air and heat seared their backs. The three of them leaped forward. For a brief instant the world turned black; then grey, then cream. Then sheer unblemished star-burst white.

A man appeared in front of them. Or perhaps they appeared in front of him. He was old, and he was well-dressed. And he was angry. He was very angry.

'Oh no!' Max heard him cry. 'Not you again!'

Epilogue

'How is old Mr Lackerty?' asked Max.

'As well as can be expected,' replied Tamara.

'Not every day three naked people turn up in his shop, I suppose.'

'Be that as it may, we have work to do,' interrupted Crayshaw, bustling around, her eyes bright with excitement. She cupped the golden glans in her big, meaty palm. 'Absolutely fascinating!' she chortled. 'Guy in a dildo, who'd have thought it?'

'But can we get him out again?' asked Tamara, waving a large, bandaged hand towards the phallus.

'Could be tricky,' said Crayshaw. 'Though Sha'ni does have an idea.'

'Does it involve a huge amount of sex?' asked Max.

'I'm afraid so,' answered Crayshaw. 'Could go on for days. Weeks, even. And then, of course, there's your training. You and Erica. We must unleash your new-found strengths as soon as possible. Find the other Hedwynne, too. They'll be around here somewhere. We can't be sure the Contessa is gone for good. No.'

Max began to undo his trouser belt. 'Better get started, then,' he said.

'Oh, yes,' said Crayshaw eyeing up the thick column of his unfurling flesh. 'And, then of course, there's the question of my fee.' She rubbed her hands together and rolled her big pink tongue around the inside of her mouth.

Max sighed. It was going to be a long, long night.

With any luck.

243

NEW BOOKS

Coming up from Nexus, Sapphire and Black Lace

The Bond by Lindsay Gordon

February 2000   £5.99   ISBN: 0 352 33480 0

Hank and Missy are not the same as the rest of us. They're on a ride that never ends, together forever, joined as much by their increasingly perverse sexual tastes as by their need to satisfy their special needs. But they're not alone on their journey. The Preacher's after Hank, and he'll do anything to Missy to get him. The long-awaited third novel by the author of *Rites of Obedience* and *The Submission Gallery*.

The Slave Auction by Lisette Ashton

February 2000   £5.99   ISBN: 0 352 33481 9

Austere, masterful and ruthless, dominatrix Frankie has learnt to enjoy her new life as mistress of the castle. Her days are a paradise of endless punishments and her nights are filled with cruel retribution. But with the return of her arch-enemy McGivern, Frankie's haven is about to be shattered. He is organising a slave auction in which lives will be altered forever, and his ultimate plan is to regain control of the castle. As the dominatrix becomes the dominated, Frankie is left wondering whether things will ever be the same again.

The Pleasure Principle by Maria del Rey

February 2000   £5.99   ISBN: 0 352 33482 7

Sex is deviant. Disgusting. Depraved. Sex is banned. And yet despite the law, and the Moral Guardians who police it, a sexual underworld exists which recognises no rule but that of desire. Into this dark world of the flesh enters Detective Rey Coover, a man who must struggle with his own instincts to uncover the truth about those who recognise no limits. Erotica, science fiction and crime collide in one of Maria del Rey's most imaginative and explicit novels. A Nexus Classic.

Devon Cream by Aishling Morgan
March 2000   £5.99   ISBN: 0 352 33488 6
Devon Cream traces the history of the innocent but wilful Octavia Challacombe as she is corrupted by the wicked Maray family. Along with the bouncy Polly Endicott and a group of other buxom Devon girls, she is cajoled and teased, first into providing her own breast milk for the Squire and then into increasingly perverse services. Her unabashed pleasure in her own sexual enjoyment lasts through spankings, bondage and ever more peculiar uses for her milk, until finally she takes her revenge. By the author of *The Rake*.

Police Ladies by Yolanda Celbridge
March 2000   £5.99   ISBN: 0 352 33489 4
Deep in the Scottish highlands a curious training academy teaches young women how to pound a beat. Restrictive uniforms, strict training and the special use of truncheons characterise the Glenlassie approach to police training – but the recruits are slowly being siphoned off by a neraby pony-girl training establishment and a unique medical clinic. By the author of *The Discipline of Nurse Riding*.

Conduct Unbecoming by Arabella Knight
March 2000   £5.99   ISBN: 0 352 33490 8
Deep in the English countryside, a group of patriotic young Wrens are doing their bit for the war effort, interrogating women who may or may not have slept with senior enemy officials. Some are willing to talk; others are not so forthcoming. And that's where Captain Cordelia Quidenham comes in. Together with her small, efficient and perfectly formed team, Cordelia applies every method of persuasion to wring information out of her quivering subjects – especially methods that involve the smack of leather on flesh. A Nexus Classic.

SAPPHIRE · SAPPHIRE

A new imprint of lesbian fiction

Getaway by Suzanne Blaylock
October 1999   Price £6.99   ISBN: 0 352 33443 6
Brilliantly talented Polly Sayers had made two big life shifts concurrently. She's had her first affair with a woman, and she's also stolen the code of an important new piece of software and made her break, doing a runner all the way to a seemingly peaceful coastal community. But things aren't as tranquil as they appear in the haven, as Polly becomes immersed in an insular group of mysterious but very attractive women.

No Angel by Marian Malone
November 1999   £6.99   ISBN 0 352 33462 2
Sally longs to test her limits and sample forbidden pleasures, yet she's frightened by the depth of her yearnings. Her journey of self-discovery begins in the fetish clubs of Brighton and ultimately leads to an encounter with an enigmatic female stranger. And now that she's tasted freedom, there's no way she's going back.

Cruel Enchantment by Janine Ashbless
February 2000   £5.99   ISBN: 0 352 33483 5

Here are eleven tales of temptation and desire, of longing and fear and consummation; tales which will carry you to other times and other worlds. Worlds of the imagination where you will encounter men and monsters, women and gods. Worlds in which hermits are visited by succubi and angels; in which dragons steal maidens to sate special hungers; in which deadly duels of magic are fought on the battlefield of the naked body and even the dead do not like to sleep alone.

Tongue in Cheek by Tabitha Flyte
February 2000   £5.99   ISBN: 0 352 33484 3

When Sally's relationship ends everything seems to go wrong for her – she can't meet a new man, she's having a bad time at work and she can't seem to make anything work at all. That is, until she starts hanging out around the local sixth-form college, where she finds the boys more than happy to help out – in every way.

Fire and Ice by Laura Hamilton
March 2000   £5.99   ISBN: 0 352 33486 X

Nina, auditor extraordinaire, is known as the Ice Queen at work, where her frigid demeanour makes people think she's equally cold in bed. But what her colleagues don't know is that Nina spends her after-work hours locked into fiery games with her boyfriend Andrew, one in which she acts out her deepest fantasy – being a prostitute Nina finds herself being drawn deeper and deeper into London's seedy underground, where everything is for sale and nothing is what it seems.

Wicked Words 2 ed. Kerri Sharp
March 2000   £5.99   ISBN: 0 352 33487 8

Black Lace anthologies have proved to be extremely popular. Following on from the success of the *Pandor's Box* and *Sugar and Spice* compilations, this second *Wicked Words* collection continues to push the erotic envelope. The accent is once again on contemporary settings with a transgressive feel – and the writing is fresh, upbeat in style and hot. This is an ideal introduction to the Black Lace series.

Nexus

NEXUS BACKLIST

All books are priced £5.99 unless another price is given. If a date is supplied, the book in question will not be available until that month in 1999.

CONTEMPORARY EROTICA

THE ACADEMY	Arabella Knight	
AMANDA IN THE PRIVATE HOUSE	Esme Ombreux	
BAD PENNY	Penny Birch	
THE BLACK MASQUE	Lisette Ashton	
THE BLACK WIDOW	Lisette Ashton	
BOUND TO OBEY	Amanda Ware	
BRAT	Penny Birch	
DANCE OF SUBMISSION	Lisette Ashton	Nov
DARK DELIGHTS	Maria del Rey	
DARK DESIRES	Maria del Rey	
DARLINE DOMINANT	Tania d'Alanis	
DISCIPLES OF SHAME	Stephanie Calvin	
THE DISCIPLINE OF NURSE RIDING	Yolanda Celbridge	
DISPLAYS OF INNOCENTS	Lucy Golden	
EMMA'S SECRET DOMINATION	Hilary James	
EXPOSING LOUISA	Jean Aveline	
FAIRGROUND ATTRACTIONS	Lisette Ashton	
GISELLE	Jean Aveline	Oct
HEART OF DESIRE	Maria del Rey	
HOUSE RULES	G.C. Scott	Oct
IN FOR A PENNY	Penny Birch	Nov
JULIE AT THE REFORMATORY	Angela Elgar	
LINGERING LESSONS	Sarah Veitch	

THE GOVERNESS AT ST AGATHA'S	Yolanda Celbridge	
THE MASTER OF CASTLELEIGH	Jacqueline Bellevois	Aug
PRIVATE MEMOIRS OF A KENTISH HEADMISTRESS	Yolanda Celbridge	£4.99
THE RAKE	Aishling Morgan	Sep
THE TRAINING OF AN ENGLISH GENTLEMAN	Yolanda Celbridge	

SAMPLERS & COLLECTIONS

EROTICON 4	Various	
THE FIESTA LETTERS	ed. Chris Lloyd	£4.99
NEW EROTICA 3		
NEW EROTICA 4	Various	
A DOZEN STROKES	Various	Aug

NEXUS CLASSICS
A new imprint dedicated to putting the finest works of erotic fiction back in print

THE IMAGE	Jean de Berg	
CHOOSING LOVERS FOR JUSTINE	Aran Ashe	
THE INSTITUTE	Maria del Rey	
AGONY AUNT	G. C. Scott	
THE HANDMAIDENS	Aran Ashe	
OBSESSION	Maria del Rey	
HIS MASTER'S VOICE	G.C. Scott	Aug
CITADEL OF SERVITUDE	Aran Ashe	Sep
BOUND TO SERVE	Amanda Ware	Oct
BOUND TO SUBMIT	Amanda Ware	Nov
SISTERHOOD OF THE INSTITUTE	Maria del Rey	Dec

Please send me the books I have ticked above.

Name   ....

Address   ....

                 ....

                 ....

                 .... Post code.......................

Send to: **Cash Sales, Nexus Books, Thames Wharf Studios, Rainville Road, London W6 9HT**

US customers: for prices and details of how to order books for delivery by mail, call 1-800-805-1083.

Please enclose a cheque or postal order, made payable to **Nexus Books**, to the value of the books you have ordered plus postage and packing costs as follows:

UK and BFPO – £1.00 for the first book, 50p for the second book and 30p for each subsequent book to a maximum of £3.00;

Overseas (including Republic of Ireland) – £2.00 for the first book, £1.00 for the second book and 50p for each subsequent book.

We accept all major credit cards, including VISA, ACCESS/MASTERCARD, AMEX, DINERS CLUB, SWITCH, SOLO, and DELTA. Please write your card number and expiry date here:

....

Please allow up to 28 days for delivery.

Signature   ....
